I0847567

THE BETRAYED BRIDE

The Perfect Poison Murders, Book 5
A Georgian Mystery

E.L. Johnson

© Copyright 2024 by E.L. Johnson
Text by E.L. Johnson
Cover by Dar Albert

Dragonblade Publishing, Inc. is an imprint of Kathryn Le Veque Novels, Inc.
P.O. Box 23
Moreno Valley, CA 92556
ceo@dragonbladepublishing.com

Produced in the United States of America

First Edition February 2024
Print Edition

Reproduction of any kind except where it pertains to short quotes in relation to advertising or promotion is strictly prohibited.

All Rights Reserved.

The characters and events portrayed in this book are fictitious. Any similarity to real persons, living or dead, is purely coincidental and not intended by the author.

ARE YOU SIGNED UP FOR DRAGONBLADE'S BLOG?

You'll get the latest news and information on exclusive giveaways, exclusive excerpts, coming releases, sales, free books, cover reveals and more.

Check out our complete list of authors, too!

No spam, no junk. That's a promise!

Sign Up Here

www.dragonbladepublishing.com

Dearest Reader;

Thank you for your support of a small press. At Dragonblade Publishing, we strive to bring you the highest quality Historical Romance from some of the best authors in the business. Without your support, there is no 'us', so we sincerely hope you adore these stories and find some new favorite authors along the way.

Happy Reading!

CEO, Dragonblade Publishing

Additional Dragonblade books by Author E.L. Johnson

The Perfect Poison Murders
The Strangled Servant (Book 1)
The Poisoned Clergyman (Book 2)
The Mistress Murders (Book 3)
The Deadly Debutante (Book 4)
The Betrayed Bride (Book 5)

The Lyon's Den Series
The Lyon and the Bluestocking

CHAPTER ONE

Faulkbourne Manor, Essex, July 1807

SERGEANT HENRY DYNGLEY was anxious. The round, comfortable chair he knew and liked seemed hard on his rear. He moved and shifted but could not settle. As he sat in the grand wood-paneled library inside his family's manor and glanced out the window, he frowned down at the offending note before him, the cause of his sudden ill will. He could picture the writer as easily as he could himself. But just reading the first few words made his stomach clench, and he'd had to force himself to keep reading.

> *My dearist Henry,*
>
> *For some tme now I have thought of you, and the promyse we made to each other many years ago. We have much to discuss. I hope it is not an imposition, but I will visit on Thursday, 9 July. I hope we will find the conversation to both our satisfaction.*
>
> *Ever yers,*
> *Honoria*

Henry's hand clenched, wishing to crumple the letter but laid it aside on his writing table instead. He glared at the offending letter. Why, now, did Honoria seek to contact him? And about a mere trifle? A child's game? They had not spoken or seen each other in more than a decade. What could she possibly want from him? And stranger still, her spelling was atrocious. She must be nearing age twenty now and she came from a good family. Surely she would know how to spell properly.

The letter was most concerning and put him at unease. He did not like it, not at all. Reading the words again made his stomach twist and his stiff collar pinched at his throat. He tugged at his cravat, loosening it, but it did little good. Honoria was back, and at precisely the wrong time. The question was, did he tell his fiancée, Poppy?

He loved her; he did. And he owed her an explanation. But Honoria Penwrith's letter could not be ignored, however much he wished it to disappear. He gazed around the solid walls of the library, its shelves holding decades of books and old periodicals from previous generations, and noted the shabby red curtains, once impressive, now discreetly tied back to hide the moth holes.

The very floorboards creaked and groaned at the merest step, and the comfortable reading chairs and sofas scattered around the large room, so delightfully soft and generous with the cushions, now appeared tattered and worn to his eyes. The small square windowpanes of cut glass were straight from the Restoration and were precious, but also were frail and needed replacing. It was a fact: the estate needed money. It had been his family's hope that he would marry a rich heiress. So why had he proposed to a poor clergyman's girl?

In a word, love.

He and Miss Poppy Morton of Hertfordshire, a tall, head-strong, young woman with a nose for finding culprits and miscreants, had fallen into company more than a year ago now when she had first become a suspect after her best friend had gone missing and was presumed dead. Working together to find the truth and clear her name had thrown them into each other's paths, and a shy but respectful friendship had led to something more, much to the consternation of his family.

The illegitimate child of Lord Hugh Blackwood of Somerset and his mistress, a woman of notable wit and beauty called "the Grace," Poppy had recently met her father for the first time, following the murder of her mother. Lord Blackwood had sponsored Poppy for a London Season, where she had befriended debutantes, one of whom decided to kill off her competition. Poppy had almost died in order to save her half-sister, and Henry couldn't bear the thought of life without her.

Against his better judgment, the condescension of his peers, and protests of his family, he had proposed and had been accepted. But it was not an easy thing, and when he had returned to the Dyngley family townhouse in London and told the others he was engaged, the reception was frosty.

Petunia, his sister-in-law who reminded him closely of a hawk, had glared at him, held her new baby close to her chest, and looked down her nose at him. She had opened her mouth to blast him with a sharp retort, but then little Arthur gurgled in her arms and she forgot Henry in an instant. His father, Sir Richard Dyngley, had asked if Miss Morton's family was in Debrett's, and at Petunia's laugh, he had quit the room to play billiards and read the paper. The only person who did seem to be genuinely happy for him was his older brother, John, the heir to the Dyngley baronetcy. He had clapped him on the back and said, "Well done, Henry. She'll be a credit to you," and poured him a drink.

That had been a month ago. Since then he had returned to Faulkbourne Manor in Essex with his family and had kept regular correspondence with Poppy, sending her boiled sweets and flowers whenever he could.

But he felt the distance keenly and did not like being apart from her for so long. He wrote to her a little of his work in the county as a local sergeant, but without her there, he felt at a loss.

At that moment John strolled into the library, looking calm and relaxed in a smart, beige patterned waistcoat, lightly tied white cravat, and tan trousers. He brushed dust from his white shirtsleeves and sniffed the air. "Ugh, I knew I'd find you here. Anywhere there's books and dust, you're sure to be found."

"I'll have the servants dust again," Henry said.

"What's that you've got? Some correspondence? Is it from Miss Morton?" John asked with a knowing smile.

Henry frowned and folded Honoria's letter away. "You recall Miss Penwrith?"

"Honoria Penwrith? Tall as a stork, beaky nose, all legs, and acne on her chin? Madly in love with you?"

"What?" Henry asked.

"God, are you still so oblivious? Trust me, Henry, I could see it even at age seventeen. She was besotted. Why?" John asked.

Henry held up the letter. "She's coming to visit in a week's time."

John's eyebrows rose. "Here? In a week?"

"Yes."

"But you're engaged. What does she want?" John asked.

"To have a discussion." He held out the letter.

John read its contents and whistled. "You've got trouble following you wherever you go."

"What do you mean?"

"Just a sense I have. I can spot trouble a mile away, and she is it. What promise is she talking about?"

Henry reddened and turned away. "Nothing. Just a childish game."

"It doesn't sound so childish to me."

"It was nothing." Henry's voice hardened.

"Very well. I'll tell Petunia. But you know how she'll be. She'll be fretting about the curtains and whether the dinner plates are spotless enough." John scratched his chin. "Still, it will do her good to have another woman around. Prepare her for when Miss Morton joins us."

The sharp staccato sound of a woman's heeled shoes struck the ground, making them pause. Petunia Dyngley entered the room, her dark eyes flashing. "Henry, there you are. I've been looking for you. John, would you give us a minute?"

John looked from his wife to Henry. "As you wish, my sweet."

Henry tried not to roll his eyes as Petunia blushed and brushed down her skirts. "Yes, well."

Her jet-black hair was curled into soft ringlets around her face, and she stood by as John passed her. She strode into the room and stood, her hands on her hips, facing Henry.

"Yes?" He set down the letter from Honoria.

"I have come to convince you to change your mind about your reckless decision. It is not too late to write to the girl and tell her all is at an end between you," she said.

"Mrs. Dyngley—" Henry started.

"Now, now, hear me out. I have thought a great deal on the matter and I see no other way around it. This sordid farce of an engagement must end. You can write to the girl and end it, and then I shall write to my acquaintances in the neighborhood and let it be known that you are single and available. I'll be bound that by the next dance in town, you will not want for partners, to be sure."

Henry felt his hands curl into tight fists. He splayed flat his hands, and instead rested them on his knees. "Mrs. Dyngley, we have spoken at length on this already. I am not changing my mind. I am engaged to Miss Morton, and will stay that way."

She talked as if he had not spoken. "I know that she has charmed you with her wit, and her face is tolerable, but there are prettier girls out there, and richer too. I shall join you, and I think at the dance–"

"You hate public assemblies," Henry pointed out.

She sniffed. "I will make an exception."

He rose from his seat. "Mrs. Dyngley, I appreciate your care for me on this matter…"

"It is not a concern for you, Henry, but for this household. Have you given no thought to what marrying this girl would mean for our family?" She stared at him with her hands on her hips.

He did not dignify that with an answer. She was being unbearably rude.

She added, "How will we support ourselves? I don't flatter myself with the fantasy that my dowry gave more than a brief respite to this family's debts. This estate needs an income, and you need to marry a rich girl. Miss Morton has brains and wit, I grant you, but money? She has nothing. How will you support a wife on your meager income? A sergeant's salary? Don't make me laugh." Her voice was cutting, cruel even.

Henry surveyed her and took a deep breath. He must keep his resolve and not lose his temper. He mustn't.

She said, "If you are too weak, I will write to the girl's family and end it. They will understand of course, as a union between you is simply preposterous. The very idea of the son of a baronet allying himself with the daughter of a whore is just beyond the—"

"Mrs. Dyngley," Henry cut her off. "That is enough. I have no desire to end my engagement with Miss Morton, and I do not want you taking any action or saying anything to ruin it. Do not write to your friends or speak to anyone with the assumption I am anything other than engaged. If you persist in pushing this, I will ask you to keep yourself to your rooms while our guests are here."

"My rooms? Confine myself away like an invalid? You're joking. This is my house."

"Then I will absent myself from your company until you see reason. Besides, you will miss seeing our new guests before the wedding."

"What guests?"

He glanced at the letter on the writing desk. "An old family friend, Miss Penwrith, is coming to visit. We have not seen each other for some years, and she wishes to renew the acquaintance."

"Does she? How old is she?"

"Twenty, I believe."

"Married?" Petunia asked.

"Not that I am aware," Henry said.

"And is she of good family and breeding?"

He raised an eyebrow.

"When is she due?" Petunia asked.

"In a week's time."

Petunia walked out, tapping a finger to her chin.

Henry penned Honoria a few lines of welcome, handed the sealed envelope to a servant to post, and took himself out to the stables for a ride. He needed to clear his head.

What sort of life was he introducing Poppy to, when not even her own future sister-in-law wanted her? At least Petunia would have Honoria to talk to about her troubles. But what Honoria wanted to discuss with him made him uncomfortable.

CHAPTER TWO

POPPY SHIFTED IN her seat, stiffening as the wooden pew creaked beneath her. Sunlight streamed through the glass windows of St Andrew's Church as her uncle finished his sermon. He glanced at Poppy, who was sat beside her aunt, rustled his papers, and said, "I announce the publication of the Banns of Marriage between Sergeant Henry Dyngley of Faulkbourne and Miss Poppy Morton of Hertford. If any of you know cause or just impediment why these two persons should not be joined together in Holy Matrimony, ye are to declare it. This is the second time of asking."

Poppy couldn't stop the smile on her face, and she beamed up at her uncle. Mr. Reginald Greene looked discomfited and looked around quickly. The service ended, he took his place at the entrance of the church to speak to parishioners.

Poppy's Aunt Rachel stood with the congregation and whispered to Poppy, "Where is Sergeant Dyngley?"

"I don't know."

"He was supposed to come, wasn't he? Why hasn't he come? Has he been delayed?" Aunt Rachel asked.

"I don't know, Aunt," Poppy said. She followed her aunt out of the pew and down the aisle. She didn't know where he was. But as she walked out of the church and felt the midday sun on her face, happiness, anticipation, and worry warred within her.

After a time in London at the townhouse she had inherited from her mother, Poppy had solved a mystery, become acquainted with her stepfamily, and become engaged, although not in that order. Almost overnight, with her mother's sudden passing, she had become an heiress, with a small but respectable fortune.

She had long had a friendship with the humble Constable Dyngley as they had solved one crime after another together, and their relationship had grown into a flirtation. Over time it had become romantic, until finally and against all odds, he had proposed marriage, and she had accepted.

She had closed up her townhouse in London for the time being and kept her maidservant, Miss Cooke, with her. She was now back in her relatives' home, the parsonage in Hertford. But she had seen Henry but once since her return, to sit beside her at church as her uncle read the banns for the first time, and then to take tea with them afterward.

After the first time it seemed like it would be a custom of his to come, but he hadn't. She felt the loss keenly, like a plaster that had been ripped off a cut. But her heart leapt when, a day later, they strolled up to the walkway that led to the parsonage to find him standing there with a bouquet of flowers.

"Miss Morton," he said with a smile and short bow.

"Sergeant Dyngley." She curtsied.

He pressed the bouquet into her hands. "These are for you. I'm sorry I didn't make it to church. Were the banns read?"

"Yes."

"One more time until we can marry," he said with a smile. "Do you like the flowers?"

She smelled them. They were wildflowers, which he had no doubt picked from a nearby field. "I love them."

"I thought you might. Hothouse flowers are very good, but I find the fresh ones from the countryside sweeter, somehow," he said.

She blinked at him. Gone was the serious expressions and talk of murder, he was practically spouting poetry to her ears. "Will you come inside?"

"I can't stay. I only came to call on you." He smiled at her.

"Is work keeping you very busy?"

"A bit. But that won't stop me from seeing you." He kissed her hand.

She blushed and looked away. He laughed and said, "It's a funny thing. Saturday, I received word from my club that the archives room had been broken into, and they wanted my help. I went to investigate and found that a number of the accounting ledgers had been messed about with, but only one actually abused, and a few pages torn out."

"Who would steal pages from an old accounting ledger?"

"These aren't just any ledgers. They are the ledgers from Whites, one of the most, well, let us say discerning gentleman's clubs in Town."

"You mean exclusive, don't you?" she asked.

He smiled. "Their accounting books are the things of legends. Just one falling into the hands of a newspaper would be devastating, for the people involved and the club's membership. But it was strange, just a few pages were missing, including some that concerned me."

"What did you do?"

"Well this was from years ago, back in 1765, so it would have been in my grandfather's or great-grandfather's time. I haven't found the pages, so I don't know the particulars."

"Was that the only thing disturbed?"

"Yes."

"And the members questioned?"

"Of course, but it's not the sort of thing a man can do in a straightforward manner. It requires delicacy. I learned nothing, but it is very odd. Very odd indeed." He patted her hand. "Anyhow, enough of that. Where will you order your wedding clothes? Here or in London?"

"I don't know. My aunt and Miss Cooke are very excited, so they have been sending out inquiries. We have received parcels of lace and ribbons…"

"Poppy. What would *you* like to wear?" he asked.

"Something special. Something nice." *To please you*, she thought.

His smile told her she had already pleased him. But her returning smile fell. "Sergeant…" she started.

"For heaven's sake, Poppy, we are engaged. Call me Henry. Or Dyngley, if you prefer."

"Henry, I…" she paused, unable to stop her smile at using his Christian name. "You are engaged to a clergyman's niece. Are you sure your family approves?"

His smile became forced. "Of course they do. John already likes you and Petunia will be happy to have a companion to keep her company while she's busy with little Arthur. My father will like you as soon as he sees you, I am sure of it."

But his eyes darted away then and Poppy felt he was lying.

"Even if it wasn't the case, it does not matter to me what they think, and it does not change how I feel about you." He raised her hand to his lips. "I mean it, Poppy."

She blushed.

"You do not think less of me for being a poor sergeant?" he asked.

"How could you think that?"

His brown eyes looked into hers and the warmth was genuine. They loved each other, she knew that.

He did not stay long, but left with a promise to send out invitations. A date was set. He encouraged her to bring her family to stay at his family's estate in the days before the wedding.

But as she watched him go and waved goodbye, she wondered how true his words really were. Petunia Dyngley was no friend of hers, and while her husband John was a friendly sort of fellow, if Henry's father was equally serious and had stern views on rank and social status, her engagement might be short-lived.

CHAPTER THREE

To Henry's surprise, wedding invitations had not yet been sent. Cornering his manservant, Geoffrey, a former acquitted felon, Henry found out a most unlikely source was behind the delay.

Geoffrey bowed his head. "Begging your pardon, Mr. Dyngley, but it were Sir Richard who told the servants not to send them."

"Why?"

Geoffrey shifted his weight on his feet, a sure sign he was uncomfortable. "I do not know."

Henry left Geoffrey in his chamber and strode to his father's study and knocked on the large wooden sliding doors.

"Come in," his father called.

Henry opened the sliding doors and walked in. The room rather reminded him of a tavern, with dark wooden paneling, comfortable cushioned chairs, and the day's sunlight streaming through the windows. His father sat facing the narrow windows, at a large, ornate wooden desk. Its surface lay covered with papers, a dirty inkstand and quill, with a large candelabra on the edge of the table.

Sir Richard Dyngley looked at him. "What is it?"

"I had hoped to send out wedding invitations today."

Sir Dyngley grunted.

"But my manservant tells me you put a stop to it. Why?" Henry asked.

"About this girl…" Sir Dyngley began. "What do we know of her? Is she of a good family?"

Henry swallowed. "She is the niece of a clergyman. She has a fine reputation."

"Petunia doesn't like her."

"Petunia doesn't like anyone," Henry quipped.

His father smiled. "She has given John an heir."

Henry's smile dropped. "Then the line is intact. You have nothing to worry about."

"Don't I? We have barely enough to live on. Our tenants are paying the same rents they were ten years ago, and now you want to get married to a girl with no income." At Henry's protest, he held up a hand. "Why would you propose to a girl with no money? We don't know the family. Why would you associate yourself with such low connections?"

Henry's hands began to clench, a sure sign he was stressed, and he forced them to stay straight and flat against his thighs. "I know her. I have known her for years."

"Petunia says she is a bluestocking."

Henry blinked. "Better that than an empty-headed fool."

"You know what I mean, Henry. What could she possibly bring to this marriage?"

Henry breathed in noisily. Did he tell his father of Poppy's parentage? Her dowry would help. The man might find out eventually, but would he refuse to give his blessing?

"Father, I…" Henry rubbed the back of his neck. "You see…"

"Ah, there you two are. So, are you excited to have the Blackwoods descend upon us?" John asked, entering the room.

"The Blackwoods?"

"Yes, Lord Blackwood and his family from Somerset. They're in Debrett's, Father," John said, crossing the room and pulling down a volume of the tome. He flipped a few pages and said, "Here. I'm sure it's them. That coat of arms looks familiar, doesn't it, Henry?"

Henry shot his brother a dark look.

"Son, why didn't you tell me this?" Sir Dyngley asked. "From what Petunia suggested, it seemed as though the girl was nobody at all. You could have told me this from the start and I would have agreed to the match."

Henry frowned. "I would hope that you would come to like Miss Morton for herself, not her lineage."

Sir Dyngley shrugged. "I do not care, as long as she is between sixteen and four and twenty, has an ounce of common sense, and comes from a good family. What did her father say her dowry would be?"

"Thousands," John interrupted Henry. "And she has her own townhouse in London, doesn't she?"

"She does," Henry admitted. "She inherited it from her mother."

"A wealthy woman?" Sir Dyngley asked.

"Of a sort. But Father, I need to tell you—"

"Come Henry, I must speak with you. This is essential," John said, taking Henry by the arm.

"John, does it need to be now?"

"Yes, absolutely. Immediately." John gripped his arm, pinching the thin sleeve of his jacket.

"Go on, you two have affairs to discuss, I am sure. I'll have a footman send out the invitations today, Henry, but mind you look them over first. I would not want to offend Lord Blackwood. Perhaps we might invite him here?"

Henry swallowed.

"An excellent idea, Father. That's just the thing. Henry will write to him, won't you?" John said.

Henry looked from his brother to his father. "Of course," he uttered.

"Come along now, I must talk with you about this matter..." John pulled him away and out of their father's study, closing the sliding doors behind them.

Standing before a billiard table, Henry turned on him. "What was that about? Why did you interrupt me? What was so important?"

"You daft fool. You're lucky I was there. Do you really think he would have given his blessing to your engagement if he knew your Poppy's background?"

Henry crossed his arms, mutinous. "He's going to find out anyway. Better now than later."

"You're wrong. You think he can't very well tell you no on your wedding day," John said. "But that's exactly what he can do."

Henry glared at him.

John shot Henry a hard look. "I am trying to help you. Think of Poppy."

"I am."

"Face it. You know as well as I do, he won't approve of her one bit." Seeing Henry's hands clench, John added, "I mean, she's pretty and smart and all. But her family, her illegitimacy, her mother. You know our father. Do you really expect him to welcome her with open arms?"

"I do not want any surprises on my wedding day. I would not want a surprise like this for him, and I think it would give rise to awkwardness and discomfort to invite the Blackwoods here, and Poppy's family, when he is unaware of the connection." Henry surveyed his brother and ran a hand through his dark hair. "I don't know what to do. I don't want to hide this from him."

"But you don't want him refusing you, either." John took a pool cue and began to line up a shot. "At least you're only the second son. I had it much worse. I hardly got a say in choosing my bride."

"Ahem."

The men turned to see Petunia, standing there, holding little baby Arthur in her arms. Her thin face looked pinched and her fine black hair looked limp as she blinked hard at John. "I was looking for you. He spoke."

"What did he say?" John asked.

Baby Arthur gurgled and dribbled on her arm. John's expression softened. "Petunia…"

"Never mind." She turned and left, her steps smacking against the hard wooden floor, and their ears.

"Damned woman. Moves like a cat," John said, missing his shot entirely. He tossed the pool stick onto the felt table and said, "Make your own decision whether to tell him, Henry. But don't say I didn't warn you. Once he knows, no amount of pleasing smiles will change his mind, no matter how smart or pretty Poppy is."

Henry watched John mutter and walk off after Petunia, leaving him alone. He picked up a yellow ball and rolled it across the table. What if his brother was right? What would he do if their father refused to sanction the marriage? And worse, what would he tell Poppy?

CHAPTER FOUR

AS THE DAYS passed, Poppy's sense of unease grew. She couldn't put her finger on why, but she knew something was wrong.

Poppy walked downstairs groggily after being helped into a plain purple day dress by Miss Cooke. She joined her aunt and uncle at breakfast, the former of which held up a letter. "We've received an invitation to your wedding."

"Really?" Poppy set down her knife and fork and reached for it.

Her uncle held it from her grasp, laying it aside. "Not at the table, Poppy. Wait until after you've eaten."

Poppy lowered her hand and glanced at her uncle, who looked at her solidly, munching on a slice of buttered toast. Since their engagement had been announced, he had offered his well wishes and muttered congratulations, but had said little beyond that. Poppy felt a curious wish to inquire as to his feelings.

"Are you looking forward to the wedding, Uncle?"

"I am looking forward to you being married and having a household of your own," he said, drinking tea.

She cocked her head at him.

"Where will you live? When the man lived in Hertford, he took a room in a stuffy little boarding house. But that is no place for a young woman, especially a married one. Have you discussed this with the constable?"

"He is a sergeant now. And no, we haven't. But we will."

"I recommend you do it before the wedding. That way if he cannot provide for you, at least we will know about it beforehand."

"Reginald?" Aunt Rachel said, pausing with her fork lifted halfway to her mouth. "What are you saying?"

"Nothing. Only that if he cannot provide for her, then we need to know. I just want her to be prepared and go into this marriage with open eyes. He is a lowly county sergeant, and cannot make much money."

"I have money," Poppy said.

"You have your mother's inheritance, and a small income from your father. Such an allowance usually ends when a girl marries, as all her assets become her husband's. It is the law."

Poppy swallowed. Her townhouse in London, her servants, the very clothes on her back… All of it would become Henry's. To do with as he pleased. She took a hasty drink of her tea and burnt her tongue.

"You would be wise to be circumspect, Poppy. Once you marry, everything reverts to your husband. Are you sure you want to be connected to such a man?" her uncle asked.

"Good heavens, Reginald. You make it sound as if Sergeant Dyngley is a vulgar fellow, when we know perfectly well he is nothing of the sort." Aunt Rachel gave Poppy an encouraging smile.

Poppy lowered her gaze. Considering her mother's choice of profession, if anything, she expected Dyngley's family to protest against her suitability as a bride.

As if reading her thoughts, her uncle asked, "And how has his family received the news of your engagement? Have they invited you to take tea with them? I have not received any invitations to dinner."

Poppy blushed. "I have not seen them since our time in London."

"Ah, yes."

Aunt Rachel shot her husband a dirty look and smiled at Poppy. "Never mind, I'm sure they're busy like we are with all the wedding preparations."

"And yet we haven't formally met them. You would think a family of such good standing would make an effort to become acquainted with the family of a new bride," he said.

With each phrase uttered, Poppy felt lower and lower. If her uncle was right, then she had reason to believe Henry's family had either overlooked the social courtesy of arranging a meeting between the families, or worse, didn't approve of her at all. And their silence was the mere proof of it.

"Reginald, really," Aunt Rachel said. "You'll frighten her."

"I mean to put her on her guard." He looked at Poppy, catching her eye. "if it was not for your fortune, do you truly think Sergeant Dyngley would have proposed?"

Poppy's mouth dropped open.

"Reginald," Aunt Rachel admonished.

"It is an honest question," he said.

"Yes, I do. We care for one another," Poppy said.

"A marriage needs more than affection to succeed," he told her.

"What is it you are looking for, Uncle? A guarantee? A written contract?"

"The articles of your marriage should have been drawn up as soon as he proposed. I am your guardian. Why have I not seen this? Why was I not consulted?" he asked.

Poppy realized, then: he was hurt. She had exchanged letters with her father and her solicitor, who were working on the articles, but her uncle had been left out of the correspondence entirely. She understood why he was in a mood.

"I'm sorry, Uncle. I'll write to my solicitor about this," she said.

"No, I will. You show a willful independence that is most unbecoming in a young woman. Have you even met this solicitor?"

"Yes." And she received money for her upkeep and expenses each month, but decided not to tell him so.

"Well, I am sure this will be sorted in no time. Now, Poppy, I have ordered some samples from London. I want your opinion on whether you prefer brocade or lace with your gown," her aunt said.

Poppy let her aunt's discussion of the fripperies smooth over the ruffled feelings and give a steady peace to the breakfast table. But Poppy felt unease in her gut.

After breakfast, she penned a letter to Henry, asking if their families might meet. She also wrote to Mr. Harding, her solicitor in London, and her father, asking about the articles of marriage.

SHE RECEIVED A swift reply, or rather swift for the nineteenth century, she thought. In the space of an afternoon she received two letters; one from Mr. Harding, with a copy of the articles for her interest; one from her father, summarizing the same and asking permission to visit, but nothing from Henry.

His absence filled her with trepidation. Why had he not called on her in weeks? Had he not received her letter? Had he had a change of heart toward their engagement and decided he had made her an offer against his better judgment? These thoughts plagued her mind as she spent the days reading, tending the vegetable patch, and feeding the chickens, or walking into town on errands for her aunt and uncle. No more was said of the Dyngleys at mealtimes, for which she was grateful. But it did not sit right with her, not at all.

The following week she received an invitation for the family to dine at the Dyngley estate in Essex. It was a simple note, with just a few lines on plain card, but its contents sent Aunt Rachel into a stir. She walked from room to room, reading aloud its words to whoever was present, regardless of their station or whether they already knew the news. "We are to dine with the Dyngleys. How wonderful. At Faulkbourne Manor. How very romantic."

Poppy exchanged a look with her uncle, who looked briefly amused, then raised his newspaper. She watched her uncle carefully. He had only sniffed and then made no mention of the invitation or the family.

When the day arrived, they took the family carriage, bought secondhand from Mr. Greene's patron, Lady Cameron, and took the road to Essex. Poppy would have offered one of her carriages, but at a stern look from her uncle, she kept quiet. She knew not why he seemed so stern or on the verge of snapping, but it was in his every movement and look. She wisely kept her mouth shut and listened to her aunt's chatter. But the journey was long as the carriage passed along the main road. They passed Bishop's Stortford, Rayne, Great Notley, then down to Cressing, Rivenhall, and finally Faulkbourne. By the time they arrived, it was very late.

They were received politely and with little ceremony. John Dyngley did the introductions, as Henry stood by, looking serious.

Poppy did her best to look demure and curtsied prettily to Sir Richard Dyngley, John, and Petunia, and offered Henry a warm smile. Her uncle stood stiffly, an expression that was matched by Petunia's, as she stood by a nursemaid who held the baby, Arthur. At the sight of him, Aunt Rachel gave up all semblance of formality and hurried toward the baby, cooing and smiling at the little one, who grabbed her nose.

Petunia's expression withered, but she bore it with good grace and began to make polite conversation with Aunt Rachel as little Arthur wiggled and smiled at her. Poppy met the serious gaze of Sir Dyngley, who came forward. "So this is the girl I've heard so much about. Miss Morton."

"Yes sir," she said.

"You look more serious than I expected. I thought all young women were light-hearted and cheery with their noses in a lady's magazine." His eyes were brown like Henry's, and his expression warm, if a trifle stern.

She smiled. "I do like magazines, but prefer poetry and novels."

"Then you will no doubt enjoy our library. Henry, perhaps you would like to show her the way." Sir Dyngley smiled and held out a hand for her to follow.

Poppy blinked. They would be unescorted. It was... questionable. But they were engaged, so... She nodded and said, "Thank you."

Henry turned and led the way, exiting the room.

Poppy followed Henry, not speaking a word as he led her down a corridor and up a flight of creaking wooden stairs that had turned dark brown with age. The steps groaned as they climbed the stairs, as Henry showed her into a large room that housed a respectable home library. The Dyngley library boasted floor-to-ceiling bookshelves, a climbing ladder, a sofa, a writing table, and comfortable chairs for any reader. Poppy instantly felt at home.

Without waiting for Henry to speak, she began looking at the books, trailing her fingers against the worn titles. Histories, dictionaries, journals, and private diaries, even old magazines. Some of the works were well used and looked a bit shabby, but she loved them on sight. There was a large atlas, rolled-up maps, and a display case in a corner of the room that held small curios and miniatures of the family. Even a marble bust of John Dyngley, which made Poppy smile.

"You like it here?" Henry asked.

"Oh yes. I love it."

"Poppy," he started.

"Yes?"

He approached her and stood a respectful distance away. He did not meet her eyes. "I need to tell you something. About my past."

She waited for him to continue.

"You see—"

They were interrupted by the polite knock of a servant. Henry turned around. "Yes, Geoffrey?"

"It's time for dinner," his valet said.

"Oh. Very well." Henry followed him out of the library, not waiting for Poppy.

She leaned against the wall of books, wondering. What had gotten into him? Where had all this stifled formality come from? Why was he being so polite, so oddly formal? They were engaged and he hadn't even kissed her hello. She rather found she missed the attention.

With a little shrug, she set her shoulders and followed the men down to dinner.

The families marched into the dining room in order of precedence, with Sir Richard leading the way, followed by Petunia and John, Mr. and Mrs. Greene, and Poppy and Henry. They were attended by servants, one of whom helped Poppy into her seat and pushed it close to the table for her. The table was already set with multiple plates and a bowl on each setting, with knives and forks. The candlelight offered a warm, golden glow to the table, but Poppy felt slightly discomfited. Here was the first meeting of their two families, and yet something was not right. She couldn't put her finger on it. Petunia's expression was glacial, John's was overly bright, and Sir Dyngley's cheeks were already flushed from wine.

Footmen soon entered the room, bearing a tureen of soup and a ladle. Poppy helped herself to fresh pea soup, admiring the rich green color.

"What delicious soup," Aunt Rachel said. "We have this at home sometimes."

Petunia shot her a glare.

Poppy added, "Yes, it is very good."

"You must have better in the parsonage in Hertford," Sir Dyngley said.

"No, not at all," Uncle Reginald said, earning a look of confusion from their host.

It pleased Poppy to no end to see that Petunia soon got green in her teeth.

As the soup was cleared away and a course of venison that John called "a bit of stag's flesh" was served, Sir Dyngley gestured for wine to be poured and he raised his glass. "A toast, to the union of our two families."

The others raised their glasses, Aunt Rachel and John more readily than the others. "Hear, hear," John said.

There was a knock at the front door of the manor.

"Good heavens, who could that be? At this hour?" Aunt Rachel asked.

"Indeed. I wonder who would come calling now when we are at dinner. Most inconvenient," Petunia said.

A servant went to the doors, and as the guests cut into their venison, a woman's voice could be heard. "No, let me in. The family is expecting me."

Poppy saw Henry's face turn pale. "Sergeant?"

Henry gave her a pained smile, and looked at John.

"Who could that be?" Sir Dyngley asked.

In walked a young woman of average height, who surveyed them all with a smile. "Hello. Oh, my goodness, I've disturbed your dinner."

"Who are you?" Petunia asked.

"Honoria Penwrith." She flashed Petunia a wide smile. "I'm Henry's fiancée."

CHAPTER FIVE

Poppy stared. Who was this foul creature? The strange woman looked about twenty and stood with soft curled locks that hung around a heart-shaped face. Her skin bore the traces of an old pox and her eyes were bright with good cheer. Her cheeks were flushed after her travels, and she wore a simple, hooded cloak over a light pink dress.

"Is this some kind of joke?" Uncle Reginald asked her.

"It's no joke. I'm his fiancée. Just ask him, he'll tell you," Honoria said.

Everyone looked at Henry, who tugged at his white cravat.

"Go on, Henry, tell them. We are engaged. To be married," Honoria said brightly.

Poppy said, "Henry?"

Henry stood and bowed. "Honoria."

"You know this woman?" Uncle Reginald asked.

"Yes. We are—"

"Childhood sweethearts," Honoria finished.

Petunia laughed aloud, shocking them all. She clapped a hand to her mouth and snickered. "Do excuse me."

"Honoria, perhaps you might—" Henry started.

Sir Dyngley rose from his chair. "Little Honoria Penwrith, all grown up. My word, it's good to see you. How is your family, your father? I have not heard from him for some time."

Miss Penwrith glanced down at her lap. "My father has been dead these past five years. A fever took him. It has been a bit lonely without him, but we make do." Honoria smiled up at him.

"I am sorry for your loss," Sir Dyngley said, "I had no idea."

Honoria waved a hand. "It was a small funeral. And you? You are all in good health?"

"We are all very well. But you've traveled all this way." Sir Dyngley turned to one of the footmen. "Prepare a room for Miss Penwrith and bring her a tray. She'll be staying with us a while."

The footman led Honoria away. Once they had left, Henry sat back down in his seat and rose again, as his father rested his hands on the back of his chair. "Well, I cannot say how odd it is that Henry's old childhood friend has come, but do not let it disturb your meal. Please, eat." He took a seat.

"But what of what the girl said?" Aunt Rachel asked.

"I am sure we will get to the bottom of it soon enough. She has travelled a long way." Sir Dyngley launched into an explanation of how the Penwriths and Dyngleys were good family friends, but after ten years or so the Penwriths had moved away.

"And was Miss Penwrith a particularly good friend of Henry's?" Petunia asked, the devil on her tongue.

"Oh yes, they were inseparable. Very good friends," Sir Dyngley said.

"I see," Petunia replied, eyeing Poppy over her venison.

Poppy shot her a look and tried to focus on her meal, but her hands trembled. Finally, she gave up trying to eat altogether and sat with her hands folded in her lap.

Two courses later, the group adjourned to a drawing room, which was a pretty sort of parlor decorated with a hodgepodge of furniture over the course of many years. Poppy felt practically faint as she followed the others through, taking a seat on the nearest sofa, and sinking into the well worn cushion. She did not look at Henry, for she did not want to know. Instead, her gaze followed Sir Dyngley and Petunia, who took a seat in a chair across from her.

Poppy glanced at her and mused how once upon a time, she would have liked to have earned Petunia's attention, rather than be the subject of her scrutiny. Now she could feel Petunia's eyes on her, watching. Was she hoping Poppy would cry, fret, tear her hair, or wring her hands? Poppy refused to give her the satisfaction. Instead, she sat quietly, primly with her back straight, her hands clasped in her lap. She could have been sculpted from ice, she thought.

Poppy's aunt patted her knee and said loudly, "Well I want to know who this young lady is. I understand she is a friend of the family, but Poppy and Sergeant Dyngley are engaged. Why is she calling herself his fiancée?"

Poppy turned red. Trust her aunt to say what she was thinking, but without any thought to social graces.

Petunia smirked as Miss Penwrith walked back into the room. She stood of an average height, with curly brown hair that needed no hair tongs or curling wrappers. Her brown hair was artfully swept up around her head and she beamed at each of them, but most of all at Henry, who looked pained to see her. She wore a pink evening dress with white lace trim around the sleeves and hem, with an old silver locket around her neck. With a rosy blush to her cheeks, now, she was the picture of prettiness. Poppy disliked her on sight.

Feeling her gaze, Miss Penwrith approached Poppy and curtsied, taking in her tall height, slim waist and expensive evening dress, a pale blue with black sheer sarcenet fabric over the blue. The effect was fetching and Poppy had hoped it would measure up against the Dyngleys' expectations and wealth. But now she didn't care. Instead, she worried. Who was this woman and why had she entered their lives now?

Miss Penwrith said, "I'm Honoria Penwrith."

"Poppy Morton," Poppy said with a small curtsy.

"And how do you know the family?"

Poppy swallowed. "Sergeant Dyngley and I are—"

"Good friends." Petunia interrupted, taking Miss Penwrith's

hand and shaking it. "Petunia Dyngley. I'm so glad to meet you."

Poppy stepped back. Miss Penwrith was delighted and shook Petunia's hand in return. "Likewise. I'm so sorry to have disturbed your dinner, but I travelled all that way and wanted to see the family."

"Not to worry, we weren't talking about anything particularly important. Come and tell me about your journey." Petunia took Miss Penwrith by the arm and led her to two available seats.

Poppy watched them and felt a dull feeling settle in the pit of her stomach. She looked at Henry, who gazed at the new arrival as though she were a problem he needed to solve. He didn't notice Poppy at all.

Poppy felt like a shy little girl, too nervous to speak up. She thought about stealing away like a thief in the night, and simply climbing into her uncle's carriage to start the long journey home. Henry and Honoria would marry, and she would remain a spinster. Then she gave herself a mental shake. They were engaged, the banns had been read twice already, and she loved him too much to lose him now. What sort of a marriage partner would she be if she simply backed away from the first pretty woman who wanted to claim him? She stood, and smoothing down her dress, approached Miss Penwrith and Petunia.

At her standing there, Petunia looked sour and ready to ignore her. But Poppy spoke up. "Excuse me, Miss Penwrith?"

Miss Penwrith turned and looked up at her. "Yes? My goodness, you are tall. I bet you can reach everything."

Poppy said, "Yes. I wonder if we might speak a moment."

"Anything you say to her can be said in my presence," Petunia said, as if she were Queen Charlotte herself.

"Very well. Miss Penwrith, I think there's been some mistake. You see, I am engaged to Sergeant Dyngley."

Miss Penwrith blinked. "Pardon?"

Poppy looked at her. The young woman was bubbly and cheerful, but also seemed rather tired from her journey. "You see—"

"I'm sorry, but I don't think I heard you correctly. I thought you said that you were engaged to Henry, which I know cannot be true. We have an understanding." Miss Penwrith glared at Poppy with dislike.

"The marriage banns have been read, twice," Poppy said.

"As if that matters. You're not married. I don't know who you think you are, but you are demeaning yourself by picking a fight with me." She turned to Petunia. "What sort of girls are you allowing in this manor? When Mrs. Dyngley was alive, she never would have let in such riffraff."

Petunia's mouth dropped open.

"Excuse me?" Aunt Rachel said, her voice cutting through the noise. "What did you just say to my niece?"

Henry and John stepped forward and separated the women. John put a hand on Poppy's arm and lightly pulled her away, while Henry stood by Miss Penwrith. "Miss Penwrith, please," Henry said.

"No, Henry. I won't believe this girl. Who is she anyway?"

"She is nothing to me, Miss Penwrith," Petunia said.

"Oh lord," John muttered beneath his breath, "Petunia…"

"She is my fiancée," Henry said.

Miss Penwrith dropped his arm. "What?"

He stood there simply, and looked at Poppy. His expression was pained, but his eyes sought hers. She smiled at him, and knew then that he was still true to her.

"No. I cannot believe this. No." Miss Penwrith backed away. "This can't be true."

"It is," he said. "And what's more, I'll thank you to stop being rude to her. Poppy?"

Miss Penwrith balked at his tone.

Poppy walked to his side. Henry met her eyes. "I am sorry for this… confusion. Miss Penwrith is an old family friend."

Miss Penwrith looked at Poppy as if she were some sort of snake. Petunia frowned and crossed her arms beneath her chest.

"But I… Henry, you promised," Miss Penwrith said.

"What?"

"You did. Do you not remember?" Miss Penwrith blinked back tears.

"Miss Penwrith, come with me. We have much to discuss," Petunia said, leading her away.

"I don't understand. He promised," Miss Penwrith said. "He invited me here. I've come here to honor the agreement…"

As the pair left, Poppy let out a small sigh of relief, but to her amusement, so did Henry and John, most audibly so.

John sank into the nearest chair and then rose to pour himself a drink. "Grand. Now what are we going to do?"

"I don't understand. Sergeant, the girl says you promised her? What is she talking about?" Uncle Reginald asked, his face stern.

Henry ran a hand along the back of his neck. "We knew each other years ago. As children, our families were very close. I think it was always assumed that the connection would continue, but her family moved away and we did not keep the correspondence. I haven't spoken to Miss Penwrith in years, not until she wrote me recently, wishing to pay a visit." He looked at Poppy. "And I am not aware of any promise she speaks of. As far as I am concerned, I am already engaged to Miss Morton, and have no plans to change that."

Poppy felt a blush come to her cheeks. He still cared for her. His feelings hadn't changed.

Aunt Rachel's face lit up in a smile. "Oh, Sergeant, you do know just what to say."

"Why has Miss Penwrith come?" Uncle Reginald asked.

"She wrote to me, asking to visit. I didn't see the harm in extending the invitation, particularly as I had happy news to share. But I did not foresee this." Henry turned to Poppy. "Excuse me."

He left the room, leaving Poppy, her aunt, and uncle with John. "Dashed awful business this, Miss Penwrith turning up like this. No excuse, really. Drink?"

"Yes," Uncle Reginald said.

"Grand." John poured a drink for himself and Uncle Reginald, and drank.

"What do you know of this girl?" Aunt Rachel asked.

"Miss Penwrith? She's all right. Good decent girl, always had a soft spot for Henry. Fancied him like mad." Seeing Poppy, he added, "But that was all in the past. Whatever hopes or expectations she might have had as a young girl, it's not real. Fantastical. And it's not like our parents signed an agreement or anything. You've nothing to worry about."

She smiled at him, and it was with some relief that she joined her aunt and uncle in their carriage and set for home. But as the carriage pulled away that evening, she could not shake the feeling they were being watched. A sense of malevolence sent chills down her spine, and despite the late hour, she had trouble falling asleep during the long journey back.

CHAPTER SIX

HENRY STOOD BY the dark windows looking out into the night. He couldn't see the fleeting carriage of the Greenes without the moonlight overhead, and that was soon overshadowed by clouds.

At that moment he was glad to be rid of Poppy's family. It wasn't that he did not like them; he had a lot of respect for them. But this was family business, and they were not yet family. He did not like Miss Penwrith's interruption of their dinner, nor did he approve of her treatment of Poppy, or her presumption. Whatever misplaced affection or promise she thought she had, it needed to be corrected, and fast.

Why had Miss Penwrith had to arrive then, at that time? Just when their families were meeting for the first time. It was all so tense, and then Petunia was being her usual dislikeable self.

As if sensing his thoughts, his sister-in-law's voice came from the doorway of the library. "Lord, what an evening. I've never been so glad to see people go."

"Are you surprised? I would have left too if I'd been so rudely treated."

"What are you insinuating?" she asked, coming up to him.

He turned to her. "Do you have to be so unkind to her?"

"I am not unkind. I am the soul of friendliness," she declared.

He tried not to laugh. "Your behavior tonight would suggest

otherwise."

She sniffed.

"Why do you dislike her? Miss Morton is a good girl from a decent family."

"Hah!"

He raised an eyebrow.

She sighed. "The girl is clever and sweet-tempered enough, but she has an impertinent willfulness and desire for independence that I do not like. You realize that any girl you marry will live here, with us. She will be my companion for years, and Miss Morton is…"

"What?"

"She's poor. She has no taste—"

"I disagree, but that can be learned."

"She has only recently come into a fortune, from her mother who was of a notorious reputation, and her father, I think, only means to assist her in society out of some misplaced guilt and sense of duty toward her dead mother. How on earth could you possibly think I would welcome such a girl with open arms into this home? Into my company?"

He gazed at his sister-in-law. Petunia was a tall, thin, hawk-nosed woman with a pinched expression, dark eyes, and jet-black hair that shone in the light. Her portrait was of a stunning beauty, but her tongue and wit were sharper than any dagger.

Did he want to subject Poppy to her company? Would they always be dueling with words at dinner, or worse, would she lose all assuredness in herself and become a weak-willed sop for Petunia to torment? He might as well see her into an early grave. No, he wouldn't wish Petunia on anyone. She sometimes showed evidence of a kind heart, but that was a rarity.

"I believe she will make me happy. We love each other. Can you not hold your tongue and be happy for us?" he asked.

She stiffened. "You really care for this girl?"

"A thousand times, yes."

Her shoulders slumped. "But what of Miss Penwrith? She

seems to be under the impression that you two are betrothed…"

"I will handle Miss Penwrith. I'll speak to her in the morning. She needs to understand that any romantic fancy she had when we were children does not hold any sort of meaning now. At least not for me."

Petunia looked at him shrewdly. "Henry, I do not think she will give up as easily as that." She crossed her arms beneath her small chest. "I do believe she will push this. What will you do if she does not back down? If she were to refuse?"

"I will ask her to leave. She will have outstayed her welcome."

"And you would kick her out into the night. And you call me cold, Henry." She turned and walked away in a swirl of skirts. She paused in the doorway and said, "Just be careful. You are an honest man, but I do believe you to be a novice when it comes to matters of the heart."

He returned to looking out the window into the night. How was Poppy doing?

THE NEXT DAY he woke up late, his sheets in a tangle. He'd had a sleepless night, spending hours pacing, attempting to read and finally sitting in his dressing gown in his room with a book by the fire in the hearth. He had eventually crawled into bed as the dawn's early rays began to glow outside of his window.

By the time Geoffrey came in to rouse him, he had maybe had about four hours of sleep, if that. He looked up groggily and washed his face from a white china washbasin on a bedside table. He dried his face with a small hand towel and dressed, pausing only to straighten his cravat in the tall mirror that stood by. He disapproved of having a valet dress a man, but knew that some members of genteel families enjoyed the practice.

He marched downstairs and was about to join the family in the dining room, only to be met by Miss Penwrith at the door.

"Oh, Henry. Good morning." She glanced at this throat and smiled.

"What?"

"Your cravat... Here, let me." She reached for it and began straightening it.

"It's already straight."

"No, it wasn't. Now it is." She smiled to herself, satisfied, and sat down to breakfast.

He frowned and took a seat beside her.

"Good morning Henry, Miss Penwrith. How nice you look," Petunia said, setting down her cup of tea. "You make quite a domestic picture, sat side by side."

Miss Penwrith smiled happily as Henry shot Petunia a level look.

"I wonder, has this manor always belonged to the family?" Miss Penwrith asked.

Sir Dyngley helped himself to a slice of toast and spread marmalade on it. "Yes. Why do you ask?"

"No reason. It is so old, I remember running around the halls as a child." She smiled sweetly at him.

"Yes, it has always belonged to our family. My grandfather won the estate in a card game, if you can believe it." Sir Dyngley winked.

"Oh my. Was he very wild?" Miss Penwrith asked.

"More like wicked. Albus Dyngley III was a rascal, a rake, a libertine and an all-around gambler. He loved women, cards and a good bet. Or at least that's how the story goes."

"What happened to him?" Petunia asked.

Sir Dyngley scratched his head. "As far as I know, he recognized a good winning when he got one. When he won the manor from some chap named Faulkbourne, he left London and settled here, into the life of a country squire. But I wouldn't go wandering the halls too much, my dear. They are likely in poor condition."

"Like much of this place," John said.

Sir Dyngley raised an eyebrow at John, and said, "Much of the manor has been left alone and needs repair. That is why my wife and I had such hopes for my sons." He looked at Henry.

"Yes, my parents had high hopes for me as well," Miss Penwrith said with a sad smile.

"All this talk is giving me indigestion. Perhaps we might leave such subjects until after breakfast," Petunia said, wiping her mouth with a cloth napkin.

"Quite right. Apologies, Mrs. Dyngley," Sir Dyngley said with an affectionate smile.

After the meal, they gathered in the large drafty sitting room to the left of the foyer. Once they were sat comfortably, Sir Dyngley leaned back in a tall wingback chair and said, "Do tell us, Miss Penwrith, why you have come. You are, of course, always welcome here. But it was rather a surprise."

"Yes, so I understand." She bowed her head and twisted a fold of her yellow skirt in her hands. "You see, my father died some time ago, and he left my mother and me very little to live on. She took on work where she could, but her health has suffered as we have had to move into lodgings which are less suited to her temperament." She met Henry's eyes. "We both suffered, in our way. Without him to look after us, my mother took on work as a servant and myself as a seamstress." She glanced down at her hands, which Henry noted were rough and worn.

"But my dear, why did you not write and tell us of your misfortune? We would have welcomed you here to stay with us until you got back on your feet," Sir Dyngley said.

Miss Penwrith shook her head. "My mother wouldn't hear of it. Over time due to her illness, her looks faded and she became a recluse from society. She would not have wanted to burden you with our little troubles."

"But what is that when there are friends of ours in need?" Henry asked.

"I agree. We wouldn't care for ceremony, we would just want to help," John added.

"You are all too kind. But no, I was busy looking after my mama and trying to support us."

"Why have you come, now?" Henry asked.

Miss Penwrith looked at him. "It is a matter of some delicacy," she said, her hand going to the silver locket around her neck. "My mother died a few weeks ago."

"Oh good lord," Petunia said, a hand darting to her mouth.

"She died of her sickness, a fever, and it took most of our savings to pay for the funeral. She had little more than a pauper's grave, no ceremony." Miss Penwrith swallowed, heat rushing to her cheeks.

"You poor thing," Petunia said.

"Her last words to me were that I might remind you of our promise, that we made together so many years ago. It was her final wish. I know I have nothing to offer, I have no money or connections. I used the last of my money to make the journey here, but I have nowhere to go. And so I am here, like a poor pauper, begging you all to take me in."

"Good lord," Petunia muttered.

"Indeed, you have suffered. You may stay here as long as you like," Sir Dyngley said.

"But what do you mean, about a promise?" John asked.

Henry gripped the wooden seat of his chair.

"Yes, what did your mother mean?" Petunia asked.

Miss Penwrith only had eyes for Henry. "You see, when we were children, I'm sure you remember, but we were inseparable. Close."

"We were good friends," Henry said.

"More than that. We fell in love."

"What?" Henry said.

"It's true. You told me yourself," Miss Penwrith said.

"I did?"

"He did?" Sir Dyngley repeated, glancing at Henry. "Son, what is this?"

"I hardly know."

"You do, Henry, don't you remember? When we were twelve, you said you loved me, and you made me a promise,"

Miss Penwrith said.

Henry paled.

"I can see you remember, even if you wish you didn't. It's true. You promised me that if we were both still unwed and single in our twenties, then you would marry me." She swallowed. "I turned twenty last May, and it was my mother's dying wish that we would end up together."

The color drained from Henry's face. If he hadn't been sitting, he would have sat down.

"Henry, you remember, don't you? That you promised to marry me? I'm here to take you up on your promise," Miss Penwrith said.

Henry stared at her.

John whistled, earning everyone's attention. "Sorry, it's just…" He snorted. "I thought I was the rake of the family."

"John," Petunia said with a frown.

"Sorry, love," he said.

"So that's why you've come," Sir Dyngley said.

"Miss Penwrith," Henry started.

"It was my mother's dying wish," Miss Penwrith said. "I have suffered such hardship. I came here with nowhere else to go. Won't you at least consider me? You loved me once. I know you did."

"Miss Penwrith, I'm already engaged," Henry said.

Miss Penwrith sniffed and tossed her head, a fine head of soft brown curls. It reminded Henry of a willful horse. "I know and I don't care. What is that girl to me? She has a pretty dress, but no manners and her family looks poor. Our families have been close for decades. Why would you turn your head against tradition, and a promise you made to me? Have you no honor?"

Henry balked as if she had slapped him. "Miss Penwrith, whatever affection I had for you years ago was… It was nothing more than an idle fancy. I had no idea what I was saying."

Miss Penwrith looked at him, no longer trying to hold back the tears in her eyes. She blinked and said, "I don't believe you.

The Henry Dyngley I know would not have said such things in haste, or by mistake. He is honorable and without fault."

Petunia snorted. "You clearly do not know him very well to think that." Henry looked at her and she shrugged. "I have yet to meet a man without fault."

Henry turned back to Miss Penwrith. "I am sorry to hurt you, but..."

"You don't understand. For weeks, as my mother's health failed her, she became fixated on this idea of us marrying. She talked of little else, until she made me promise, once she had gone, that I would see you and remind you of your promise."

"Well, you have done that," Henry said.

"Henry, don't be so callous," Petunia said. "The poor girl has come all this way with nothing more than a hope of seeing you. Do not be so unkind."

"That is not the Dyngley way," Sir Dyngley said.

"What would you have me do? I am already engaged. We cannot marry," Henry said.

"Break off whatever understanding you have with this other girl. She looked poor, she'll understand. She should know better than to aim so high as this family," Miss Penwrith said, with an air of aloofness.

Petunia looked upon her with approval, whereas Henry shook his head. "No. I am engaged to Miss Morton, and that is the end of it. I am sorry you came all this way for nothing, Miss Penwrith, but nothing will change my mind."

"Then allow me to prove you wrong, Henry. At least allow me that chance," Miss Penwrith said.

"To do what?"

"Prove to you that we belong together. We are meant to be together, Henry, trust me. Our parents saw it. Let me stay and show you that."

"No. Stay as long as you please, but do not interfere with my engagement."

"You owe me, Henry," Miss Penwrith told him.

"I don't. Whatever I promised was a childish fancy. I do not love you, Miss Penwrith. I care for you as a sister, nothing more."

Miss Penwrith batted away tears and spoke with confidence. "You'll see. You may not believe it with your head, but you know in your heart it's true. I'll prove it to you, Henry. I'll show you."

"And I'll help you," Petunia said.

Henry stared at Petunia in dismay.

CHAPTER SEVEN

THE NEXT DAY was Saturday, which for Poppy meant running errands, paying calls to the sick and delivering parcels of food to the poor, and tending to the garden. The wooden fence adjoining the back garden was old and had rotted, and needed mending. Poppy had had Miss Cooke purchase some wooden posts, nails, and a hammer, and that morning had begun digging out the rotted posts one by one and hammering them in. It wasn't an easy business, and in the summer heat, made for sweaty work.

Poppy was hammering a post into the ground as her uncle whistled a jaunty tune. He was up on the roof of the parsonage, looking at the shingles. She hummed tunelessly along until her uncle yelled and fell.

She whirled around in an instant. "Uncle!"

He grimaced in pain and held his left leg, where a piece of white bone peeked from his torn and bloody leg.

"Oh my god," she breathed. "Wait here."

Poppy got Miss Cooke, Betsy, and her aunt. They built a makeshift stretcher and gently as they could, moved her uncle inside to rest on the sofa in the sitting room. He groaned and turned pale.

In minutes, Poppy had saddled their horse and rode to town, returning with the doctor. A short time later he had cleaned the wound, giving her uncle a hard knot of wood to bite into. Her uncle fainted, and Aunt Rachel fretted with worry.

"Leave it for now. I need to work. He'll wake soon and I'll give him some medicine to dull the pain." The doctor reset the bone, fixed a splint to his leg and tied it tightly with cloth wrappings so Uncle Reginald could not move it. "There. He will need to rest."

"For how long, Doctor?"

"Weeks. A broken leg is no small thing. Complete bedrest for a month, then we'll see about giving him crutches to help him walk." He gave them all a serious look. "I warn you, do not push Mr. Greene back into physical activity too soon. He needs rest. When I attended him the bone was poking out of his skin. I have seen more than one healthy man succumb to infection and disease through such an ordinary ailment as a broken bone, so do not take this lightly."

Aunt Rachel's hand darted to her mouth. "But Doctor, what about church services?"

"He should abstain for now. Is there someone else who can do them?" the doctor asked.

"Yes, there is. A Mr. Ingleby in Waterford," Aunt Rachel asked.

"Better send him a message."

"Oh, Doctor, what about officiating weddings?" Miss Cooke glanced at Poppy.

"He won't be doing any officiating for at least six to eight weeks. Not until he's healed."

Poppy's expression fell. Her wedding was to be soon. Where would she be without her uncle to preside over it? It was to be his great part in the ceremony. Her shoulders slumped, then she straightened. She felt selfish and ungrateful. Her uncle had fallen off a roof, he could have died, and yet here she was thinking about her wedding. She gave herself a little mental shake to be more thoughtful of others.

They took more instructions from the doctor and made lists

of medicines to prepare from home to care for him, but judging from her uncle's pallor and sweaty head, he wasn't going anywhere, and most certainly would not be present for her wedding.

THAT SATURDAY THERE was a dance, and after some time looking after her uncle, Poppy was excited. Mr. Ingleby had readily agreed to conduct services for him and spent time working on sermons at her uncle's instruction. Their little sitting room had become a makeshift bedroom and study for her uncle, and Poppy could use the break.

She had received a note from Henry saying the Dyngleys would attend the dance, and hoped she would too. She decided to wear one of her pretty summer dresses, a light and airy pink muslin dress with round cap sleeves and a white wide embroidered ribbon around her high waist. She matched it with a pair of mid-length pink gloves and satin pink dancing shoes. Miss Cooke arranged her hair in a comely style, mostly coiled atop her head aside from a single thick lock of hair she curled to hang by her shoulder. The effect was becoming, or so she hoped. She wanted to look her best, and so even let Miss Cooke dab a bit of rouge on her lips and cheeks, and a touch of kohl to her eyelids.

Then Poppy realized, this was a simple country dance. It wasn't a ball, or a private assembly. She was dressing as if she were a debutante back in London, where even when going out on a simple errand, people dressed well.

Miss Cooke was just tying a necklace to her neck, when Poppy said, "Stop."

"Miss?"

"I forget we're not in London. The people at this dance will be more casually dressed, and not in anything so fine as this." She touched the delicate folds of her soft faded pink dress, feeling the light layers of muslin.

Self-doubt plagued her thoughts. She was nothing but the niece of a country clergyman, and the illegitimate daughter of a lord and his mistress. Who was she to have pretensions and dress in finery, when her own background was so shocking?

"You forget yourself, Miss, if you don't mind me saying," Miss Cooke said.

Poppy looked at her maid in the reflection of her small round looking-glass. "These people know me as my uncle's niece. If I show up dressed in finery, they will think I'm showing airs above my station. Or that my aunt and uncle are starving themselves in order to afford me nice clothes and jewelry."

"They do not know of your mother?"

"They believed, as I once did, that she died in childbirth. Any word of my father has long since faded from their memory. As far as anyone knows, I am my aunt and uncle's ward, and they have been kind enough to raise me."

"Poppy, stop feeling sorry for yourself." Aunt Rachel stood at the entrance to her room. "Miss Cook, I will finish getting Poppy ready." She stood by as Miss Cooke curtsied and left the bed-chamber. Aunt Rachel entered and sat on the edge of Poppy's bed, her hands resting on the plain patterned coverlet. "For far too long, your uncle and I have cared about what other people think. But that is over now. We only care about you. And as far as I'm concerned, you wear what you like. People can think whatever they please."

Poppy turned to face her. "But, Aunt, it's a country dance. Aren't I overdressed?"

Her aunt took in the sight of her hair, her makeup, her pretty dress, down to her shoes. "Remove the gloves, perhaps, and the ribbon from your hair, if you are so desirous of not attracting comment. But, Poppy, I think you should not seek to hide yourself. Your mother never did so and she was very popular."

Poppy lowered her head at this. It was true. The few moments she had had to know her mother, the older woman had possessed an independent self-awareness, a comfort with herself and who she was, and as a result moved with a grace that was statuesque and serene. Poppy envied her mother's self-possession and rather wished she could have some of her self-confidence. If she were to show up at the local dance in her finery, would the townspeople not laugh? Or worse, wonder if she was making her relatives starve and go without in order to dress well?

Poppy exhaled and looked down at her dress.

"There is nothing wrong with looking pretty, Poppy," her aunt said. "And besides, your mother left you a small fortune. She would want you to enjoy it."

"But Aunt…"

"No. You have had enough trials lately. Take this opportunity and enjoy it, for once you are married, there may be rather fewer chances to attend country dances."

"What do you mean?"

"Well, we know Sergeant Dyngley to be a good, honest sort of man. But he always seems so serious. He doesn't know how to enjoy himself, I think. He's always off chasing down a criminal or solving a crime, and it makes me wonder if you aren't allying yourself with a man whom you'll be forever waiting for, instead of one who will want to wait for you."

Poppy blinked. "I wouldn't want him to wait for me. I hate being late to engagements."

"That's not what I mean. Will he put you and your happiness above his profession? Or will he leave you to attend balls and assemblies alone while he is off working?"

"I don't know. But, I daresay catching a criminal is more important."

"You say that now, but when you have avoided going to multiple social engagements, you might see things differently. Are you sure you care for him? Enough to marry him?"

"Yes."

"His family is titled, but that horrible woman, Mrs. Dyngley. You're liable to see her every day. And what was that nonsense about Miss Penwrith, calling him her fiancé?" Aunt Rachel asked.

"I don't know. An honest mistake, I think."

"An honest man does not go around promising marriage to

multiple young ladies," Aunt Rachel said.

"Aunt?"

"I know, you love him. I just want you to be aware of the realities of the match. Who's to say he isn't some young buck who likes to fall in love, and conveniently disregards the girls he's left heartbroken?"

"Dyngley isn't like that. He wouldn't."

Aunt Rachel surveyed her niece. "I'm sure you are right. I just want you to be certain before you go promising yourself away to him and his family."

"I'm certain, Aunt."

"Very well. In that case, you don't need to worry about what anyone says or thinks. Just enjoy yourself at the dance. I have no doubt that any number of men will have wished they had proposed to you before the sergeant."

Poppy smiled. She wasn't so sure.

That night at the dance it was like any other evening in town. A simple country dance, with the same ordinary faces Poppy had grown up with and known all her life. Except that she was older, tall like her mother, and as she gazed around the room, eyeing the dancing couples, she rather wished she were shorter, or at least that she might not tower over all the men present.

To be fair, there were a few taller gentlemen there, but many more who were not, and some even stood almost a foot shorter than her.

"I can guess what you are thinking," a voice said.

Poppy turned around. There stood a man she had never met before in her life, and she felt the poorer for it.

It was a gentleman, of near or around her age and height, with light brown hair that held a glint of auburn, fair skin and a smile to his round face. His hair was coiffed with care and he wore a light gray jacket, a waistcoat embroidered with silver thread, and dark breeches, over white knee socks and smart black dancing shoes. His light blue eyes caught the light and sparkled, and his grin made her want to laugh.

"I'm sorry?" she said.

"I know what you're thinking."

"Is that so?"

"Yes. You are looking out at all these couples and thinking to yourself, good god! It's not quite the assembly at St James's, is it?"

Poppy smiled. "I have never been."

"Haven't you? I could have sworn I'd seen you there. And I always remember a pretty face."

Poppy blushed in spite of herself. "Have we met?"

"No, but I'm hoping to rectify that. Would you do me the honor?" He held out a hand.

Poppy swallowed. She didn't even know his name. But why not? She accepted his hand and allowed him to lead her into the next set.

As an ordinary country dance began, she soon became aware that they were attracting some attention, or at least he was. "Do you always ask girls you don't know to dance?"

"Do you always say yes?" he asked.

She snorted. He'd caught her there. "Sometimes. If the company is pleasant."

His grin widened. "And how are you finding it so far?"

"Polite enough," she said as he clasped her hand, turned her, and let go. "But I will not be swayed by your charms, however polite."

His face lit up. "What a delight. Tell me your name, so I might find out who I am charming."

"But we have not been introduced," she said. "That's for the master of ceremonies to arrange."

"Then please do point him out, so that I might know who it is I am dancing with. There's a shortage of statuesque beauties in the room."

Poppy blushed and laughed at him. "You seek to tease me."

"Hardly. I am simply commenting on the company." He smiled.

The dance soon ended and she curtsied, leaving his side

quickly. Where was Dyngley?

She was stopped by a hand on her arm. "Miss Morton, isn't it? You move fast, don't you?"

Poppy stared at the hand gripping her and frowned at the source. "What do you mean? Oh. Hello, Miss Penwrith." She pulled her arm free of Miss Penwrith's grasp.

"You know who that was you were dancing with? I bet you don't even know him. The Dyngleys wouldn't take kindly to see you dancing with strange men."

"I don't see what business it is of yours who I dance with," Poppy said.

"Hah, I should have known you'd be rude. And common, too. You'll dance with just anyone, won't you?" Miss Penwrith's face was nasty.

Poppy frowned at her. "Miss Penwrith…"

"What? I just think you should pay better attention to who you're spending time with. If I was engaged to Henry as you say to be, I would never even think of dancing with another man."

"Well, then, there we differ. Excuse me," Poppy said, pushing past her. She came face to face with, "Henry."

"Poppy." He bowed.

He looked stunning. He wore a dark suit jacket over a slate gray waistcoat, navy trousers and smart shoes. His cravat had been skillfully tied at his throat, and his dark hair in the dim light looked almost black, at odds with his pale skin. His expression was curious. "I was hoping to see you," he said, "May I have the next dance?"

"I would be delighted." She took his hand and felt a tingle at the warmth of his touch. He led her into the next set, a slow, stately dance of couples in a line.

His hand was warm as he led her in the formation, and neither of them said a word. At first she felt discomfited, and wondered if she had something wrong, or had annoyed him. Then she realized that he gazed upon her with pleasure, and there was something to be said for simply enjoying the moment.

"I have not seen you since that dinner," he said.

"No. I imagine you have been busy with your guest." She paused, ignoring his raised eyebrow. "I have already spoken with Miss Penwrith this evening. I trust she is well." Two spots of color appeared in her cheeks, and she avoided his eyes.

He squeezed her hand for a second longer than was necessary before letting go. "She is just an old friend, Poppy. Whatever affection I might have had for her was little more than a child-hood fancy." Seeing her expression, he added, "My feelings for you are unchanged. Will you not believe me?"

"She called you her fiancé."

"She was mistaken." He twirled her around. "And I shall inform anyone who entertains that notion. Loudly and with great decorum."

She laughed. His dark eyes danced as they met hers. "I mean it, Poppy."

Then he froze and dropped her hand. "Henry? Henry, what is it?"

He stiffened, his hands flat against his thigh. "That man is staring at you. I feel like I've seen him before."

Poppy turned around. "Oh, him? I danced with him earlier. He is—"

"Enchanted," the young man murmured, taking her hand. Behind him stood the local master of ceremonies who said, "Miss Morton, allow me to introduce Mr. Rupert Faulkbourne."

Henry cocked his head. "Faulkbourne? As in Faulkbourne Manor?"

The man kissed Poppy's hand and released it, executing a neat bow. "The country estate of an old relation of mine. Do you know it?"

Henry gave a curt nod. "I do."

"How wonderful." He turned to Poppy. "I am delighted to make your acquaintance, Miss Morton. I had no idea Hertford-shire girls were so pretty."

Poppy gazed down, wary of the warming blush on her

cheeks. Then she glanced at him quizzically. "Faulkbourne? I know that name."

Henry gave her a warning look.

"It is a pleasure to meet you, sir. Now if you'll excuse us, we were dancing," Henry said, taking Poppy's hand and leading her away.

Poppy looked back to see Mr. Faulkbourne watching them, a slight frown on his features that was quickly replaced with a pleasant expression. "What was all that about?"

"I do not like him," Henry said.

"You've only just met."

"You did not seem unappreciative of his attentions."

"He was being polite. We had danced together once already. To ignore him would be rude," she said.

His brown eyes narrowed, and he led her to a place in the set, bowing to her, his face stern.

They did not speak during the dance, which suited her very well. He had no right to dictate who she could and could not talk to in polite company. She frowned at him right back.

The couple next to them talked about all manner of things, being of a good humor. Unfortunately, Poppy and Henry's firm silence made their company rather uncomfortable, and so they had to make do with polite smiles for the remainder of the dance. Once it had ended, Poppy walked away from Dyngley and into the crowd. As she entered the grand side parlor to procure a drink from a passing servant, she was cornered by a familiar face.

"Mrs. Dyngley, hello." Poppy gave Petunia a polite curtsy.

"The proper greeting is good evening," Petunia corrected her. "I saw you dancing. Have you no sense of propriety? You say you are engaged and here you are dancing with other men. But then, perhaps you have come to your senses."

"My senses?" Poppy repeated.

"Yes. You have no doubt seen Henry's preference for Miss Penwrith and have decided to step aside gracefully and release him from this farce of an engagement."

Poppy snorted. She was rapidly losing her patience with Petunia. "Mrs. Dyngley, I do not believe our engagement to be a sham, nor do I have any intention of breaking it."

"You have already danced with another man."

"Only because he asked me, and I had not yet seen Henry in the crowd. I assure you, if I had, he would have been my preferred dance partner."

"What will it take you to see reason? You are not suited for each other," Petunia said in her face.

"That is not for you to decide," Poppy said.

"You take an uncivil tone with me, but it is you who will see the error of your ways, trust me."

Poppy balked. "He proposed to me. And I will dance with whomever I choose. We are engaged and have danced twice tonight already. If I were to dance any more with him it would cause comment, and I have no wish to attract unwanted attention." *I have so much of it already*, she thought.

"You are presumptuous to think our family will allow the match. His father has not given his blessing and without it, you will not be married."

"But the banns have been read. One more week and it will be official." Poppy rued the words as she said them aloud. She would not put it past Petunia to try and cause trouble.

"That does not matter. Once Sir Dyngley hears of your odious background, he will laugh and that will put an end to it."

"Why are you telling me this?"

"To save you the embarrassment of a public censure. I pity you, Miss Morton. You have had a hard life, and it is not your fault your mother and father came together as they did. But you will not tarnish my family's name, and I swear I will do everything I can to prevent this farce of a marriage."

Poppy rolled her eyes and spoke with a bravado she did not feel. "I appreciate the concern, but I am confident in my relationship with Henry. If he wishes out of our engagement, then he must say so. Otherwise, I will see you on our wedding day."

"Hmph. You are the most addle-brained, flighty, self-absorbed girl I have ever met. Will you not see reason?"

"Do you worst, Mrs. Dyngley. You cannot hurt me more than I already have been. I have faced murderers, pimps, and prostitutes. What can you do?" Poppy turned on her heel and left Mrs. Dyngley fuming behind her. A wave of warmth came over her in triumph, but as she walked away, she wondered... She had dared Petunia to try and stop her marrying Henry. What if the woman took up the challenge?

CHAPTER EIGHT

T HAT SUNDAY AT church, Poppy sat in a pew with her aunt, as Mr. Ingleby gave his sermon, stepping in for her uncle as he rested at the parsonage. In the pew to the left and behind them, sat Petunia and Miss Penwrith, to Poppy's surprise.

"What are they doing here?" Aunt Rachel asked, but Poppy shrugged. "I don't know. Your guess is as good as mine."

Miss Cooke and Betsey sat next to them in the pew. "Looks like trouble to me," Miss Cooke whispered.

"Nonsense, it's fine. They're just here to attend the service," Poppy said.

"If that's true, then I'll eat my hat," Miss Cooke replied.

"You're not wearing one," Betsey pointed out.

"Don't matter. It's a figure of speech. Besides, I'm peckish. I'll eat yours if you're not careful."

Betsey clutched her straw hat in alarm and Miss Cooke grinned. "Only joking."

Mr. Ingleby glared at them and Aunt Rachel said, "Hush girls."

The sermon finally came to an end, when he began to read the weekly community announcements and the banns. But as he rustled his papers and said, "And now, for the third week, the wedding banns of Miss Poppy Morton and Sergeant Henry Dyngley. If anyone here knows of any impediment to this union—"

"Stop!" Miss Penwrith shot up in her pew, standing. "This cannot happen. I protest."

Mr. Ingleby dropped his papers, sending them flying. "What?"

"This marriage cannot take place," Miss Penwrith said loudly, amidst gasps and mutters from the congregation.

Poppy stared. "No." She felt physically ill.

Miss Cooke and Betsey stood by Poppy, who began to feel faint.

"What are you saying? What sort of trouble are you causing?" Aunt Rachel rose to her feet, her hands on her hips.

"Only the truth," Miss Penwrith said, her nose in the air.

"What is the meaning of this?" Mr. Ingleby asked loudly.

Petunia stood and said in a tight voice, "The girl is right." She heard a gasp and seeing she was the center of attention, turned pink with embarrassment. "Perhaps we might speak in private, Reverend."

"Yes. We will." Mr. Ingleby ended the service quickly and waited outside the front of the church, impatience on his round features until the last nosy parishioner had greeted him and left, before he turned back inside and shut the church doors.

"Now, what are you saying? This is a very serious accusation, Miss," Mr. Ingleby said.

"I am perfectly serious. Sergeant Dyngley cannot marry this girl, because he is already engaged to me," Miss Penwrith said.

"What?" Mr. Ingleby looked at Poppy, who was pale. "Miss Morton, is this true?"

"No. She's lying."

"I swear I am not. Bring me a Bible, I will swear on it. I will swear on a stack of Bibles, I will—"

"Perhaps you might leave the swearing for when we are outside church, Miss Penwrith," Petunia said. "Tell the good reverend what you told me."

"Yes, of course." Miss Penwrith drew herself up and looked Mr. Ingleby straight in the eye. "The fact is that Henry Dyngley is engaged to me. He promised me so years ago, and it was the final wish of my mother that we might finally be married."

Mr. Ingleby waggled a finger and said, "Whatever promise he made to you is a matter of hearsay. He was promised to Miss Morton, and she has accepted him. Unless you have written proof of a prior engagement, there is nothing more to be said."

Miss Penwrith burst into tears. "B-but it's the truth. He promised me."

"I believe the girl. Why would she have come all this way if it were not?" Petunia added.

"I do not know," Mr. Ingleby said, as Aunt Rachel boomed, "To cause trouble, of course. She's had nothing on her mind but breaking up the two of them and it's no different today."

"You have every reason to want our families to be joined, so I hardly think you are an objective point of view," Petunia muttered.

"What on earth are you talking about?" Aunt Rachel asked.

"Let's see, the fact that Sir Dyngley is a baronet, and you are the sister of a whore? A fact that has been hushed up until now, but it is only a matter of time before Henry's father learns of Poppy's poor origins. A fact which I am inclined to tell him myself. There, now, what do you have to say to that?" Petunia said.

"Only this, that if that is true, and Sir Dyngley disapproves of our girl, then he is no gentleman at all, and I do not want the connection," Aunt Rachel said.

Poppy fretted, her hands darting to her mouth. "Aunt, no."

Aunt Rachel ignored her. "You think you are so smart, marrying into such a titled family. But I didn't think your grand estate was that grand at all."

Petunia gasped. "How dare you?"

"How dare you?"

The women faced each other, Petunia's eyes narrowed, Aunt Rachel's cheeks flushed with anger.

"Ladies, please," Mr. Ingleby said. "You have said quite

enough, madam. Please leave. I will speak with the sergeant and get to the bottom of this."

"Pray, where is he? He's not here. Why wouldn't he be here, if not to support his bride?" Petunia asked rudely.

Eyes turned to Poppy. "I don't know."

"What a shame he couldn't be bothered to come, you could have asked him yourself. But never mind. I'm sure he has a good reason to miss the reading of the banns." Petunia smirked. "Come along, Miss Penwrith. I'm sure Henry will make an appearance for you." She swept out of the church, tugging Miss Penwrith by the hand.

Once the doors closed behind them, Aunt Rachel sagged into a chair. "Well, what rude people. I'm almost hopeful they don't become our relations, although I must say, even so, why did you not speak up, Poppy? Surely you could have given them a piece of your mind."

Poppy felt fragile inside, like a piece of glass with a hairline crack that was very close to splintering. She didn't know where Henry was, or why he hadn't turned up. Petunia's words had shocked her as if she'd slapped her face, and she felt her tongue dull and heavy like lead in her mouth. She couldn't speak, not even a word. All she could do was stand there and listen as Petunia spouted her hateful words. She couldn't even bear to look at Miss Penwrith, whose eyes had glowed at the situation. Even as the girl had wept, Poppy had spotted a smile forming at the corners of her mouth.

"I am sorry I did not speak up. I did not know what to say." She gripped the wooden back of the pew beside her, so hard the wood creaked.

"Well never mind. Their interruption was enough to disturb anyone. We'll soon know the truth of it. Besides, a promise made as children holds no weight legally, even if it happened."

Poppy joined her aunt on the slow walk back to the parsonage, her boots trudging along the dirt road and the miniature pebbles and stones, causing dust to stain the hem of her dress.

The sun was bright and shining and she was glad of the shade her bonnet cast over her face. It allowed her to avoid the gaze of anyone watching.

Henry paid a call later that afternoon, not long before the dinner hour. He was received, but with little cordiality. "Well, Sergeant, I suppose you've heard about this ruckus your sister-in-law and her little friend caused at church today. A poor showing indeed. Not at all what I would expect from your family," Aunt Rachel said.

Henry gave her a deep bow. "I can only apologize. I had no idea they would stoop to such lengths. It's unpardonable."

"You're darn right it is." Uncle Reginald waved a cane in Henry's direction from the sofa. "I wouldn't tolerate such behavior in my church. If I'd been there—"

"Yes, yes, dear. The question is, Sergeant, what are you going to do about them? This sort of disturbance cannot go on. We were humiliated at church, when this should be a happy time for you both. When I think of this, on top of the fact that nothing is settled. We haven't even sent out invitations," Aunt Rachel said.

"Then let's do it. We will organize the invitations and send them out for… Well. Considering Mr. Greene's injury, we should wait of course until he is well. Six weeks from today perhaps?" Henry said.

"Marry in six weeks…" Poppy said, looking at Henry.

"We'll do it. I'll do it. We'll be rid of their interruptions once and for all," Henry said. "If that is agreeable to you, Miss Morton."

"Yes." She nodded, feeling shy and demure.

"Oh Poppy, there's so much to do. We haven't chosen your wedding dress, yet, or decided what flowers you'll hold, or where you'll stay on your wedding night…" Aunt Rachel began.

Poppy glanced at her aunt, seeing her get excited, and looked up to see Henry watching her. He smiled at her, one of his warm, charming smiles meant just for her, and she felt right again. All would be well; she just knew it.

"Would you care for some tea, Sergeant?" Aunt Rachel offered.

"No, thank you, Mrs. Greene. I'll just be going. If Miss Morton might walk me to my horse?" he asked.

"Very well," Uncle Reginald said, watching him through narrowed eyes.

Poppy and Henry rose, and she led the way out of the room and into the narrow corridor that led to the front door of the parsonage. As she walked outside and he closed the door behind him, he touched her hand. "Poppy?"

"Yes?"

"Are you all right?"

She looked down and bit her lip. She couldn't hide her emotions from him, nor did she want to. "Yes. I'll be happier once we are married, to just put an end to all of this trouble. When we saw them at church my maid suspected trouble, but I didn't think that Mrs. Dyngley would get involved too. It was… awkward."

"I'm sorry about that." He took her hand and pressed it to his chest.

She could feel the warmth of his shirt, and instantly felt uncomfortable. It was an intimacy and one she was unprepared for. She'd never touched a man before. She tensed as he smiled and released her hand.

She blushed and he said, "I'll be staying in town for the time being. With my relations causing trouble, I don't want to be far from you."

She brightened at this. "We'll be together soon enough in a matter of weeks."

"Maybe that's not soon enough for me." He raised her hands to his lips, kissed it and let it fall. "I'm staying at the boarding house in town. If anything happens, send a note to me there."

He walked off to his horse, mounted and waved, before trotting away.

Once he left, leaving small clouds of dust in his wake, the door opened behind her, revealing her aunt. "Just think, Poppy, in just a short time you'll be Mrs. Henry Dyngley!"

CHAPTER NINE

Henry fancied a warm meal, and rode to the Crosskeys Tavern in the center of town. As he sat down with a plate of steaming hot sausages and mashed potatoes, he heard the doors open and a familiar pair of voices nearby.

"There he is!"

Henry looked up and was soon joined by Petunia and Miss Penwrith. He did not bow or invite them to join him, a social slight he hoped would not escape their notice.

If the ladies noticed, they did not say so, and instead sat down across from him in the small wooden booth that sat beside a window. Miss Penwrith looked unhappy with her surroundings and looked around with distaste, but Petunia had no such qualms. "Well, Henry, I hope you're happy. We have done our part to help."

Henry looked up from his wooden plate. "Help? By which you mean interrupting a church service and embarrassing my fiancée?"

Miss Penwrith stiffened and sat down. "No Henry, by telling the truth. We only did what was right. You are engaged to me."

"No, I am not," Henry said.

"You are."

He cocked his head at her and said with a measure of sarcasm, "Forgive me, since we haven't exchanged a word these past ten years. How are we betrothed?"

"Do you not remember? Down by the little pond, when we were children. I was complaining that my dress was ugly and I feared nobody would like me. You took my hand and said that no boy in his right mind wouldn't like me, and to prove it, if we were both single by the age of twenty, then you would marry me," she said.

He blinked. "That was a long time ago. I had forgotten that conversation, if it even happened." He cut his remaining sausage with a two-pronged fork and knife and said, "But it does not matter, for I am not single. I am engaged to Miss Morton."

"Hah," Petunia said.

"Stay out of this, Mrs. Dyngley."

"But Henry, don't you see? She is all wrong for you," Miss Penwrith said, reaching across the table and touching his arm.

He pulled his arm away.

"From what Mrs. Dyngley tells me—"

"No doubt my sister-in-law has told you all sorts of things about my betrothed. But it matters not, for she is the one I have chosen to marry, and that is the end of it." He set down his knife and fork with a loud thump, making the thick table rattle.

Miss Penwrith shut her mouth and stared at him. "You refuse to see reason."

"I am being reasonable. It is you who are not."

"Ugh, why must you be so dramatic, Henry," Petunia said. "Come to your senses. Miss Penwrith is only trying to do what's best for you and to save you from an imprudent marriage. Why must you be so difficult?"

Henry glared at Petunia. "I think I am the best judge of what an imprudent marriage constitutes, Mrs. Dyngley, but I bow to your greater experience."

"What?" Miss Penwrith asked, confused.

Petunia's mouth shut with a snap. She glared back at Henry through narrowed eyes and said, "Your future husband insults me, Miss Penwrith. Henry, I beg you to reconsider. Miss Morton is not the right sort of girl for you, and you know it. She may have some money hidden away, but it doesn't matter. How can you look your father in the face and honestly tell him you're going to marry the daughter of a whore?" Her voice rose.

Miss Penwrith gasped. "Henry? Is this true?"

"Now it is Mrs. Dyngley who is being insulting." Henry gave up on the idea of finishing his meal and leaned back against the hard wooden back of the booth, the wood creaking comfortably. He liked this pub. It would be nice if it weren't for the company. Now even his half-eaten sausages looked forlorn.

"I cannot let you do this."

"You won't have to. In no time at all, it will all be over," he said.

"What do you mean?"

"We have set a date. I am to be married in six weeks' time, or thereabouts once Mr. Greene is better. And once the banns have been read again." He drank his beer.

"Is this a joke?"

Henry shook his head. "No. and I'll thank you both not to interfere."

"But what about the contract?" Miss Penwrith said. At their expressions, she added, "The one drafted between our mothers. Years ago. I told my Mama what you said, she told your mother and they wrote up a contract."

Henry froze. He could hear the blood roaring in his veins. "Our mothers drew up a marriage contract?"

Miss Penwrith nodded.

"I don't believe it. She would have told me, or my father. I wouldn't be the last to know."

"I do not think my mother ever thought we would need it. But you should know of it, your mother kept the contract amongst her things."

"Since her death, my father has kept her rooms closed. No one goes in there." He spoke dully and looked at the table, covered in ring stains from cups and tankards.

Miss Penwrith shivered. "Then it would probably be there."

Petunia said, "Well let's go. That will determine it once and for all."

"No. You will not go nosing around my mother's room like out of some gothic novel," Henry said.

Petunia crossed her arms beneath her chest, a mutinous expression on her face.

"There is no point," Henry said, "even if it is true, it cannot be a binding contract. Parents cannot simply contract their children away, not amongst families of our sort. And even if it were true, I cannot imagine our mothers found witnesses or a notary to officiate such a document. This is little more than an outdated agreement between two women who hoped their children might one day marry." He looked at Miss Penwrith. "Please, accept the facts. Whatever closeness we had ended a long time ago. I am engaged to another woman. Let me marry her in peace."

Miss Penwrith's shoulders slumped, and he could see the will to fight abandon her. "Even if she is the daughter of..."

"Miss Morton cannot be blamed for her mother's profession," Henry said.

"And her father?"

"Was unaware of her existence until recently."

"The mother's shame was too much for her to bear, I imagine," Petunia started, "I think–"

"Enough." Henry rose from his seat. "The matter is settled."

"It is anything but. Do you really think your father will approve of your marriage once he learns of her background? Perhaps he has already guessed something is amiss. Why else would she not use her father's surname?" Petunia said, rising. She placed her gloved hands on the table and glared at him.

"And let me guess, you plan to be the one to tell him," Henry said.

"Someone should. He needs to know what sort of girl you're bringing into his household."

"Why do you care so much about this?" he asked.

"Because I want one of us to be happy. It might as well be you. I don't want to see you make the wrong choice. Not like I did," Petunia snapped, her eyes glassy as she shuffled Miss Penwrith aside to exit the booth. She stalked away and slammed the door of the pub shut behind her.

Henry alone faced Miss Penwrith. "Do you even remember me? It was so long ago."

"Of course I do." She fingered the locket around her neck.

"When you first saw me, you commented on my appearance. What did you say?" he asked, remembering it well, for it was the first time he'd interacted with a girl near his own age.

"Why I… said how handsome you look. Of course."

"You commented on my ears and said they were too big."

She laughed prettily. "Well, silly, I do remember but didn't want to hurt your feelings. Can you blame me for wanting to spare you?"

He shrugged. "I just don't see how we have any real connection. We hardly know each other anymore."

She blushed and said, "I know. And I understand you think you are in love, Henry. But you must see we are doing the right thing. Mrs. Dyngley is right. And if you will not see that, I will just have to…" She paused. "I am not to blame for what may happen. I trust you will see things my way in time." She left Henry to his now cold sausages and mash.

THE NEXT DAY Henry received a note from Poppy. It read:

My dearest Henry,

I have thought on the matter and wish to end our engagement. I no longer wish to marry into a family so unwelcoming. I hope that in time we can be friends.

Best of luck,
Miss Morton

Henry read the note, again and again, his hand shaking. What was the meaning of this? Hardly thinking, he threw on a jacket, saddled his horse, and rode to the parsonage, the letter stuffed into his jacket pocket. He slipped off his saddle, loosely tied the horse's reins to the large tree that stood in the front yard of the parsonage, and knocked boldly on the front door.

A few minutes later Miss Cooke opened it, fixing him with a hard glare.

"Who is it?" Aunt Rachel called.

"It's Sergeant Dyngley," Miss Cooke said in a stern voice.

"Bring him in."

Miss Cooke stood aside and let him in. he strode inside, finding his way to the blue sitting room.

Poppy sat on the sofa, holding a note in trembling hands. Her face was pale and she looked up. "Oh, Sergeant. Hello." Her voice wavered.

"What is the meaning of this, Sergeant Dyngley?" Aunt Rachel demanded, her hands on her hips. "How dare you show your face here? On second thought, I am glad you did. Perhaps you can explain this." She ripped the note from Poppy's hands and shoved it in his face.

Henry took the paper and read:

Miss Morton,

It pains me to have to tell you this but our relationship is at an end. Any romantic feelings I had for you were a passing fancy, and I have now renewed my engagement to my dearest Honoria, whom I love dearly. I am releasing you from our engagement with immediate effect. I trust you will appreciate this is the best for both our families considering the diffrinces in our stations and social spheres. I hope you will not mourn me for too long. There are some good farmers and stablehands you might find to your liking insted.

Best of luck,
Henry Dyngley

He tossed the letter to the floor, his hands trembling. It was insulting beyond compare. It even had spelling errors. "This is an egregious falsehood. I am shocked."

"Are you? I wonder at your coming here. Pray, have you had second, no, third thoughts?" Aunt Rachel sniped.

"Aunt, enough." Poppy stood and said, "If I might, I would speak with the sergeant alone."

"I'm not sure…" Aunt Rachel said.

"Please."

"Very well. I'll be in the kitchen if you need me." Aunt Rachel swept from the room in a swirl of skirts, but not before fixing Henry with a glare. Uncle Reginald glared at Henry and with the help of crutches, hobbled from the room.

Once they were alone, he said, "Miss Morton—"

"Henry. Please, sit down."

He sat in the hard-back chair reserved for visitors, and she sat across from him, smoothing down her skirts.

"Ever since the arrival of Miss Penwrith, I have felt smaller. Diminished. Her interference and Mrs. Dyngley's attempts to prevent our marriage have bothered me so much that I felt weaker and more subdued about our relationship. Almost sick."

He looked at her with concern.

"But now I realize that with their interrupting the reading of the banns, and now this, these are nothing more than cheap ploys to take us down. And I for one, will not stand for it." Her voice was calm and sure.

"Poppy?" he asked.

"You wish to marry me, yes?"

He nodded.

"Why is it that they are so against me as a bride? Is it my background? My mother? The fact I am a ward?"

"It is everything. But none of that matters to me," he said.

She gave him a soft smile, almost gentle. "If we are to be together, I don't want any of this nonsense hanging over our heads. This should be a happy time."

"What would you have me do?"

"I don't imagine any convincing will change Mrs. Dyngley's mind. Your father, I am guessing, is unaware of my background."

"Yes," he said.

"Then let us tell him. Let him decide whether to approve of our engagement."

"Poppy, I'm not sure that is wise," he said.

"Let me tell him to his face. I would be honest. That is the way forward."

"And if he refuses to sanction the match?"

She gazed at the letter he'd tossed on the floor. "Then at least I would know, and we wouldn't have to hide anything. Is that what you are afraid of, that he might disapprove of me?"

Henry didn't want to speak it. But he was afraid, and his silence was telling.

"If your father does disapprove, then I do not know what I will do. Would you still want to marry me if that is the case?"

Henry thought on this. He knew in his heart, yes. But to face his father's disapproval... He had always been the good, reliable son. The stable one, not like his elder brother John who drank, gambled, womanized and diverted himself with little amusements, when there were tenants to look after and debts to pay.

"I would rather marry you poor, than Miss Penwrith rich," Henry said, conscious that her aunt and uncle were listening just outside the room.

"We must be practical. What if my father were to speak to your father? Would that help him consent?" Poppy asked.

The rules for marrying were that the age of majority was twenty-one. If a minor wanted to marry and had not reached their majority, they either needed permission from their parents or a special license to marry. Couples who wished to avoid this could also travel to Gretna Green in Scotland, which had no such restrictions, but to have procured such a marriage would not come without a certain infamy.

"What do you want to do?" he asked.

"It is clear that Miss Penwrith's attempts to separate us–" She nodded to the letter on the floor. "Will not stop unless she is forced to leave or we are married. But if she and Mrs. Dyngley are so disapproving, let them do what they will. We simply do not have to invite them to the wedding."

Aunt Rachel burst into the room. "A fine idea, Poppy, but how do you know they won't do more to prevent the marriage from happening?"

"They likely will. We will just have to think ahead of them," Henry said, "Whatever it takes. I will not let anyone stand in the way of our happiness."

"My thoughts exactly," Poppy said with a smile.

TOGETHER HENRY, POPPY, Miss Cooke and Aunt Rachel drew up a list of people to invite, and they split the sending of invitations, which went out the next day. The ceremony would be held at the Dyngleys' private family chapel, which might sound rather small, but was perfect for their purposes, as it would only hold a certain number of people, which prevented the happy couple from inviting too many.

CONSCIOUS OF THE Dyngley family's financial struggles, Poppy refused to buy a new dress just for her wedding. It seemed like an unnecessary extravagance, and one that Petunia might be offended by.

"If it's that horrid woman you're thinking about, don't. This is your wedding," Aunt Rachel advised.

"At least let us decorate it some," Miss Cooke suggested.

"Very well."

Poppy took out her best dress, a light pink silk concoction with small cap sleeves, matching pink satin shoes for dancing and a pair of elbow length gloves. She stood by as her aunt and maid debated what ribbons to use for her hair, what necklace would go best around her neck, and what sash to accentuate her waist.

LATER THAT WEEK there was to be a dance at the assembly rooms. Dyngley had paid a call at the parsonage and sat with them a little, before asking if Poppy might attend. She blushed and said yes, to which he replied, "I am most glad to hear it."

He did not stay long, but rose and asked if Poppy might escort him to his horse. Aunt Rachel and Uncle Reginald exchanged a brief look before agreeing, as they were engaged.

Poppy led the way out, before she uttered an undignified squeak, as Henry took her hand and rested it in the crook of his elbow.

"Sergeant, what are you—?" she asked.

"Ssssh." He winked and led her down the path toward his horse, as if they were a courting couple. She realized they were and her cheeks warmed at the thought.

"You blush, Poppy. What are you thinking about?" he asked. "Is it perhaps the thought that you will become Mrs. Henry Dyngley in a matter of weeks?"

She laughed. "A little. Only that I am so used to us speaking formally, it feels almost improper to hear you use my Christian name."

He patted her hand. "I am proud of you, you know."

"What do you mean?"

"You have borne Miss Penwrith and Petunia's tricks and ill-will again and again, and you have been strong throughout. There are some ladies without half your mettle who have thrown a fit, or broken down into hysterics, or at the very least, thrown me over. I am not the first suitor who has come your way. Why haven't you?" he asked lightly.

His light tone betrayed him, for he was always serious. It was one of the things she liked about him. She knew then that he spoke seriously, and honestly wanted to know.

She curled her hand around his elbow tighter. "Because I love you."

Their eyes met, his dark brown eyes searching into hers. What they looked for; she didn't know. She met his gaze unflinchingly and smiled.

He slowly lowered his head and kissed her then, gently, pressing his lips to hers.

She closed her eyes and felt the kiss warm her, more than a fair summer's day. They kissed a moment longer and then he broke off the kiss, a twinkle of mischief in his eye.

"What is it?" she asked, a little breathless.

"We're being watched."

She glanced to her right, back at the house. Sure enough, the curtains were open before the windows and her aunt stood there, waving. Poppy snorted. "So it seems."

He tugged her along to his horse, and looked disappointed when she removed her hand from his arm.

"Where will we live, when we are married?"

"First, I thought we might go to Bath for a week, just us. Bring your maid and I'll bring Geoffrey, my valet. I think a husband and wife should have some time alone first."

"And then?"

"Well… We could live at your townhouse in London, or we could sell it and we could live somewhere else."

Sell her mother's home? She had only just taken ownership of it. She looked away.

"You do not wish to sell?"

"I don't know. I have not been there very long." She paused. "It feels wrong to let go of the place, when she has recently passed. It was her gift to me, as part of my inheritance."

He put a hand on his horse and rubbed its back, making it wicker quietly. "Poppy, you know that you are marrying a man with no money. I have but a small income, hardly enough to live on. And every penny of that goes to my family, to support the estate. I could remind you that when we are married, all of your property and finances go to me."

Her eyes widened. "You would force me to sell? My mother's home."

"No, Poppy, I only meant–"

"I understand you perfectly. That once we marry, everything I own belongs to you. And you ask why I have not thrown you over. Well, Sergeant, now I am wondering that too. Good day." She turned and walked away.

"Poppy," he called after her, "come back."

She ignored him and slammed shut the parsonage door behind her.

"Damned woman." He climbed atop his horse and rode off, nudging it with his heels angrily.

CHAPTER TEN

POPPY WAS FURIOUS. She railed at Henry's callous words and high-handed manner. At that moment she disliked the very look of him. She repeated his words and told her aunt, her uncle, even the maids how she felt.

"Yes, Poppy, we are all aware of how you're feeling. Now please, eat your peas," her aunt said, at dinner.

Poppy flushed pink and drank more wine.

"What will you tell him at the dance on Saturday?" her aunt asked.

"I don't know."

"Well if you're going to break it off with him, a man's got a right to know," her uncle said, not without some pleasure in his face.

"I'm not breaking it off with him, Uncle."

"Aren't you? Even when he wants to use your money and sell your mother's house to fund his lifestyle?"

"It's not like that, Reginald. He wants to use it to build a life for them both," Aunt Rachel said, cutting into her slice of pork. "It's romantic."

Poppy wasn't so sure.

THE DANCE ON Saturday came quickly, and as it was a regular country dance, not a ball, Poppy was disinclined to dress with any finery. She looked much like a simpler version of herself, in an ordinary black and white check dress with a black sash around her waist. As she let Miss Cooke dress her hair with a black ribbon, her aunt walked into the room.

"Lord, Poppy. You do look a bit morbid. Why all the black?"

"I was thinking of my mother."

"Well it's a dance, not a funeral. Miss Cooke, please change the ribbons in her hair and the sash at her waist. It's too dark. I don't want people thinking she's still in mourning."

POPPY FROWNED AS her maid quickly changed out the ribbon and sash for something lighter. She reached for the small compact of rouge and began to dab a tiny bit on her cheeks, and let her maid touch a bit on her lips. She'd gotten used to wearing makeup now, and to her surprise, she rather liked it. Her uncle would never have condoned the use of cosmetics, but she found she didn't care.

After her mother's death, when she had first explored her mother's townhouse in London, she had found her mother's boudoir, where her dressing table was covered with bottles of perfume and cosmetics. Since then she felt closer to her mother, even if it was by putting a dab of rouge on her cheeks. She smiled at the thought.

SHE JOINED HER aunt and uncle that evening to attend the assembly room in Hertford, and as the carriage pulled up to the smart brick building in the center of town, Poppy was struck by the noise, a contrast to the peace and quiet of the parsonage. The clatter of horses' hooves and turn of carriage wheels outside, as well as dogs, servants, footmen, including some standing by at the entrance to help ladies down from their carriages, all made for a minor cacophony of sound. Lanterns and torches lit up the growing evening darkness, and inside the trim building windows she could see the silhouettes of men and women, talking and dancing to the strains of music. The sound of pipes, a drum and strings could be heard slightly above a general noise of talk, chatter and laughter.

THEY WALKED INSIDE and were instantly ushered into the large hall, brightly lit with dozens of candles that added a warm glow to the room. The makeshift ballroom was tightly packed with dancers and people standing off to the sides, making an awful crush of people.

"Good lord, it's hot. And we've only just arrived," Aunt Rachel said.

Poppy agreed, wishing she'd brought a fan. The room was indeed warm, and with so many dancers about, she looked to see if there was anyone she recognized.

It wasn't long before her aunt left her to chat to the other older people present, and she stood alone, pinned back by the throng of people.

THEN SHE SAW him, standing in a group of people, gazing over the heads as if looking for someone. Henry looked dashing as ever, in a smart blue suit jacket over a starched white shirt and ruffled collar. Tall as she was, she could see little more of him aside from his face and dark hair. She would recognize those piercing eyes anywhere, and when they landed on her, her heart skipped a beat.

His eyes narrowed and his lips pursed as if an angry retort lay on his lips, ready to speak, when his expression softened and he inclined his head formally.

So that was to be it, then. Formal civility, with no attempt at affection. Very well, two could play at that game. She inclined her head and then turned, bumping into a man. "Oh, I'm sorry."

"WHY, IT'S MISS Morton," Mr. Faulkbourne said.

"Hello."

"What a pleasure it is to see you again." Mr. Faulkbourne's

face lit up in a smile. "There's no one I'd rather bump into here."

Was it her imagination or did his smile not reach his eyes?

"That is very kind of you. And are you enjoying the dance?"

"I am now." His eyes twinkled with mischief. "Is that your beau over there?"

"Where?" Poppy turned.

"The dark-haired fellow who is looking so angry at you."

"Oh." Sure enough, Dyngley's expression was as dark as a storm cloud. "Yes, I suppose so."

"You suppose? What a funny predicament to have. I would never leave a good-looking young lady such as yourself in any doubt of our relationship. You are either civil acquaintances, friends, or something distinctly more." He looked at her pensive face. "You clearly need cheering up. What's wrong? Did you two have a tiff?"

"Something like that."

"Well, never mind. Come, let me distract you." Mr. Faulkbourne took her by the hand.

"What are you doing?"

"Leading you to dance. A little dancing never hurt anyone," he said with a smile, and soon they were in the queue for the next set.

A quadrille began to play, and as she and Mr. Faulkbourne began to dance, Poppy felt all the troubles and stresses of the day start to leave her. As they looked at each other and held hands as the rules dictated, she found herself smiling naturally, and returned his grin.

Once the dance ended, she curtsied and faced Henry, who stood before her like a dark statue.

"Sergeant Dyngley." She curtsied.

"Miss Morton," he said, looking at her with barely restrained annoyance. "And Mr. Faulkbourne, what a surprise."

"Not at all, dear fellow. It is a dance, you know. But perhaps you might find the air a bit more appealing." He looked at Henry. "I say, I'm in town and heard my family's old manor is still around. I don't suppose you happen to know who lives at the old place now, do you? Faulkbourne Manor?"

"I happen to, as a matter of fact."

"You do? What, by yourself?" Mr. Faulkbourne smirked.

"My family does. The Dyngleys," Henry said.

"By Jove, that's a laugh. And here I thought the old place had crumbled into dust. I'd heard it was in a very bad state. Do you really live there?"

Henry's face turned red. "Yes."

"Say, I don't suppose I could visit? See what you've done with the place?" Mr. Faulkbourne said.

"No."

"I wouldn't want to bother you, of course. It's just that my father is unwell, and it would cheer him up to no end to hear how the old family haunt was doing. Are you sure?"

"Quite," Henry said stiffly.

"Sergeant…" Poppy said.

"If you'll excuse me, sir. I would like a word with my fiancée." Henry led Poppy away into the crowd.

They were soon swallowed up by the warm bodies, which Henry pushed through until they stood behind a pillar. It offered a small bit of shadow, but hardly any privacy.

"Sergeant, that was rude," Poppy said.

"I don't care. The man is insufferable. What is he thinking, stealing you away for a dance one minute and asking to visit my house the next? It's presumptuous."

Her cheeks blushed. "He didn't steal me away."

"I didn't see you protesting."

"It was just a dance." Their eyes met, and she said, "Perhaps it is well we are not married. I would not want to have an argument every time another man asked me to dance."

His mouth firmed into a hard line. "At least then I do not have to worry about you making a fool of yourself."

"Excuse me?" She tugged her hand from his and put her hands on her hips, glaring at him. "I don't know what you mean."

"You are throwing yourself at him. Why? Just to tease me? To annoy me? It's working."

"If anyone is annoying, it is you, for coming up with all of these absurd ideas. The man asked me to dance, Dyngley, and I didn't say no. He cheered me up, although now my good humor is gone, thanks to you." She frowned at him.

He uttered a sound and ran a hand through his dark hair, mussing it. "I am... I am sorry. I don't know why it bothers me so. Something about him strikes me as odd. Wrong, somehow, and then to see you with him..." He cast his eyes to the floor.

"It was just a dance, Henry. It meant nothing."

"Poppy... What I said earlier..." Henry took her by the shoulders and pulled her toward him. He kissed her, in the slim shadow of the column, surrounded by people.

Like before, his kiss thrilled her, down to the tips of her toes. This felt soft and gentle like a butterfly's wings, but without the heat and passion she'd expected. This was more of a longing, a wish to touch her, to not lose her.

She opened her eyes, unaware she'd closed them, and broke off the kiss. "Henry... You go too far. Kissing in public? What will people say?"

"Nothing, if they know what's good for them." He blushed, looking past her shoulder at someone. "And if they don't, then I suppose most everyone will know that we are engaged, if they do not already."

She laughed a little. "I'm still mad at you, you know. A kiss won't change my mind."

"No, but..." He paused. "Miss Morton, understand me when I say that when we spoke earlier, I never intended to hurt your feelings. I only meant–"

"You meant to impress upon me the reality of our relationship; that we are not equals. And that once we are married, everything I own belongs to you." She almost spat, her voice rigid with anger. "Ever since we met, you have treated me with the utmost courtesy, respect, and honesty a woman could hope for.

You treated me like I was intelligent, and not one of these fanciful girls that fainted at the first opportunity."

"I have never wanted a girl like that," he muttered.

"But now, just when I have lost my mother and come into a fortune, you want to control all of that."

He looked at her mutely.

"Henry, how could you?" She meant to move away, when quick as a snake, he grasped her wrist. She said, "Let me go."

"Ah, Miss Morton, there you are. Chatting with our furious sergeant, I see. You'll never guess who I just met, who says she is acquainted with you both." Mr. Faulkbourne stood back and revealed Miss Penwrith, who looked at Henry with delight, and Poppy with suspicion.

Miss Penwrith wore a faded but pretty brown dress with long sleeves, and a low scoop-neck cut that revealed a flat bosom. Poppy could well understand, for she too was tall, thin and for the most part flat-chested, but she didn't mind.

Miss Penwrith said, in a breathy voice, "Hullo Henry."

Poppy's mouth shut like a trap and she breathed in, mentally trying to calm herself. She would not let Miss Penwrith get under her skin.

"I gather you two know each other," Mr. Faulkbourne said.

"We are engaged," Miss Penwrith said.

"Engaged? Why, then I offer my congratulations," he said politely, and then looked at Poppy. "How odd, I thought that… Never mind."

Henry colored with embarrassment and said, "Miss Penwrith is mistaken. We are good friends."

Miss Penwrith's face faltered and she blinked away sudden tears. "Oh Henry, don't say that. Anyone would think you didn't love me at all. Just wait until I tell Mrs. Dyngley." She flounced off in a flurry of brown skirts.

Henry sighed and his shoulders slumped a fraction. "I'd better go after her before she makes a scene."

"So you are engaged, then?" Mr. Faulkbourne asked.

"Of course not. She's making up tales, like she always does." Henry frowned. "That's going to get her in trouble one day."

"What do you mean?" Poppy asked.

"One of these days someone is going to take issue with her lies, and they won't tolerate her falsehoods in public. I wouldn't mind seeing her gone, I must admit." He gave himself a little shake and said, "Excuse me."

As he disappeared into the crowd, Mr. Faulkbourne asked Poppy, "Well. I never knew there was such drama to be seen in this town. Is it always like that?"

Poppy gave a little smile. "Sometimes."

"And what do you make of your sergeant and the darling Miss Penwrith?"

"Only this, that Sergeant Dyngley is right. If she continues to make up stories, then she's going to land herself in trouble." She frowned in the direction they left.

At that moment she was met by her aunt, who said, "There you are, Poppy. I think we should leave."

"Why? We've not been here long."

"No, but that woman, Miss Penwrith, is telling anyone who will listen that she is engaged to Sergeant Dyngley, and that he is carrying on with you behind her back."

"What?" Poppy stared.

"It is true, I overheard it myself. Although why she would want to paint herself as a victim and her so-called fiancé a philanderer is beyond me. My dear girl, do you want to leave? I'll call for the carriage," Aunt Rachel said.

"Allow me," Mr. Faulkbourne said.

"Who are you?"

"Mr. Faulkbourne, at your service, ma'am." He bowed.

"Well, that's very nice of you, but completely unnecessary. Do call on us sometime, we're at the parsonage in town. Poppy, where are you going?" Aunt Rachel asked.

"I want to speak with Miss Penwrith." Poppy pushed her way to the front, where Miss Penwrith was speaking to Henry.

A small crowd was forming on the sidelines, watching them argue. Henry said, "You are telling lies about my betrothed. This must cease this instant."

"It is not lies; it is the truth. We are engaged and I refuse to hear anything different. You just don't want to admit it. You're trapped under her spell, Henry. Why can't you see that?" Miss Penwrith sounded so earnest, she seemed convincing, earning a few nods from one or two people.

"I have cast no spell," Poppy said, moving through the people to face Miss Penwrith. "It is you who are mistaken. Sergeant Dyngley proposed to me recently, and I have accepted. The banns have been read. We are free to marry, and we are going to do so."

"Over my dead body," Miss Penwrith snapped, lunging forward. She threw herself at Poppy and slammed her to the hard wooden floor.

Shrieks and cries filled the air as Poppy saw stars dart across her vision and pain stabbed the back of her head. "You witch!" she cried and scrabbled as Miss Penwrith pinned her from above, her rough hands curling around Poppy's neck.

"Get off!" Henry cried and pulled Miss Penwrith off, but not before she raked her nails down Poppy's left cheek, marring her fair skin.

"Poppy!" Aunt Rachel cried, shoving her way through.

"You are a nuisance. I should arrest you for assault," Henry said, hauling Miss Penwrith back.

She stood up straight and spat at his feet. "You know nothing of the pain I feel. It kills me inside, seeing you two carry on as if everything is fine. When really the truth is plain to see. You are poor and need money, and she wants your title. I mean to save you, Henry, from the likes of her."

"Save me?" He pinned her arms behind her back and held her fast. "If I have to kill you myself, I will. Miss Morton and I will be married, and you will return home, if I don't put you in a jail cell first."

Poppy slowly sat up, feeling pain in the back of her skull and then gingerly touched her left cheek. She felt something warm and wet there. Her pale fingers came away with little specks of blood and she tensed. "Oh no."

She instantly felt embarrassed, to be sitting on the sticky floor in a now dirty and slightly torn dress, with blood dripping down her cheek. She must look a fright.

Mr. Faulkbourne and her aunt helped her to her feet. "Are you all right?" he asked.

Poppy bit her lip and nodded. Tears threatened to blur her vision but she blinked hard and put on a brave face. The stresses of it all were getting to her, and part of her just wanted to cry like a child. But she would not. She'd rather die than show that Miss Penwrith had gotten to her.

"I'm fine. But I will take my aunt's advice and call it a night. I've had enough excitement for the evening," Poppy said.

"I should say so." Aunt Rachel took her arm. "Sergeant, we are pressing charges. I want that girl arrested. You saw what she did to my niece. All of you did." She glanced at the onlookers.

"I'm not going to jail! She's the harlot! Harridan! Slut! You should be ashamed of yourself, Miss Morton, carrying on like you're some prize chicken when we all know you're nothing but a cheap slut, just like your mother." Miss Penwrith's voice carried, and now silence reigned. Even the music had stopped.

Poppy shook off her aunt's hands and marched over to Miss Penwrith, ignoring the drop of blood that dripped down her chin. She looked at the woman's pale face, seeing Miss Penwrith's eyes bright with wicked delight. "You are nothing but a spoiled young woman who likes to cause trouble. If we were men and could duel, I'd challenge you to pistols at dawn."

Gasps sounded.

"As it is, this will do." Poppy slapped her, hard.

Miss Penwrith shrieked as if Poppy had committed bloody murder. "You selfish, horrible woman. You're nothing but a whore! A slut! Mrs. Dyngley told me all about–" She continued screaming obscenities as Henry hauled her away and out of the assembly.

Poppy let out a small sigh of relief. She this time gratefully accepted her aunt's arm, and held her head tall, and was quiet as they silently made their way out of the room. Poppy felt people's eyes on her, but this time the sensation was rife with suspicion. They did not trust her, for what if Miss Penwrith's assertions were true?

Chapter Eleven

S OMEONE WAS BANGING on Henry's door. He muttered a foul curse into his pillow and got up, throwing the light bedcovers off of him with an angry retort on his lips. He was usually a heavy sleeper, and disliked waking in the early hours of the morning, but thanks to Miss Penwrith, he'd had no peace.

"What is it?" He threw the door open.

"A message for Sergeant Dyngley, from Mrs. Petunia Dyngley, of Faulkbourne Manor." A messenger stood there with a note clutched in his hand.

Henry took it from the man and paid him a coin, then shut the door in his face. He sat on the bed and tore the note open. It was written very ill, not at all like Petunia's normal ladylike writing.

Henry

Miss Penwrith is dead. Come home at once.

Petunia Dyngley

Henry cursed and threw the note away. He should have known she'd make a nuisance of herself, and of course had chosen the most public place to do it in. He rose stiffly and sat on the edge of the bed, resting his hands on his knees. He pulled out the battered tin piss pot beneath the bed and stood and relieved himself, then poured some tepid water from a jug into a small ceramic basin that stood on a night table. He washed his face in the water and ran his wet hands through his dark hair, combing the locks with his fingers into some semblance of respectability. He wiped his hands on a small wash towel and dressed quickly, putting on a light gray suit jacket, dull sandstone-colored waistcoat, and matching gray trousers.

He thought back to Miss Penwrith's behavior the previous night at the assembly rooms. He was so embarrassed, and shocked. She'd insulted and attacked Poppy. It was strange. So unlike the girl he'd grown up with. And all because she believed she was engaged to him, from a forgotten promise he made to her years ago. It didn't bear thinking about, and yet, this needed to stop.

After her outburst and what with Poppy and her family leaving, he had taken Miss Penwrith aside and said, "I hope you're pleased with yourself."

"I got rid of her, didn't I? Did you see the blood on her face? She's so weak, even a little scratch is too much for her."

"You should be ashamed. I am shocked at the way you've behaved," he said.

She shrugged and looked up at him through her eyelashes. "What are you going to do about it, Henry?"

He grabbed her arm. "You're going to spend the night in a jail cell."

"No, Henry! Don't. She's sorry, aren't you, girl?" Petunia said.

"Oh yes, 'course I am. So terribly sorry," Miss Penwrith said, without a trace of sincerity.

"You assaulted my fiancée. Have you nothing to say for yourself?"

Petunia put a warning hand on Miss Penwrith's arm. "Don't say anything. You've caused enough trouble tonight."

The young woman shot Petunia an angry look and shut her mouth.

"Let me take the girl home," Petunia said.

"She belongs in jail."

"Please, Henry." Petunia looked him dead in the eye. "Think of what this would do to your father. He cares for her family. It would break his heart to see her led away like a common criminal, and after all she's been through."

Henry frowned and said, "Fine. Take her away this instant."

Miss Penwrith said, "You can't make me. You'll be sorry if anything happens to me. Just wait and see! Then you'll come running."

"Only if you were dead," he said rudely, and took pleasure in seeing shock cross her face.

He saw Petunia standing nearby, looking ill at ease. "Mrs. Dyngley, take her away from here. Right now."

Petunia opened her mouth to protest, then shut it. She nodded and motioned for Miss Penwrith to follow her.

Henry had escorted them both out, waiting for them to climb into one of the Dyngley family carriages. Miss Penwrith smiled at him, ignoring his frosty glare.

He didn't care; he was going to set her straight in the morning and send her away. He didn't care that she had nowhere to go; he'd be damned before she came anywhere near him or Poppy again.

His thoughts back in the present, he wrote a quick note of apology and concern for Poppy, and sent it via a messenger, then rode out to his family home, his horse easily making good time as the roads were dry. The day was warm and his horse was tired by the time he arrived at Faulkbourne Manor, but he didn't care. He dismounted and handed the horse over to one of the groomsmen with orders for it to be cared for, and marched inside, the loose gravel crunching beneath his riding boots.

Once inside the grand house, he quickly sought out Petunia, who stood in the foyer, wringing her hands. "Oh Henry, thank God you've come. I don't know what to do."

"What happened? Did you call a doctor?"

"Yes, of course. That was the first thing I did. But the man hasn't arrived yet. I sent a messenger to you immediately."

"Tell me what happened," he said.

"This way." She led him up the stairs, practically flying up the grand staircase he knew so well and took him down the right corridor toward the guest rooms. "We came home, and she was in a very bad state. She kept saying she would prove it. She couldn't believe you'd reacted so abominably—"

"Me?" he said.

"Her words, not mine," Petunia said, hurrying along. "And then once we got back, she pleaded she was tired and ran up to her room. She cried a bit in the carriage home but tried to hide it. I ignored it, of course."

"You didn't try to comfort her?" Henry asked.

"Not when the girl was trying so hard to hide her emotion, no. I wanted to give her the peace of mind that she was crying quietly and to herself. For her to realize she had an audience would have made it infinitely worse." She glanced back at him. "Lord, Henry. Where is your heart?"

Back in Hertford, he thought, shaking his head. Petunia's coldness toward others never ceased to amaze him.

Soon they were at Miss Penwrith's room, and were joined by the doctor, a local gentleman whom Henry had rarely met more than a few times in his life. Dr. Thornburg was a man with a long face, tufts of whitish gray hair around his ears, and a gnarly brow and beard that desperately wanted trimming. His beady black eyes surveyed them all and he went to Miss Penwrith's side, assessing her and taking her wrist.

"Is she…" Petunia asked, holding herself by her sides.

"She is not dead, but she is not well, either. Who gave her that draught?"

They looked to the small night table beside her bed. On it was an ordinary cup that lay on its side. Henry picked it up and sniffed it. It had an herbal odor and smelled like a bitter tea.

"I do not know. Mrs. Dyngley?"

"I've no idea. She was in a bad state last night, but went straight to her room. I didn't think she'd had anything to drink."

"And nothing before then?" the doctor asked.

"No, nothing. I mean, perhaps she had a glass of wine at the dance, but so did a lot of people." She fretted. "You don't think it was poisoned, do you?"

The man shook his head. "I think it was this draught that did it. Was she in the habit of drinking before bed?"

"How should I know? A woman's toilette is none of any of our business," Petunia snapped, a sign of her unsteady nerves.

"Let us call up the servants and see what they have to say," Henry said, "Doctor, can you confirm? Is Miss Penwrith—"

Miss Penwrith's chest rose and fell and her eyes fluttered. She let out a whispery moan. "Henry…"

"Miss Penwrith! You're alive!" Petunia moved past Henry and stood by her beside, taking her hand. "Are you all right?"

Henry breathed a sigh of relief. Miss Penwrith coughed, her eyes slowly opened and she said, "Oh Henry, you've come. I knew you would come."

"Miss Penwrith, what happened?" he asked.

"I'm sorry?"

"That's it. The girl can barely lift her head. Henry, we are going to address the servants. Someone will pay for this. They could have killed her," Petunia said.

"But…" Miss Penwrith said weakly as Petunia patted her hand.

"There now, don't trouble yourself. Just rest. We'll get to the bottom of this."

Petunia and Henry marched downstairs to the kitchen, to find their cook, Mrs. Piggott, and the housekeeper, Mrs. Ewing, were standing before the pantry.

"There you both are, just the women I wanted to speak to. What in the world is the meaning of this?" Petunia demanded.

The women inclined their heads. "Mrs. Dyngley?" Mrs. Ewing asked. "We heard the young woman took ill. Is she all right?"

"No, she is not. The girl almost died. Which one of you did it?"

Mrs. Ewing stiffened and looked at her colleague. "Begging your pardon, Mrs. Dyngley, but neither of us did anything to hurt the girl."

"She was poisoned with a foul drink. Which one of you did it?" Petunia asked.

"Neither of us made her a drink, ma'am. After dinner we closed up for the evening and the staff were all in their beds by half-ten," Mrs. Ewing said.

"If one of the girls had gone nosing about in my pantry they'd get a stiff smack, and they know it, ma'am. When we came down this morning, the doors were open and bottles were out," Miss Piggott exclaimed, hands on her hips.

"What was taken?"

"Some leftover tea, sugar, honey, poppy and valerian root. Was one of you hard of sleeping, ma'am?"

"No. What is valerian root? Is it dangerous?" Mrs. Dyngley asked.

"Only if you take too much. But that with the poppy, it's a bad combination. No one should be nosing around taking those out. They're liable to kill themselves if they're not careful," Mrs. Piggott said.

"You keep poisonous substances in your pantry, where anyone could get at them? I am disappointed, Mrs. Piggott. Sorely disappointed," Petunia said.

Mrs. Piggott turned red and bowed her head, furious but conscious of her place.

Henry stepped in. "Perhaps you might keep the more dangerous items locked away, to prevent any further mishaps."

"We will, sir. This is the first time this has happened," Mrs. Piggott said.

Henry nodded. "I'm sure it won't happen a second time. But who would have done such a thing?"

The ladies exchanged a glance but said nothing.

"Mrs. Dyngley, perhaps you might check on Miss Penwrith and see if she knows anything," Henry said.

"But I—very well." Petunia left in a huff, and they could hear her sharp steps echoing as she stomped up the stairs. Once the door connecting the upstairs and downstairs shut, the cook and housekeeper instantly relaxed.

"Fix you a spot of tea, Master Henry?" Mrs. Piggott asked, wiping her hands on her apron.

Henry smiled. He'd known these ladies since he was a child. "Not right now, Mrs. Piggott. Have you any idea who would try to hurt Miss Penwrith?"

"Not the faintest. Although she did make herself known."

"What do you mean?"

"It's the strangest thing. I never met such a harsh taskmaster. If I didn't know any better, I'd say she'd been in service."

"What makes you say that?" Henry asked.

"Well, it's just… The young Miss Penwrith, when she was a girl, she was a sweet thing. So meek and shy, and her eyes always did grow big at the sight of you, Master Henry. She did admire you so. To us, even the scullery maids, she was always saying her *please* and *thank yous*. A far cry from the Miss Penwrith today, let me tell you."

Mrs. Ewing shot her colleague a look and said, "She's developed some pride since we last saw her, Mrs. Piggott means to say."

"High opinion of herself, more like, and I don't need you to talk for me," Mrs. Piggott said, shooting Mrs. Ewing a dirty look. "Your Miss Penwrith made it clear she expected you to propose marriage to her any day now. She had some not very nice things to say about Miss Morton, and treated us like we was dirt. Ordering us around, telling the girls to clean her room, press her clothes, shine her boots. She's fond of saying that once she's lady of the household, she wouldn't tolerate any laziness on our part. We almost came to blows when she hinted my kitchen was dirty." She blushed, as if remembering who she was talking to. "Anyway, we spared Nelly to look after her, but she wasn't too keen after a day, that's fer sure."

"Where is Nelly now?"

"She's just had her breakfast. I imagine she's gone to look in after Miss Penwrith."

"I'll speak with her. Thank you, ladies," Henry said.

As he left, he overheard Mrs. Piggott say, "Such a shame he's as good as betrothed to that Penwrith girl. I'd settle her hash if I could."

"Hush, Miss Piggott," Mrs. Ewing admonished.

HENRY WENT BACK upstairs and entered Miss Penwrith's room, where he saw her sitting up in bed with a cup of tea in her hands, attended by Petunia, the doctor, and a maidservant he presumed was Nelly.

Nelly was a young thing, thin like a stick, with greasy dark hair, acne on her chin and a dollop of a nose, as if God had wiped a speck of sugar on her face when making her. She looked as if she had a sweet temperament, but then her eyes gave her away, especially as she listened to Miss Penwrith's tale of woe.

"And then the girl had the audacity to slap me, can you imagine?"

"No, miss," Nelly said, her eyes wide.

Henry knew from her excited look that the girl was a gossip and made a mental note never to trust her with any of his secrets. He cleared his throat and said, "How are you feeling?"

"Oh better, now that you're here." Miss Penwrith turned to Nelly. "You may go. Fetch me a fresh pot of tea." She held out her teacup and Nelly took it and left.

Henry disliked the ordering tone of her voice.

"What did you learn from the servants, Henry?" Petunia asked.

"Not much. Only that they did not disturb the pantry or make anyone any drinks after dinner last night."

"How can you trust them? They're only servants. They'd say anything to escape a scolding," Miss Penwrith said.

Henry's eyebrows rose. "I have known these women since I was a boy. So have you, Miss Penwrith. Do you not remember?"

She blinked and waved a hand, airily. "How am I to remember one from another, especially when I only met them years ago? You are too trusting, Henry."

"We will need to find out who did this. None of us are safe," Petunia said.

"Oh… Um…" Miss Penwrith looked away.

"Do you know something?" Henry asked.

"Well, it's just…"

"Do you know who did this to you?"

"No one."

"What do you mean?" Petunia asked.

"No one did." Miss Penwrith turned pink around the cheeks. "Where is that girl with my tea?"

"Miss Penwrith, you think no one gave you that drink. Why is that?" Henry asked, approaching the bed.

"Why, because no one did. I…uh…" she mumbled something.

"What was that? I couldn't hear you."

"I made it myself," she said louder.

"You did? Why?" Henry asked. "Why would you try to hurt yourself?"

"I didn't. There's no need to make such a fuss. I was feeling tired, and I couldn't sleep, so I helped myself to an old remedy my Ma used whenever she couldn't sleep. It was easy."

Henry looked askance at her. Ma? She never used to call her mother that.

"Why didn't you tell us this earlier? You made me look a fool in front of the servants," Petunia said archly.

"I never told you to question them. You assumed they were at fault."

Petunia shot Miss Penwrith a hard look.

The doctor packed up his things. "You very nearly put your-self in danger, miss. You could have hurt yourself. It's not right, women to be messing about with medicines. They have properties that can be deadly."

Petunia shot him a basilisk gaze, ready to argue, when Henry said, "Well, I am glad Miss Penwrith is all right."

Miss Penwrith smiled brightly at him.

"Come, let us allow her to rest," the doctor said.

"But I—" Petunia started.

Henry extended his hand to her, and she frowned and took it, rising from Miss Penwrith's bed. "I shall check in on you later."

As Henry led the doctor and Petunia out and down the stairs, the doctor said, "I did not want to alarm you, but when I sniffed the bottle, it smelled strongly of valerian. It's used in sleeping draughts. She is lucky. Such a strong dose could have killed her."

Henry paid the man and saw him off, to find Petunia waiting for him. "What do you think she was about, dosing herself like that?"

"Did she seem tired when you returned last night?"

"Not so much. Distressed, maybe. I was tired. That's the last time I take her out without John by my side. Not that he would do anything, but he can be a comfort when he tries. Henry…" she paused.

"What is it?"

"What she said last night. About making you sorry. Do you think she… did this to herself? To get your attention?"

Henry frowned. "I hope not."

Petunia shook her head. "When I think of the scene she caused at the dance, and then that horrid attack on your little friend, and now this. Making me look a fool in front of the help. It's rude. It's so unladylike. It's despicable. It's almost like she's causing trouble on purpose."

He let out a breath. "I must go. I need to check on Miss Mor-ton."

"Oh. Yes, of course. Was she very hurt?" Petunia asked.

Henry paused, his eyebrows rising. "She was bleeding. I will pass along your well wishes for her recovery."

"No, don't. She and I were never friends. I see no need to be disingenuous now." Petunia turned and left, leaving Henry staring after her.

CHAPTER TWELVE

P OPPY'S FACE WAS sore. She had woken and removed the
bandage Miss Cooke had administered the night before,
cleaning the scratches given to her by Miss Penwrith. The water
in her ceramic basin on her writing table was thankfully clear of
blood, unlike the water used to clean her wounds yesterday
evening. She'd felt like a heroine out of a gothic novel as Miss
Cooke had gently dabbed at the scratches on her cheek. The
lamplight played shadows on her lady's maid's face and seeing her
sorry expression made Poppy shiver.

Whatever had made Miss Penwrith attack her so, she knew
the woman was no lady. A well-earned slap was nothing
compared with bloody streaks down her face. But she had felt
such righteous anger at the time. Now all she felt was regret and
embarrassment, at giving in to Miss Penwrith's insults and
responding in kind. Her aunt had brought her swiftly home and
was full of loud mutterings and consternation about her plight,
concern for her dress and hair, but her uncle said not a word.

That morning after breakfast, he asked her to come see him
in the sitting room. As she joined him and shut the door, she felt a
disturbing feeling in her gut, like a pastry that had sat too long in
the sun. Was she in trouble?

"Sit down, Poppy," he said.

She sat and faced him. Her uncle, a rotund man of some sixty years, peered at her from his horn-rimmed spectacles and he laid his quill and papers aside. He sipped a cup of tea Betsey had made earlier. "Do you really want to marry Sergeant Dyngley?"

"Yes, Uncle. I thought we had been over this. We love each other."

"A youthful passion can quickly fade when faced with reality. Think about it, Poppy. The woman who would be your sister-in-law has made it clear she despises you and all of us, despite your money, good breeding, and charm. The men in the family seem civil enough. But this Miss Penwrith, with her outrageous behavior and assertions. She makes every effort with Mrs. Dyngley to throw doubt on the suitability of your engagement to the sergeant and seeks to blacken your name. How can you countenance allying yourself with such a family?"

She opened her mouth to speak when he held up a finger. "I am not finished. Let me remind you that we have kept the circumstances of your mother, and her relationship with your father, a closely guarded secret. But your sergeant knows, and it is a miracle that no questions have been asked by Sir Dyngley. I think it only a matter of time before he wonders at your relationship with the Blackwoods. What do you plan to tell him?"

"The truth."

He wagged a finger at her. "Unwise. The man has his pride and his principles, he would no sooner hear of your dubious background than turn you out onto the street. And if you and Sergeant Dyngley marry in secret, you can kiss any help from him goodbye. He will not welcome any young couple into his home, no matter how smart or charming they are."

She frowned at him.

"Where will you live?"

"At my mother's townhouse in London," she said.

"And then? The sergeant is based in Hertfordshire. He cannot go gallivanting around the county all day and then ride to spend the nights back in London with you."

Her shoulders slumped. "What do you suggest?"

"Aside from breaking off the engagement?"

She raised an eyebrow at him.

"I would urge you to consider giving up your mother's townhouse. Sell it, and the bad memories it holds. You cannot convince me that you hold it dear."

"But I do." And she did.

"How will you survive? A newly married couple must have an income to live on."

"I have my annuity from Papa, and my dowry from my mother," she said.

"That will only go so far. Especially for a young man like the sergeant, who is used to a finer lifestyle."

She felt deflated. "What would you have me do?"

"Think on these things and discuss the practicalities with the sergeant before you marry. And think of a way around Sir Dyngley, should he learn of your origins. He may forgive his son for marrying beneath him, but he will not readily accept a young woman who tricked his son into marriage, especially when she has not the grace or manners to acquit her."

She blinked back a tear. "Why are you saying these things? You sound like Petunia Dyngley."

"I say them because they are what the Dyngley family will think once you enter their sphere. They will assess every ounce of your person, and when they are not dissecting your ready opinions and amateur attempts at solving crimes, they will dismiss your views as uneducated and declare you have no manners. I know I seem harsh, but it is because I want you to be prepared for the household you are entering. They are not nice people, these Dyngleys. I would not see you marry a man only to become miserable and downtrodden. I love you too much for that." Her uncle cleared his throat. "That is all I wished to say."

She rose, nodded, and left the room. She had much to think about. With all that he had thrown at her, would her and Henry's love be enough?

A FEW HOURS later brought her the man himself. She recognized the jaunty hoofbeats of his horse anywhere, and within moments of his arrival, she fretted and patted her hair. Today she wore a light blue and white patterned check dress with a blue sash about the waist and a light blue ribbon in her hair. Her skin was pale, but for her left cheek, which still bore the red scratches from the night before. They itched. She held up a hand and wished for a plaster, or a mask, or something, to hide them so that Henry might not see Miss Penwrith's handiwork and be disgusted by her.

Her aunt was in the kitchen with Betsey and Miss Cooke when Sergeant Dyngley knocked on the front door. Poppy opened it and within a moment, wanted to throw herself in his arms. But she didn't dare, for her breeding and decorum demanded she act with modesty. Instead, she curtsied and said, "Hello Sergeant."

He smiled at the formal tone. "Poppy. May I come in?"

She stood aside and felt his gaze on her cheek. She met his eyes and for an instant, thought his hard frown was for her.

"Are you all right?" His hand drifted to her cheek.

"I am well." She exhaled a little breath, and his hand fell to his side.

His gaze dropped to the floor. "I can only apologize for the actions of Miss Penwrith."

"Is that the sergeant?" Aunt Rachel called from the kitchen. She bustled out, wiping her hands on a floury apron. "Hello Sergeant, do take a seat in the parlor, I'll join you both in just a moment."

Poppy and Henry shared a smile as she accepted his hat, set it aside and led him into the blue drawing room.

Once they were seated, Henry began, "I wanted to let you know that Miss Penwrith has taken ill."

"Oh my word," Poppy said.

"Rather, she has made herself ill. She made herself a sleeping draught, possibly to calm her nerves—"

"Her nerves? What about ours? I lay in bed sleepless the entire night thanks to her," Aunt Rachel said, coming into the room with all the grace of a royal British navy ship.

"She made herself ill."

"Good riddance to her," Aunt Rachel said, sitting down on the striped sofa beside Poppy. "Couldn't have happened to a better person."

"Aunt," Poppy started.

"It's true. You were up late with Miss Cooke tending your wounds thanks to that ungodly woman. You've seen her face, Sergeant."

"Yes," Henry said gravely.

There was a sharp knock at the door of the parsonage, and Miss Cooke went to answer it. A moment later she returned to the blue sitting room. "A Mr. Faulkbourne, to see you, Miss Morton."

"A visitor for Poppy?"

Miss Cooke stood aside as Mr. Faulkbourne entered the room and bowed. "Ah, I see I am not the first." He held out a bouquet of flowers to Poppy.

"Oh, how kind." Poppy accepted the bouquet, unaware of Henry's dark look. "What are these for?"

Mr. Faulkbourne laughed. "Have you never received flowers before? They are to cheer you up after your war wound."

Poppy's hand drifted to her cheek.

"Do not trouble yourself on my account, I had expected you to be laid up in bed like a grand lady. Although it does not look so bad as it did last night. That was very brave of you, Miss Morton, to withstand that girl's attack like that."

Henry cleared his throat.

"I didn't see you there, my good man. I forget, did you say you were with the constabulary?"

"Yes. A sergeant."

"And is that vicious woman sitting in a jail cell?" Before Henry could speak, he added, "I ask because I am confused. You see, I stopped by the jail earlier and did not see her there. Why might that be?"

Henry's face clouded. "The woman took ill and is resting at home. She is an invalid."

"I see. And what convinced you of her innocence? Her attack on Miss Morton was after all, seen by dozens of witnesses." Mr. Faulkbourne's voice took on an even tone.

"Yes, why wasn't she taken in?" Aunt Rachel asked.

Henry coughed. "My sister-in-law pleaded her case. She begged to be able to take her home."

"After she attacked my Poppy?" Aunt Rachel declared. "Why?"

"I agree. Why should you accept the word of your sister-in-law over this girl's flesh and blood." Mr. Faulkbourne paused. "Oh, I see it now. I understand."

"What?" Poppy asked.

"Well, it's obvious. Never mind. I'm sure the constable was acting in his best conscience," Mr. Faulkbourne said, "No doubt he did what he thought was best."

"What do you mean by that?" Poppy asked quietly.

Henry blushed. "The girl was taken away and became ill. They thought she had almost killed herself this morning."

"Oh, well. These grand ladies," Mr. Faulkbourne waved a hand airily.

"Never mind that," Aunt Rachel said. "I would know your meaning, Mr. Faulkbourne."

"Well... Only that in some parishes, when there are altercations or matters of disagreement, there is a certain way of doing things. One rule for the members of the genteel and aristocracy, and another for the lesser sort. More common folk," Mr. Faulkbourne said, with an attempt at delicacy. Or was it false sincerity?

"My word." Aunt Rachel shot to her feet. "Well Sergeant, I think you'd better go."

"Aunt," Poppy started.

"No. I've heard enough. Sergeant, thank you for your visit."

Henry rose. "I came to inquire after Miss Morton's health."

"She is fine, as you can see. I only hope that that wretched young woman Miss Penwrith is plagued by her own conscience for doing such a thing."

"Aunt…" Poppy started.

"And you Poppy, with nothing to say for yourself. Why not?" Aunt Rachel put her hands on her hips. "I have raised you to speak your mind, not to be a meek little milksop."

"I know that the Sergeant acted the way he thought was right. I trust him, even if I do not always agree with his actions," Poppy said.

Henry shot her a grateful look.

Poppy said, "Thank you for the flowers, Mr. Faulkbourne. I'll just put these in some water. Excuse me." She left the room.

Henry said, "I must be going anyway. I just wanted to pay my respects. I hope to see you all at the manor tomorrow."

"The manor?"

"For our wedding preparations. We wished to extend the invitation after our dinner was interrupted and felt a few days' stay might be pleasant."

"May I come?" Mr. Faulkbourne asked.

"Yes, of course," Aunt Rachel said, shooting Henry a level look. "What's one more to the happy party?"

"As you wish, madam." Henry bowed and left.

Mr. Faulkbourne did not stay long after.

Poppy put the water in flowers in the kitchen and set them again on a table in the sitting room by the window, just as the sound of a carriage was heard outside.

"Oh, who is that? Not more visitors. Unless that girl has come to apologize, I have no interest in seeing more people, not at all," Aunt Rachel said, sitting back on the sofa.

Moments later Miss Cooke answered the door. Voices were heard, and she soon introduced, "Lord Blackwood and Mr. Blackwood."

"Father. James," Poppy said with a smile, and rose.

Lord Blackwood entered, and his smile fell. "Poppy, what's happened to you? Your face…"

James followed him into the room. "Poppy?"

Poppy's hands darted to her cheek. "A misunderstanding at a country dance."

James's eyebrows rose up to his forehead. "And I thought duels were dangerous."

Poppy smiled. "It is nothing. I am glad to see you both."

The men smiled. Lord Blackwood and James bowed to Aunt Rachel. "We thought we might visit you and stay a night in town before you all descend upon Faulkbourne Manor," James said.

"Oh?"

He pulled out an invitation from his slate gray suit jacket's pocket. "We received it just the other day. I am happy for you, Sister." He pulled Poppy into a close hug.

Poppy grinned and loved the attention, relishing his touch. Even if James was only her stepbrother, or distant half-brother, she loved him as dearly as if she'd known him her entire life.

Aunt Rachel said, "You will stay for dinner, won't you?"

Poppy stepped back from the hug and saw Miss Cooke's wince at the idea of so many mouths to feed. "I rather feel like dining out. What do you think, Aunt?"

"A fine idea," Lord Blackwood said. "I have a longing for the cottage pie served at the Red Lion Inn. Do they still make it?"

"I would think so. We should find out," Poppy said, matching his smile.

"Agreed. Shall we meet there say at six o'clock?" he asked.

"Excellent notion. I say, Poppy, show me around the place. I want to see where you grew up," James said.

Once they were alone, he stood by and chatted as she pointed out the upstairs rooms, where her uncle poked his head out of his office and nodded, then went back inside and shut the door. At the sound, Poppy said, "He's working on a sermon."

"Ah," James said. "I imagine that takes some work."

"I suspect it does. How to prevent the parishioners from falling asleep is the task, I suspect."

The siblings shared a smile and Poppy led him outside. As she walked him around the yard with the new fence and the chickens, James said, "I had another reason for wanting to get you alone from the others, Pop."

"Pop?"

"I'm trying out a pet name. What do you think?"

"I don't know." She laughed and saw his cheerful grin had faded. "James? What is it?"

"Well..." He rubbed the side of his neck. "I'm unable to make this little trip to the manor with you all, as I've got to actually check on our accounts in London. But Father will be with you, and I'll be there for the wedding. It's why I wanted to speak with you alone, to warn you."

"About what?"

"You know my mother doesn't know about you."

"No."

"We had to hide the reasons for our going. The invitation arrived and Susan almost saw it, but I hid it from her in time. Neither of them knows where we have gone. They think we've rode to London, to check on Father's accounts."

"I'm grateful you came. Even if under a veil of secrecy," she quipped.

He laughed. "There's another thing. What do you know of Tom Harris? Do you know the man?"

She blinked. "Tom? Yes, I know him. He helped me when I was working as a companion. We're friends."

"When were you working as a companion? I—Never mind. How well do you know him?"

"Pretty well, I suppose. Why?"

"He's been writing letters to Susan."

"What?"

"It's true. Ever since we came back from London after you and Susan had met that lunatic debutante, Susan's been acting very secretive. She's normally rather scowly–"

"Scowly? Did you just make that up?" Poppy asked.

"Yes. What do you think? It's a good variation of the word, I think, and it suits Susan well. She's often scowling around the place. Anyway, she's different. She's… Humming. And dancing when she thinks no one is watching. And she has these letters. I found some in her room."

"James," Poppy admonished. "Those are her private correspondence."

"I know, and I'd normally never do something like that. I just… wanted to know why she's been acting so strangely."

"You think it's these letters?"

"Definitely. There was a dance in London we were invited to, and we never say yes, but all of a sudden she was wild to go. She almost threw a fit when Father said he didn't fancy going. None of us could understand why she wanted to attend so badly. When Mother said we'd just go another time, Susan was almost in tears."

Poppy blinked. "How long has this been going on?"

"Since we came back from London."

Weeks, Poppy realized. "And now?"

"She was happy to see Father and me gone, but angry when she found out we were going to London without her." He slipped his hands inside his pockets. "I don't like to think of what might happen if she goes to London and finds we're not at the family townhouse. She'll know we lied about where we were going and she might come here."

"Do you really think so?"

He nodded. "She knows of our connection. I just hope she doesn't tell Mother. I wouldn't want anything to ruin your wedding, Pops."

"Pops?" Poppy repeated.

"Just trying it. What do you think?"

She shook her head. "You don't actually think Mrs. Blackwood would come, do you?"

"Lady Blackwood, and I wouldn't put anything past her, especially where Father is concerned. Before she fell ill recently, she watched my father like a hawk. If he looked too long at any young woman, she assumed he was cheating on her." He rubbed his right cheek. "It's not what you'd call a happy marriage, exactly. But they do love each other. In their own ways."

"Why are you telling me this?"

"To put you on your guard. If Mother or Susan turn up, don't question why or make pleasantries. Run," he said seriously.

CHAPTER THIRTEEN

HENRY RODE BACK to the boarding house, where he collected his things and paid his bill. He disliked Mr. Faulkbourne intensely, even more so now that Mrs. Greene had invited him along to his home. The woman had no shame. Who was she to go around inviting people to others' homes? It was not to be borne. And yet he knew, just as patiently as his horse trod the dusty roads that led out of Hertford, that he would accept it and more, for the love of Poppy.

He wheeled his horse around and trotted back through town, until he reached the parsonage. Once there, Poppy answered the door.

"Sergeant? Did you forget something?"

"Yes." He pulled her out of the parsonage and shut the door behind her, tilting her head up into a kiss. He kissed her lightly, passionately, trailing his fingers down her neck. He felt her stiffen and then relax into the kiss, like a swan easing its wings. He pulled her to him, feeling her soft warm body touch his. He released her and stepped back with a smile, seeing her eyes flutter as she gazed up at him with surprise.

He took her hand and kissed it. "I did not want to leave you for a time without saying goodbye, properly."

"And is that how the Dyngleys say goodbye?" The left corner of her mouth quirked in a smile, her cheeks turning pink.

"It is how I choose to say farewell to my fiancée," he said.

Their eyes met, and he knew that all was well between them.

"You don't need to worry about me, Henry," she said, "I'm fine."

He gazed down at the angry red scratches on her cheek, a visible reminder of Miss Penwrith's anger. The ugly sight of it made up his mind. "I will leave you now. When will you and your family come to Faulkbourne?"

"In a day or so. Are you sure it's all right that we come and stay?"

"Yes, we have plenty of room. Unless you'd rather..." his voice was hesitant.

"What, Henry?"

He swallowed, feeling a lump in his throat.

"If it is Miss Penwrith you are referring to, I do not care." Her dark brown eyes met his. "The fact is, I feel sorry for her."

"You do?"

"Yes. She clearly loves you and is hurt and angry by the fact that you love someone else. It must cut her to the quick. She knows her behavior is wrong, but I almost wonder if she cannot help herself. She wants your attention so badly. Her little jibes and digs at me, I see now it's all that she has left, to rail at me."

He looked at her. "You are so composed, even after all she has done."

Her smile was kind, and earnest, her fair skin and blushing face rather lovely, despite the angry red scratches on her left cheek. "Her actions were done out of a misguided affection, and that I cannot be harsh about. I cannot blame another woman for loving you when I love you so myself."

His heart felt full, and he squeezed her hands. "Poppy, I meant to tell you, I–"

"Who is that at the door?" A familiar voice called from inside the parsonage. "Poppy? Are you outside?"

Poppy looked at Henry and gave his hands a light squeeze. "We will see each other again soon."

He kissed her right cheek, his lips on her just as the parsonage door opened to reveal Mrs. Greene. He released Poppy's hands.

"Well, Sergeant. Come back to pay another call, have you?" An eyebrow quirked.

He opened his mouth to speak and laughed. Nothing came to mind, and she had caught him. "Not exactly, Mrs. Greene. Just that I did not want to return home again without saying a proper goodbye to Miss Morton."

"Yes, well, I think you've done that now. Go on, Sergeant, we'll be seeing you soon."

He touched his hat and bowed. "Ladies."

"Do not worry, Sergeant, nothing would stop us from making sure Poppy is ready for her wedding day!"

HENRY RODE OFF, feeling the women's eyes on him. He covered the distance easily enough, and soon the familiar sight of Faulkbourne Manor came into view. He loved the sight of the green fields, the small tenant houses, little more than a scattering of homes with small, fenced yards and piping chimneys in the approach. He rode into the main courtyard and dismounted, passing off his mare to a groom. He was met by his valet, Geoffrey, who bowed. "Sir. May I offer you a drink?"

"No, not now. Where is Mrs. Dyngley?" Henry asked.

"In the parlor, with Miss Penwrith."

Henry's eyebrows rose. "She has not left?"

"She is feeling better, it seems, sir." With a pointed look at this travel-worn appearance, he asked, "Would you not care to freshen up after your journey?"

He rubbed the side of his face, feeling a bit of stubble on his chin. He glanced down and his boots were covered with dust from the long ride. He walked into the parlor, where Petunia sat with Miss Penwrith.

His former childhood friend rose to greet him. "Henry, good morning. I am feeling much better, as you see."

He ignored her. Perhaps rudeness would inform her that he

was displeased with her. It seemed to work, for her face fell at the slight.

"Mrs. Dyngley," he said.

"Henry," Petunia said evenly.

"I want her out." He turned to Miss Penwrith. "Miss Penwrith, you are leaving. At once. Pack your things."

"No!" She shot to her feet. "I am still unwell." Her hand drifted to her forehead.

"Henry," Petunia said, "You're being rude. Let's talk about this before you do something rash."

"There will be no discussion. She has assaulted my fiancée." To Miss Penwrith, he said, "That is it. You are lucky I don't throw you in jail. I am already being questioned as to why I didn't the other night."

"Henry, no!" Miss Penwrith came forward and took his hand, pressing it to her chest. "How could you do such a thing?"

He snatched back his hand, causing her to misstep. "I want you gone. Get out. You have outstayed your welcome and abused our hospitality. You are no longer welcome here."

Miss Penwrith blinked back tears. "Is that really all you care about? Kicking me out of your home? I have nowhere else to go."

"It's true," Petunia said, putting aside her sewing.

"I do not care. She may go anywhere she wishes, as long as it's not here."

"Henry, you're being unreasonable."

"Me? She assaulted Miss Morton. You saw it," he said, his voice hardening.

"Yes, I did. And she's very sorry. Aren't you, Miss Penwrith?"

"Yes, I am," Miss Penwrith said immediately, her expression earnest but wary. "Honest, I am."

Petunia cocked her head at her for a second. "There, you see. It was no harm done."

"She clawed Miss Morton's face. She drew blood. I will not dismiss this as easily as you seem to want to. You would not be so quick to overlook her assault if it had happened to you."

"No, but I am a woman of good breeding. I dare say Miss Morton is of a more common stock. She can bear a scratch or two."

It took every ounce of Henry's self-control not to address Petunia with some very foul language.

"Miss Penwrith is my guest, and she is welcome to stay on and keep me company. I need female company after Arthur's birth. She can help me look after him and act as a sort of companion to me," Petunia said. "I will brook no opposition on the matter."

He served her with a look he normally reserved for hardened criminals. She ignored it entirely and gazed back at him.

He turned to Miss Penwrith. "Stay out of my way. I am expecting guests here within a few days. Do not be a nuisance."

"I won't." She nodded.

"And do not even come near my fiancée. Do not touch her, do not talk to her. If you enter a room and she is there, I want you to walk out again. If you do not abide by this, then I will hand you over to the authorities and put you in jail myself. Am I making myself clear?"

She mumbled something.

"Am I clear?" he growled.

"Yes, Henry," she said meekly.

He strode out of the room in a huff, anger in his every step. His dirty boots struck the polished floors as he returned to his room and stripped down to his trousers and undershirt. There was a slight knock at his dressing room door and he whirled around. "What?"

"Henry," Petunia walked in and shut the door. "I know you are displeased—"

"That's one way to put it," he said, and sat down on his bed. "What do you want, Mrs. Dyngley?"

"If this girl means so much to you, why do you not make her your mistress?"

He gaped at her.

"I understand that what I say shocks you. But think on it. She has no society, no connections."

He glared at her.

"And until recently she had no fortune to speak of."

"She does now."

"That would only be a drop in the ocean to what the estate needs and you know it," she said, "I swear I cannot see what hold this girl has on you. But think of it. Her mother was a mistress. That sort of profession, I mean…"

He stared at her. "You're never going to understand, are you?"

"I understand that she comes from a different sphere, and she is beneath you. You think you love her now, but what will happen when her money goes away, and all you are left with is her country ways? They will not seem so charming, and you will resent her. Believe me, Henry, I do not speak these words out of a means to hurt you or her, but to guard you against your meaner self. It is inevitable. I do not want her to run into my rooms crying and whining because you do not love her anymore."

He was tired from the ride and felt it then. Could she be right? "What would you have me do?"

"At least do not treat Miss Penwrith with such incivility. She needs our help and has nowhere else to go."

"That is unfair to Miss Morton and her family. They are due here in a few days. It is insulting to expect them to be here and have to face Miss Penwrith."

Petunia frowned. "Then we shall put them in separate corridors. With any luck they will only encounter each other at mealtimes." she paused. "Do you really mean to go through with this, Henry?"

"Yes. Why is that so hard for you to understand?"

"I've never understood why anyone would seek out the company of those beyond their own social sphere, especially those of a lower sort. What is the attraction?"

"I hope you never find out," Henry said. "On second thought, perhaps there is a stable boy I might introduce you to..."

She turned red, squawked in alarm and ran from the room. Henry laughed and called for Geoffrey to run him a bath.

Once he was clean, Henry felt better. He'd dressed and ran a comb through his damp hair, he walked down to the servants' hall, where he sat with the housekeeper and cook in the housekeeper's private parlor.

"It's true then, that there's to be a wedding," Mrs. Ewing said in a polite tone.

"Yes. I am marrying Miss Morton."

Mrs. Piggott's eyes widened. "So, you're not to marry Miss Penwrith then? Praise the Lord."

"Mrs. Piggott?" he asked.

The housekeeper shot her colleague a dirty look, and the cook turned pink. "Begging your pardon, sir. Just the scullery girls getting up to gossip, you know how these silly chits are."

"What were they saying?"

"Nothing. They're saying they heard Miss Penwrith taken ill, and you gone to her bedside, that you're announcing your engagement to her any day now."

It was all Henry could do not to roll his eyes. "They are mistaken. I am to marry Miss Morton."

"Yes, Master Henry."

He explained the wedding preparations that needed to be done, and spoke with the butler, Mr. Newell. The man looked rather odd, with thin cropped hair, slightly narrowed eyes and a thin angular face. For as long as Henry had known him, he had seen the man as very polite and civil, but detected no warmth there.

Still, it was soon settled, and Henry spoke with the staff at length over the flowers and decorations to be had, the cake to be made, the meals needed for the wedding breakfast, and the rooms that needed preparation for guests.

IN NO TIME at all, the arrival of Poppy and her aunt, along with

Miss Cooke, set things astir. Lord Blackwood came in a carriage which looked very grand, and Mr. Faulkbourne arrived, on the invitation of Mrs. Greene, but no one seemed to mind. Then strangely enough, there came another rider, which turned out to be Tom Harris. He had packed a bag and looked a bit travelworn, but was received with great cordiality as another of the guests, particularly when he showed his invitation. He took in the view of the great manor house with interest, but seemed to be slightly distracted, as if he were looking for someone.

True to her word, Miss Penwrith stayed out of sight, only venturing out during mealtimes. When she and Miss Morton were in the same room together, she soon left, and took to wandering the gardens.

Lord Blackwood soon befriended John and Sir Dyngley, and took to spending time playing billiards, cards, or reading in the library. Tom soon joined their merry bunch, along with Mr. Faulkbourne, who after a brief period of awkwardness, took pains to ingratiate himself in the company, and whose cheerful temperament and good manners made him a welcome addition.

Petunia made it clear that Miss Penwrith was perfectly welcome in her company, and they soon seemed to have their own society, which served to exclude Poppy.

Henry did not care for this sort of social clique but was soon distracted by the number of things left to do before the wedding. Petunia wanted no part in any of the planning, as a sign of her protest against the match, so it was left to Henry to work with the servants and go over plans for the meals and decorations. It was a busy time, and as such it left him little time to check on Poppy.

POPPY AND HER aunt stayed together. Mrs. Greene wandered around the gardens and stayed in the parlor or worked on her sewing while Poppy read books in the great library. Henry had just opened the library door to say hello, when all of a sudden they heard the most dreadful commotion, a baby crying, a woman pleading and the slam of a door. As a group they got up to see, and went down the hall, where they passed a woman in a servant's uniform, hurrying away. Poppy and her aunt knocked and came upon Mrs. Dyngley with a crying little Arthur in her arms.

"Mrs. Dyngley?" Poppy asked.

"Oh, what do you want? Can't you see I'm busy?"

The baby cried and waggled his arms, his face red.

"What's happened?" Poppy asked.

"Another wet-nurse gone. That's the third this month." She held the child at arm's length, her angular face pinched in worry. Arthur cried louder.

Henry winced at the sound, as Aunt Rachel swooped in and took the baby, holding him in her arms. She bounced the child and burped him and he hushed.

Poppy and Petunia stared in amazement as Arthur quieted.

"What did you do?" Petunia asked.

"I'm the wife of the local rector. I've looked after a few babes in my time." Aunt Rachel smiled.

Petunia relaxed and exhaled a sigh of relief. "That's excellent news. You can look after him, then."

Aunt Rachel's mouth dropped open.

Petunia rose and said, "Thank you very much, Mrs. Greene. I can hardly think when he is crying like that." She touched her nose and said, "And I believe he has soiled himself. Please do change his nappy. You'll find his things in the nursery."

"Where are you going?" Poppy asked.

"I am due for my afternoon walk. I need it for my health, the doctor said." Petunia sailed out of the room.

"Well, that's a fine kettle of fish. And to think, that was the first nice word I've had from her since we've arrived," Aunt Rachel said.

Henry stammered, "I'm sorry about this. I'll see about hiring another wet nurse."

"Oh, don't worry, I don't mind looking after children. I never had any of my own, not really, so it's nice," Aunt Rachel said, making faces at little Arthur. He laughed and pulled her nose.

CHAPTER FOURTEEN

POPPY WAS WALKING in the gardens when Petunia found her. "Hello, Mrs. Dyngley."

"Miss Morton. I will walk with you a little."

The pair walked through the gardens, which were set out in orderly quadrants. They currently strolled in the flower garden, where wild roses grew along the stone walls. Bright pink roses that reached high into the sky, so high their branches intertwined with the trees above, and yellow roses with red inside petals. Small yellow cowslips peeked in a row, their tubular clumps of light cheery yellow petals looking like miniature bells that turned up to seek the sun.

As they walked on, they reached the manor's vegetable garden, where green and red leafy stems of rhubarb grew, their leaves larger than the width of two hands.

"For my part, I am relieved to have had the opportunity to speak with you alone, away from the others. I have spoken with John, and he says that it is no great matter to marry below one's station. That if there is love, that is all that is needed. To him I say a man must provide for his wife, for love will not feed them when they are hungry. He laughs at me and calls me a pragmatist. What do you think?"

Poppy took a moment to smell one of the low-hanging pink roses, conscious of insects walking along its petals. She released the rose and said, "I think both your arguments have merit. Without love I would not expect it to be a happy marriage, but neither do I think a married couple can have nothing to live on. There must be an income, and economy, for a match to work."

"My point exactly. And what is your thought on the matter of different stations? Do you think it is possible for a person to marry beneath them and be happy?" Petunia asked.

"I wouldn't know."

"But you are to marry soon. Surely you have thought on it."

Poppy gave a tiny snort and said no more. She was not of Henry's station, she knew that. To hear it mentioned so openly surprised her.

The ladies did not say more, for their attention was distracted by the arrival of a carriage. "Who could that be?" Petunia asked. "More guests? It's practically time for supper."

They walked out of the gardens and around the house to the main courtyard, to see the carriage that had pulled into the dusty round entrance. The pair of horses that had pulled the carriage stood with their sides heaving, as if they had traveled at speed, and as groomsmen and footmen came forward, the doors to the carriage opened and a tall, thin woman with a face like a stiff prune came out, bellowing orders.

"Who is that?" Poppy asked.

"What a fearsome-looking woman. I'd hate to be on the foul side of her," Petunia said.

They watched as the woman was joined by a younger woman with ash blonde hair.

"Oh no," Poppy said softly.

"What is it? Do you know that young woman?"

"I'm afraid I do."

As if by magic the women heard her, and both the new arrivals turned and saw them observing them from the garden.

Poppy watched with dread as her half-sister Susan followed the fearsome woman, who approached with a mighty glare, as she fixed her green, snake-eyed gaze on Poppy and Petunia.

"Excuse me. Are you acquainted with my husband, Lord Blackwood?"

"Yes," Petunia said.

The woman raised her nose high as if Petunia were a pile of dog refuse and slapped her across the face.

Poppy stared in disbelief, her mouth dropping open as Petunia did what any well-bred woman would do: she shrieked bloody murder. Poppy stood in front of the strange woman with her arms spread wide. "Stop this."

People came pouring out of the building as the older woman lunged at Poppy, reaching for her like an unholy wraith.

Poppy stumbled and fell back to the ground, scrambling back on her hands and feet. The grass was wet beneath her skirts, and she could feel the wet blades soaking into the fine material of her dress. But none of that mattered now, for the foul woman had stepped on her hem and she was trapped. Poppy tugged and tried to get back but she was stuck. "Let me go."

"You foul, wicked creature," the older woman snapped at Petunia. "How could you do it? And have the audacity to invite my husband? Have you no shame?"

"What on earth are you talking about? You senseless harridan!" Petunia cried.

The woman standing over her was tall and thin, with short, curled hair that was fading to gray, thin dark eyebrows that had narrowed angrily, and a low, small bosom that drooped. She wore a fine gray dress that had seen better days but was worn and well-loved, for it bore the traces of many washings and patched-up marks. Its fine threads frayed and dust had collected at the hem. She wore thick boots that were suitable for traveling but not for walking.

"Mother, stop!" Susan's voice called out. She ran toward them, followed by John, Henry, and Lord Blackwood.

The woman ground her booted heel into the hem of Poppy's dress, looking her dead in the eye. "You are interfering where you do not belong. Let a muddy skirt be the least of your troubles, girl."

"Get off me," Poppy said, tugging at her dress.

The woman smirked as Susan ran up and pulled her away. "Mother, what are you doing?"

"Restoring justice in this den of inequity. Where is your father?" The strange woman asked.

"Den of iniquity? Excuse me, but that's my home you're talking about. Who are you, madam, and why are you trespassing here?" John demanded, walking up to them. He held a hand out to Petunia and helped her to her feet, frowning at her muddied hem. He put an arm around her shoulders and held her close.

At that moment the clouds opened with rain, and within seconds the air was filled with a downpour.

"Let's go inside," John said loudly, and he led the way through the gardens and back into the house.

Once standing inside the marble foyer of the house, John said, "All right. Would someone mind telling me what is going on? You, madam. Who are you and why are you attacking my wife?"

"Who are you?" The woman demanded. She reminded Poppy of a picture of an ostrich she had seen, with a very long neck, wide eyes, a sloping nose, and short hair curled around her head.

"I am John Dyngley, and this den of iniquity you are standing in is my home. Mind telling me what you're doing here? Preferably without your fists." He stood protectively by Petunia, who glared at the stranger.

"I am Lady Amelia Blackwood. You, sir, have in your company a woman of ill repute. I demand that you remove her from this house immediately."

John blinked. "That is quite a charge. What proof do you have of her guilt?"

"Proof? I do not need any, for it is written upon her face. Can you not tell that she is a woman of ill-gotten gains?"

Everyone stared at the woman.

"Mother..." Susan started. "It's not what you think." She reached for Lady Blackwood's arm, but was shaken off.

"Really? And when I find a note in your father's things to his darling Poppy, what am I to think?" She glared at Petunia with a blazing look of righteous fury. "I have long suspected that my husband dallied elsewhere, but to do it with such a woman, and so brazenly, under your noses. Tell me you were not aware of this solicitous assignation."

John blinked again. Petunia scoffed and uttered, "I am not Poppy, you nitwit. I am Mrs. Dyngley. That is Miss Poppy Morton." She held a hand to her cheek. "Do you always go around hitting people rather than saying hello?"

Lady Blackwood had the grace to blush. "I apologize. But I might ask you why you are spending time in the company of such a woman."

Down the staircase came Lord Blackwood, who stopped short, his hand frozen on the wooden banister. "Amelia."

"Hugh."

"What are you doing here?"

"I might ask you the same thing. Imagine my surprise, when I am told to my face that you and James are to go to London, only to find notes—"

"Notes? You were interfering in my things?" he asked.

"That is of no import. What I found was horrid. Simply horrid."

"What is all that noise?" Sir Dyngley walked in from the other room with Henry and Aunt Rachel, who held little Arthur. "You've woken Arthur up from a nap. What is all this? I can hardly hear myself think." He looked at the sour-faced woman. "More people? Who are you?"

"I am Lady Amelia Blackwood. And I demand that you throw out this young woman at once." She jabbed a finger at Poppy.

"I wish I could," Petunia muttered.

"Mrs. Dyngley," Henry snapped.

Sir Dyngley waved a hand. "What is the matter here? I heard an awful shriek from outside. Was it an animal?"

"No, it was not." Petunia glared at Lady Blackwood. "This

woman attacked me, mistaking me for Miss Morton."

"What is the meaning of this?" Henry asked. "Miss Morton, are you all right?"

"Who cares for her when it is I who have been struck?" Petunia said.

"Amelia, what are you doing here? Susan?" Lord Blackwood asked.

"I found your notes, Hugh. The letters between you and your harlot," Lady Blackwood practically spat. "And when I brought this evidence to our daughter, why, she knew all about it."

Poppy breathed in. "You found our correspondence?"

Lady Blackwood laughed. "Is that what you call it? I can scarce believe you speak of it so innocently, when it is the proof of my husband's guilt. And adultery." She sniffed.

"Now hold on, just a minute," Aunt Rachel said, bouncing the baby in her arms. "My Poppy has done no such thing. You've got the wrong end of the stick, er… Lady."

"Have I? Then I am a fool, for I seem the be the last to know of this."

Sir Dyngley scratched his head. "Would someone please tell me what is going on?"

"Let us get out of these wet things first. Come down for tea in a quarter hour," Petunia said. She called for the servants and ordered them to prepare a room for the new arrivals.

ONCE GATHERED IN the dining room, Poppy looked around. The long table could easily seat fourteen or more, but she counted herself, Susan, her father, on her right, and her aunt on her left. Next to them sat Miss Penwrith, Lady Blackwood, Henry, Petunia, John and Sir Dyngley. Poppy felt slightly grateful that it was not the entire household come to witness this conversation, for she feared it would be uncomfortable.

Petunia opened her mouth, when Sir Dyngley spoke, his even voice cutting across her. "It is pleasing to me that we are all gathered here together to celebrate the joining of our houses.

And now we are graced by Lady Blackwood and her daughter. I bid you both welcome."

"Hah! A fine way to put a pretty face on this den of sordid activity," Lady Blackwood said.

"I beg your pardon?" Sir Dyngley's voice was chilly.

"Amelia," Lord Blackwood admonished.

She shot him a dirty look.

"Perhaps you might say why you came here unannounced and seem intent on dismissing our home," Sir Dyngley said.

Poppy saw then that the man appeared old, but he was not forgetful or befuddled, and one would be wise not to dismiss him due to his age.

"I apologize, sir. She—" Lord Blackwood started.

"Do not apologize for me like I am a child. I am your wife," Lady Blackwood snapped.

"Then act like one," Lord Blackwood said.

She shot to her feet. "I followed you here, to this place, and—"

"Madam," Sir Dyngley said.

"Lady Blackwood," she told him.

"Lady Blackwood, am I to understand you believe there is some impropriety here?"

She blinked. "Are you so blind you cannot see what is happening right under your nose? Or in this case, your roof?"

"What do you mean?"

She took a deep breath. "For years, I have long suspected that my husband has been… unfaithful. His regular trips to London, his having seen plays and exhibitions, with never a thought that I might like to attend. He has been neglectful, sir, but that is not the worst of it."

Sir Dyngley's eyebrows rose. "No?"

"No. I have found correspondence between my husband and that woman." She did not even dignify Poppy's presence with a look.

"But that is only natural," Sir Dyngley said.

"Natural? You mean to say you condone this sort of wicked behavior?"

Sir Dyngley glanced at Lord Blackwood. "Would you care to explain?"

Poppy's father looked down, his expression a mixture of embarrassment and regret. "Amelia, Miss Morton is my daughter."

Lady Blackwood hissed, "No. It cannot be."

"It's true, Mama," Susan said.

She glanced at her daughter with venom. "I am shocked. I suspected Hugh of foul deceit, but you? You knew of this? And you kept this from me?"

Susan hung her head.

"Then Miss Morton is… Illegitimate," Sir Dyngley said.

Miss Penwrith simpered, earning sharp glares from Henry and James.

Poppy's head snapped to Sir Dyngley and blushed. Petunia looked pained.

"Yes, she is. Her mother came to us years ago and asked us to raise her. We raised Poppy as our own. And we've no shame of it. She's a good girl, with a smart head on her shoulders," Aunt Rachel said, her voice loud.

"So, you mean to say you knowingly cheated on me, you are an adulterer, and this girl is your illegitimate child," Lady Blackwood said.

Petunia held up a hand. "Good Lord, must you repeat it? This revelation is bad enough."

Lady Blackwood shot her a look.

"Miss Morton's birth means little to me. And as far as I am concerned, this has no bearing our on engagement," Henry said, earning a grateful smile from Poppy.

"Henry you are being obtuse. You cannot expect to bring such a woman into our family, especially under the guise of such… low origins," Petunia said.

"I don't understand," Tom piped up. "Is it that Lord Blackwood slept with another woman or that Miss Morton is illegitimate, that is the problem?"

"That is not the entire matter," Miss Penwrith said.

Poppy's heart stuck in her throat.

"Miss Penwrith, now is not the time for your tales," Henry said.

"Oh, I think it is. You see, Sir Dyngley, they mean to pull the wool over your eyes. They make it sound as if Miss Morton's mother was a woman of equal standing, but I assure you she was not."

"Girl, you know not of what you speak," Aunt Rachel warned.

"But I do. Mrs. Dyngley told me everything." Miss Penwrith shot Petunia a triumphant smile. "Do you want to know what she said?"

Poppy met her father's look of alarm. "Perhaps we might continue this conversation in private," Lord Blackwood started.

"Miss Morton's mother was a whore. She was Lord Blackwood's mistress. She's been whoring herself out for years until a madman killed her."

"You little witch, I hope you die." Poppy flew out of her seat and lunged at Miss Penwrith.

"Poppy!" Aunt Rachel cried, her arms full of Arthur.

Miss Penwrith screamed and backed away, falling out of her chair, as she hit the floor.

Poppy screeched and scrabbled, halfway across the table when James and Henry pulled her back, their hands grabbing hold of her. She was pulled back and pinned with her arms behind her back like a common criminal, hair tangled around her face as she glared at Miss Penwrith. "I hope you are pleased with yourself."

"What has come over you, Poppy?" Aunt Rachel asked, holding Arthur close to her chest. "Have you lost all sense?"

"You saw it! You all saw it, she tried to kill me," Miss Penwrith said, pointing at Poppy. "Oh I've hurt my wrist. It hurts…"

She moaned and clutched her right wrist.

Arthur started crying, loudly, enough so that Aunt Rachel rose from her seat and walked out the door, hushing and cooing at him.

Lady Blackwood helped Miss Penwrith up from the floor. "A fine example of the sort of girl this Miss Penwrith sought to warn you against. We have seen her true colors. But then I would expect nothing less from the daughter of a whore." She raised her nose and gave an indignant sniff.

Poppy looked at the woman with a viper's glare. "Do not call my mother that."

Lady Blackwood scoffed.

"Sir Dyngley…" Petunia started.

"You are right. We cannot allow such a connection into the family," Sir Dyngley said. "I had thought it odd that Miss Morton did not take your surname, and that I could not find her family in Debrett's."

Lady Blackwood sniffed loudly.

"If it was as simple a thing as allying ourselves with the Blackwood family, that would be different altogether, but this… And for you to try and hide this girl's nature and true origins from me." His face clouded. "This is wrong. Lady Blackwood and Miss Penwrith are entirely correct. It is deceitful and dishonest. This marriage cannot take place."

Pain flashed across Lord Blackwood's face.

A gasp emitted from Poppy. She felt the blood drain from her face, and blinked back tears. "No. Please."

"For what it is worth, I am sorry." Sir Dyngley rose to his feet, and looked a bit unsteady, enough so that John reached out to support him. "This engagement is cancelled. There will be no wedding."

"No. Sir Dyngley, please reconsider."

"My mind is made up. I might inquire, Lord Blackwood, why you were so keen for this match to take place. Were you perhaps looking to offload your wayward daughter on a noble family? We may live in reduced circumstances but we have our pride. I will not be false and say that your girl's dowry was not a temptation, but even I am unwilling to overlook what her low birth would mean for our family."

He frowned at the party, his eyes resting on Lord Blackwood. "I am disturbed by the knowledge that it took this girl and your wife to come all this way in order to show me the truth." He sighed and looked weary. "Excuse me. I trust Miss Morton and her family will not be staying."

A tear rolled down Poppy's cheek.

"And neither will we. Hugh, Susan, we are leaving. Right now," Lady Blackwood said, right as a streak of lightning cut across the sky.

CHAPTER FIFTEEN

HENRY FELT A dark pit settle in his stomach as Poppy quit the room without a word. It was as if he had been punched in the gut, and all the air had gone out of his lungs. "Father, think what you are saying. I do not care about Miss Morton's birth, or her mother. That matters not to me. I love her. Is that not enough?"

Lady Blackwood snorted. "Who will want to socialize with you, boy? Who in their right mind would want to dine with the daughter of a whore?"

"Hold your tongue, Amelia," Lord Blackwood said.

"And you have much to be grateful for. You are lucky I have stood by you all this time and do not ask for a divorce. Any court in England would grant it, I am sure."

"Amelia, stop it. You don't know what you are saying."

"Can we focus for a minute? I am sorry that young Henry has been disappointed in love, but what now?" Petunia asked.

People looked at her. "I imagine people will go home, my love," John said.

"No. I do not accept this," Henry said.

"The matter is decided, there is nothing more to be done. Now I am weary. Excuse me," Sir Dyngley walked out of the room.

Henry followed him out. "Father—"

"Enough, Henry. I have made my decision. You do not have my blessing. Do not trouble us both with protesting. I am angry enough with you."

Henry stared at his father. "How could you be so cold? You have met Miss Morton. You liked her."

"That was before I knew the circumstances of her birth. Did you really expect me to rejoice in your choice of a wife, when you worked so hard to hide her true nature from me?"

Lord Blackwood entered the corridor, a tall figure, his face drawn with concern. "Sir Dyngley, I—"

"I have heard enough. I do not need to hear your arguments again. You may attempt to pay her way through life, sir, but I will not allow her to be admitted into this family. You and your wife, son, and daughter are welcome to stay the night."

"Thank you. But Sir Dyngley, please reconsider. She is my daughter. Poppy is a good, sweet girl. She cannot be blamed for the indiscretions of her mother and I."

"No. That is not her fault. But the fact she went along willingly to this farce casts aspersions on her character. I blame you, her, and everyone else for trying to fool me into accepting a girl of her stock. We are of noble blood, much like yourself. I do not judge you on your choice of women, so do not be judgmental of mine," Sir Dyngley said and slowly walked up the wide wooden steps.

"Father, please," Henry started, but a hand on his arm revealed John, who gave a mute shake of his head.

"Leave him be. All this has been stressful on him. Let him rest and we'll speak to him again later. It's been a long day."

Henry frowned at his brother, but he knew he was right. He watched Sir Dyngley disappear upstairs and turned to his sibling. "What am I to do, John? I love her."

John exhaled and gave a little sigh. "I know. But is it not better to have loved and lost, than never to have loved at all?"

Henry blinked at him. "That was profound. Where did you hear that?"

"Some dead poet, I'm sure. Someone will write it. It's clear enough." John scratched his chin. "Come away, Henry."

"I can't. What am I to tell her family? What should I say to her?"

"I doubt you'll need to say anything. Miss Morton was there. You should go to her. I'll speak with Petunia and urge Miss Penwrith to stay out of the way. If you wanted to absent yourself from company tonight, no one would blame you."

Henry felt drained and looked at his brother. His eyes felt dry and itchy, and he rubbed them. "I'm fine."

John gave him a knowing look. "You're not. I've known you all my life, remember? I know when you're all right and when you just think so. Moreover, I'd bet money that Miss Morton's not all right at all, not even a little bit. She's come here with her family. They all thought this was going to happen. You should be by her side."

Henry turned to go when he was cornered by Petunia. She opened her mouth to speak and he swept past her. He did not want to stay and hear any more abuse of Poppy.

Rain beat down on the windows, a sure sign of a storm. The afternoon sky that had looked so bright and promising had darkened and was almost the color of slate rooftops or stone, like that of a grave. The very thought made him shiver as he searched in the dining room, the parlor, and then dashed up the stairs to the guest rooms. He found Poppy sitting on the bed in her room, while Miss Cooke hurriedly packed a valise and her Aunt Rachel fussed and marched to and fro around the place.

At his appearance in the doorway, Aunt Rachel paused. "A fine thing for you to turn up. You've broken her heart. Get out."

Henry shifted on his feet, but refused to budge. "Not until I see Miss Morton."

Aunt Rachel stood in his path, her arms crossed over her chest. "You've seen her enough. Now go."

"Please, may I just have one word with her."

She frowned at him. "What for? So you can plead and make pretty promises and give her hope all over again? Meanwhile your family demonizes her and abuses us all. She's done nothing to deserve such ill treatment and we are going as soon as we are packed."

Henry's eyes went out to the tall form sitting on the edge of the four poster bed. "Poppy?"

She ignored him.

He pushed past Aunt Rachel who sniffed, loudly, and went to his knees before Poppy, taking her hands in his. He saw her face then, and it was pale and bloodless, her eyes already rimmed red from crying.

"Please, say something. Talk to me."

"There is nothing to say." She did not meet his eyes.

He rubbed her cold hands. "I'm sorry. I'll fix this. I will."

"It's over, Henry."

He felt ice jab into his heart. "No. You don't know what you are saying."

"Isn't it true enough? Our family hid my base origins from your father, who Mrs. Dyngley knew only too well would refuse the match once he learned of it. I suppose I should thank her. I wouldn't want a father-in-law who despised me."

"Stop that. He doesn't despise you."

"You're right. He just thinks I'm lesser, of a more common sort, and unsuitable to join your family. Somehow I think that is worse. Like I'm no better than the help." She glanced at Miss Cooke. "Sorry."

Miss Cooke shook her head and kept packing.

"I am sorry I lost my temper and caused such a scene. I don't know what came over me. Please give my apologies to Miss Penwrith. I hope she is not too injured."

"No. Stop this, Poppy. Just stop." He let go of her hands. "Will you not look at me?"

"What for? Just seeing you hurts," she said.

He stood and ran his hands through his hair. "Please, Poppy. Don't give up on us." An idea came to him. "Run away with me."

"What?" her head snapped up. "What did you say?"

"I mean it. Run away with me. We'll go to Gretna Green right now and be married in a matter of hours. We will do it. I will marry you, no matter what my father says. He will just have to get used to the idea of having you as a daughter-in-law."

Poppy's eyes filled with tears.

"Oh Sergeant, think of what you're saying," Aunt Rachel said. Even Miss Cooke had dropped a handkerchief and stood staring at him.

"I assure you, Mrs. Greene, I am thinking clearly."

"You mean it? You would have us run away?" Poppy asked.

"This instant. Pack a bag and we'll go within the hour," he said.

The wind howled outside. Rain whipped against the windowpanes with the slap only hard rain can have. It sounded grim, and Henry fought off a shudder.

"No."

"What? But Poppy, think."

"I am. I want to be with you, Henry, I do. But to go against your family's wishes. To ignore the opinion of your father, when we have nowhere to live. I would not start a relationship with him by having the first impression be that I am not only low-born and wayward, but I have dragged you into a shoddy elopement. He will think me a fortune hunter."

"Hah. There is no fortune to be had."

"A social climber then."

He shut his mouth.

"My answer is no."

"But Poppy…" Aunt Rachel started. "This may be the only way you can be together. Would you throw that away?"

"I would marry Henry honorably or not at all. I will not start a marriage by running away, in secret."

Henry growled. "Damn your pride, Poppy."

Poppy started, and Aunt Rachel gasped. "Sergeant, such language."

He continued as if she hadn't spoken, his eyes only for Poppy.

"You're as bad as my father. You have such morals. Can you not be so rigid and uptight for once?"

She stared as if he'd slapped her. "You propose we elope, then call me uptight?"

"Your mother would not have balked at such an invitation."

Her eyes blazed and she rose to her feet. "Think hard before you mention my mother in conversation, Henry. She made her own choices, but I am sure she acted honorably. How else would she have kept my father entranced for so many years?"

"I can think of a few ways," he quipped, and instantly regretted it.

Her face was all aflame, first pink and now red. Her voice shook and she pointed to the door. "I would like you to leave now, Sergeant."

He bowed, stiffly. "Miss Morton. I ask you that take the time this evening to reconsider."

"I don't need to. You have my answer."

He bowed, she curtsied. Both turned away. He quit the room and almost tripped over Nelly standing outside, uttering a foul curse.

Poppy sat at the small vanity table and gazed out the window until she was left alone.

WITH THE RAIN pelting the windows and Sir Dyngley keeping to his bed, John sent word to all the guests that the roads were unsafe and everyone should stay the night. Dinner was a quiet affair, with Miss Morton and her aunt having trays sent up rather than join the others.

Henry was beastly, ignoring all attempts at conversation, not speaking a word to anyone. He took too much food and sawed into his lamp chops with a harsh ferocity, his fork, and knife screeching against the plate. He drank too much wine and felt heady, bashed a few balls at billiards, and sent them flying across the room before he returned to the library, where he failed to read anything, he found himself gazing outside the window, watching the rain lash against the windows with growing ferocity.

He walked down the corridor to his room, when he spied a note slipped beneath the door. He picked it up. It read:

I have changed my mind. Meet me at midnight. I will wait for you inside the carriage.

—P

Henry's heart rose in his chest. She had changed her mind. She loved him. She really loved him. She was going to run away with him, and they would be together, finally. Man and wife. Sergeant and Mrs. Dyngley. He felt light, and his muddled wits faded in an instant. He rubbed his hands together, there were things to do.

THAT NIGHT, SHORTLY before midnight, Henry crept downstairs. He had packed an overnight bag with money and clothes and had penned a note to his family, that he'd left on his dressing table. Geoffrey was instructed to find it the next morning. Meanwhile, he had enlisted the valet's help in arranging for the carriage and horses to be fed, watered, and rested in time to pull the carriage that night.

He stepped outside the house and shut the door behind him, only to get pelted with rain. His face and hat were soaked, and even his heavy wool coat was drenched. He grimaced and made his way to the carriage and flung open the door, throwing himself inside. Poppy was already there, dressed in dark clothing.

"Hello, my love."

She bowed her head coquettishly.

He slammed the door shut and tapped on the roof to the driver. The man set off, with heavy rain pelting against the roof and windows.

He sat back when Poppy launched herself at him, landing on his lap with a force that made him grunt. He took her in his arms.

She wore a veil over her face, and she lifted it just enough to lean in and press her lips to his.

They felt rough. Chapped. But he didn't care. She was his Poppy, and he wanted her too much to give a damn.

He pulled away. "You changed your mind, then?"

She nodded, squirming in his lap.

He reached to stroke her hair but got tangled in the veil she wore. He coughed and said, "What made you decide to run away with me?"

"I…"

The carriage came to an abrupt stop, sending her rocking.

"What was that?"

"Ignore it. I want to be with you," she purred, her voice muffled through the veil.

"No, we've stopped. I want to know why."

He could hear the driver climb down from the driver's seat.

In a moment, the door to the carriage opened, revealing the driver holding a lantern. "Sorry sir, but the road's washed out. It's not safe to be traveling."

"What? Oh very well," Henry said.

The driver took them back to the house. Henry could hear voices outside, including a woman's saying, "Who is that?"

The door to the carriage was opened.

"Who is that? Henry, is that you?" Petunia asked, holding a cloak over her head to keep away the rain.

Henry squinted in the light that shone in his eyes. "Yes, Mrs. Dyngley, it's us."

"Us? Who are you traveling with? Someone is in there with you?" Petunia asked.

Henry stepped out, getting a face full of rain. "Yes. Come along, Poppy, we've been found out."

He held a hand out to her in the carriage, but she didn't move.

"Poppy?" Petunia said, "Henry, the girl went to her bed hours ago."

"No she didn't, she's here with me. We were going to—never mind."

In the dim light, he saw John and Petunia exchange a look. "Henry, are you all right? Have you been drinking?"

"Of course he has, you saw him at dinner. He drank like a fish," Petunia said.

"Not now, darling. Henry, come out of there. It's pouring rain and we're all wet. As a matter of fact, Petunia, take the others and go inside."

"Come on, Poppy," Henry said, holding a hand to her. "It's all right."

"Henry, what are you talking about? Miss Morton is—oh. She's right here," Petunia said.

Henry looked from her to the carriage. "Of course, she's here. She is in the carriage. She's been there with me the entire time."

"No, Henry, she hasn't," Petunia said, looking at him with a strange look.

Henry looked past her to see Poppy standing in her nightgown with a robe belted around her, her face pale and her long hair plaited in a braid that hung over her shoulder.

"But then... Who...?" He turned slowly back to face the woman in the carriage, who finally shifted toward him and the carriage door.

"Hello lover," Miss Penwrith said, stepping into the light.

CHAPTER SIXTEEN

POPPY LOOKED ON in horror as Henry stumbled back, as if in a daze.

"What? What are you doing here? You're not Poppy…" he said.

"No. How you could mistake me for her is anyone's guess, but then you have been drinking." Miss Penwrith stepped fully out of the carriage. Her bodice hung low, revealing an expanse of chest and her hair was in disarray.

Petunia gasped at the sight. "Henry, what have you done to Miss Penwrith?"

"Nothing, I swear."

"Don't lie, Henry, it's unbecoming," Miss Penwrith said.

"Miss Penwrith, are you all right? Did he hurt you?" John asked.

"He didn't hurt me at all. He might have been a little rough in his attentions but it's nothing I can't handle." She blushed and looked up at John, the beginnings of a smile on her face.

"Henry you know what this means," John said.

"That I am a fool."

"More than that. Come everyone, let's get out of the rain. Edmund, take the horses back to the stables and see that they're made comfortable and dry," John ordered, and the man leaped to do his bidding, keen to be out of the pouring rain.

Poppy stepped back into the shadows of the dimly lit foyer and was soon joined by the others. She clutched her robe tightly around her.

Henry took off his damp hat and stood to the side as John said, "Henry, you have to marry Miss Penwrith."

"No."

Miss Penwrith looked pained.

"You must. You have been seen in a compromising position. Her clothes are disarranged, and her hair. We all saw you both coming out of the carriage, unaccompanied. Where were you going?"

"To Gretna Green. To be married," Miss Penwrith said.

"Not to you. I thought she was Poppy."

Poppy breathed in noisily. "So you thought I'd jump in a carriage and steal away in the middle of a storm."

Henry looked at her, his eyes bleary. "Yes. I thought you'd changed your mind."

"You actually asked this girl to run away with you? Oh." Petunia threw up her hands and rolled her eyes. "Never mind. What's done is done."

"She's right. Henry, you two must marry, and soon. If word gets out…"

"What do you mean?" Henry asked.

"You are being willfully dumb. You have compromised Miss Penwrith's virtue. It is clear you have had your way with her, even if you thought she was someone else," Petunia said, a slim eyebrow raised at Miss Penwrith, who shrugged.

"What has your role in this been, Miss Penwrith?" John asked.

"Why, I was in the carriage, waiting for him. I gave myself to him, and he took full advantage. He was quick to do so." She looked at Henry. "And now we are engaged."

Henry stiffened. "No, it cannot be."

"It is."

"But how did you know to even be here?"

She sidled up to him. "I heard you proposing to run away

with Miss Morton, and her refusing you." To Poppy, she shot a look that said, *You missed your chance, and now he's mine.*

Miss Penwrith continued, "I wrote a note offering to come away with him tonight at midnight, and he joined me. Were it not for the rain we would be well on our way to Gretna Green now."

"But the note, the note underneath my door said you'd changed your mind. It was signed 'P'. P as in Poppy," Henry said.

Miss Penwrith shrugged a pretty shoulder. "A little subterfuge never hurt anyone."

Petunia's mouth dropped. "You willingly impersonated that girl in order to entrap him?"

For a moment Miss Penwrith wilted, then her eyes grew hard. "We all do silly things for love. I am no different."

"But Miss Penwrith, this is dishonest. You admit to pretending to be Miss Morton in order to trick him into the carriage. You seduced him."

"I am tired of all these accusations. So what if I did? It is done now, and I am compromised. We both are. We are either engaged, or I go to town and tell everyone how the son of Sir Dyngley stole my honor and refused to do right by me."

Petunia looked ready to faint. John turned pale. Henry stood stiff as a poker, and Poppy's heart went out to him.

"I wish you were dead," Henry muttered.

Petunia gasped. "Henry, don't say such a thing."

"It's true." He looked at Miss Penwrith with bloodshot eyes. "Better that than… this."

"We will apply for a special license. Immediately. First thing tomorrow, once the rain lets up," John said.

"Do what you like. I don't care anymore." Henry turned his back. He moved to walk away and stopped before Poppy. "Can you forgive me?"

She looked at him. "Can you forgive yourself?"

He looked back at her, his red-rimmed eyes hard and unforgiving.

Before she could open her mouth, he took her few seconds' silence to be a judgment, a dismissal of him and his character, and he walked on, his shoulders slumped. Every step he took was dogged and tired as if he had climbed a mountain, rather than creaking wooden stairs.

Poppy watched him go. She had refused him, and now she felt bereft because of it. He was honor-bound to marry another woman. She wanted to cry and tear her hair out, but she could not. Her features felt as if carved from marble.

"What are those two doing here? Susan, come away from him," Lady Blackwood said, eyeing Susan and Tom standing together, so close they were almost touching hands.

Susan left Tom's side and walked over to him. "What did I miss? I was lost in the house and he was helping me find my way, then we heard voices."

Lady Blackwood raised an eyebrow at her and she blushed.

Tom put his hands in his pockets and leaned against a podium, looking rakish as usual. He glanced at Poppy and gave her a look that said, *Everything all right?*

She gave a minute shake of the head and bid the others good night. She walked quickly upstairs and back to her room. She did not wish to see their faces anymore, particularly Miss Penwrith's, which looked positively triumphant.

IF THE RAIN was bad the previous night, the following morning it was worse. Poppy had slept little the previous night, lying awake and crying silent tears into her pillow. Henry was lost to her. That was all there was to it. Henry, gone and stuck getting married to that wretched woman, Miss Penwrith. There was no justice in this world, she thought, in the early hours of the morning. In the end, she had slept fitfully, tossing and turning. The only comfort was that the rain was so loud, it drowned out any sobs she might have uttered.

Despite wishing she could be like a grand lady and spend the day in her room, her stomach growled, and she was determined to find breakfast. She pushed the light sandstone-colored curtains aside and looked out the window. Rain fell steadily, misting against the glass window panes, and the entire grounds appeared wet and muddy. There would be no traveling home today, she was sure of it.

With the aid of Miss Cooke, she dressed in a plain slate gray dress, that had pretty embroidery around the bodice, short sleeves, and hem. But she had lovingly worn it so many times it was now faded and after many washings, the threads were free and looked a bit straggly. Her brown hair she wore in an ordinary bun with a few wispy hairs teased to hang about her ears and neck, which rather gave her a bookish appearance.

She walked downstairs to the sound of voices. The smell of toast, jam, porridge, and ham filled her nose, and she went in search of the source. She entered the dining room and conversation stopped. There sat John, Tom, Lord and Lady Blackwood, Susan, as well as Mr. Faulkbourne. Poppy paused at the entrance and said, "Good morning."

Then feeling their eyes on her, she walked to the serving area set up for self-service and helped herself to a plate of toast, marmalade, and butter, along with a cup of tea. The men busied themselves by eating, drinking tea or reading the morning papers, but set them down quickly as they were old news.

"Is there none of today's papers to be had?" Lord Blackwood asked.

"No, sir. None. The roads are washed out. It's not safe to be traveling. We're stuck here, I'm afraid," John said.

Susan and Tom shared a look.

"Does that mean we can't leave?" Susan asked.

"Susan," Lord Blackwood said.

"Yes, my dear, that's correct. I hope that's not too onerous. I promise you there are diversions to be had," John said.

"Like what?"

"Well, we have billiards, and a good library, and… We could always play charades, or if you have needlework to do, the parlor is very comfortable, Petunia tells me."

Susan's mouth curled up in a half smile. "I see. What a shame I did not bring my needlework with me."

"That's all right. I'm sure we could find some to keep you occupied," John said.

Susan looked less enthused by this. Mr. Faulkbourne mentioned, "We could always go ghost hunting."

That caught people's attention. "Ghost hunting? What do you mean? That there are ghosts? Here?" Lady Blackwood asked.

"That's what I heard," Mr. Faulkbourne said, winking at Susan.

"What ghosts?" Susan asked as Sir Dyngley entered the room and sat down at the head of the table.

"Ghosts? There are many. Well, really only two. Isn't that right Father?" John asked.

"This manor is full of old ghosts. But there are two you should watch out for," Sir Dyngley said with a smile.

"Do tell, Sir Dyngley," Susan said, her face eager and expressive like a child.

"Well," he started, getting a brief twinkle in his eye. "When my grandfather and Sir Faulkbourne, Mr. Faulkbourne's great-grandfather I expect, had their infamous card game at the club, they were both betting high stakes. I think my great-grandfather couldn't believe his luck when Sir Faulkbourne bet his manor house over a turn of the cards." He looked around the room, catching Mr. Faulkbourne's eye.

"It all could have ended very differently. But the bet, the stakes, and the winning hand were documented and witnessed by the other members of the club. Both men had had too much to drink, but both were gentlemen, and the matter was closed. Both loved a good bet. Sir Faulkbourne cleaned his family out within a matter of days and they removed themselves to London. But he couldn't part with the place. He stayed on and couldn't say goodbye. The legend goes he walked from room to room, pacing, until he found himself on top of the roof of the house, in the east wing. There as the sunlight began to fade, he saw the carriage of the Dyngley family approach, and knew his time had come."

"You mean…" Susan started.

"He threw himself off the roof of the manor house and broke his neck in the fall. He would rather die than hand over his family home to a bunch of outsiders," Sir Dyngley said.

Mr. Faulkbourne nodded in sympathy.

"So now his ghost wanders the corridors of the house, particularly the east wing. And if you look up at the rooftop at night, when the moon is full, you might see him, reliving his final moments before his death."

Poppy shivered. "What a gothic tale."

"Indeed. It does rather chill one to the bone, doesn't it? Now, you ladies should stay away from the east wing, as it's fallen into disrepair over the years, and isn't safe," Sir Dyngley said, pouring himself a cup of coffee. "It's strange. I haven't thought of that story in a long time and yet, I can still see the man throw himself off the roof."

"You witnessed his death?" Mr. Faulkbourne asked.

"Yes. I was but a child at the time. It was ghastly."

"How horrible. That must have been terrifying," Lady Blackwood said. "And you, just a boy."

"I didn't know that had happened to you, Father," John said.

"It's not something I'd normally talk about," Sir Dyngley admitted. "I had nightmares for years. My mother screamed and refused to set foot in the house. It was days before we came back and even then, my mother was afraid to let me go near the roof."

There was a pause as people digested this, and for a few minutes, only the gentle clinks of utensils against plates and tea cups could be heard.

"And the other? You said there were two ghosts," Susan said.

"Miss Blackwood, really." Petunia shot her a look.

Susan looked contrite for a moment, but then it passed.

"I would like to hear about this too," Mr. Faulkbourne said.

"Oh yes. The other is the ghost of Minnie Woods, a local girl.

She was a kitchen maid here when I was growing up." He looked at Lady Blackwood. "You don't mind if I tell the story?"

She offered a polite smile. "You are a good storyteller, Sir Dyngley. I too, love a good ghost story, and you have me quite curious to find out what happened to this maid. Do tell."

He smiled wider and set down his coffee. "The story goes that Minnie was an innocent girl who fell in love with the wrong man. She was thrown over by a footman, who knocked her up with child. But when she demanded he look after her, he laughed and went after other women in the household. Apparently, he was a looker, quite popular with women. Minnie disappeared and was never heard from again. But it was so sudden, and no one had seen her go. She didn't even stay long enough to ask for a reference. I remember that confusing my father. He'd said she was such a good, kind girl." Seeing he had a rapt audience, he said, "In any case. It was thought that during a cold night, when the wind is still, you can hear her calling out Freddy's name, moaning for the young footman who had been her ruin."

"Did the constabulary not investigate this?" Lady Blackwood asked.

"Somewhat, but not as meticulously as they might today. My guess is they did a cursory examination of the household staff at best, and the whole matter was hushed up. Then over time, she was forgotten about. Until the nights when they could hear her call…" His voice was quiet and still.

Silence fell upon the group, and Poppy shivered again, as did Susan, who said, "I love a ghost story. It makes me shiver."

"That's not the worst of it. Freddy left not long after."

"He disappeared too?" Susan asked.

"No. He was fine. But within a few weeks, he left our employ. I think the womenfolk turned against him when he didn't support Minnie," Sir Dyngley said.

"Where is he now?"

"I don't know. Once my grandfather gave him a reference, we didn't hear from him again."

"Where did he go?"

"No one knows. I suspect it was thought that he couldn't stay in a place where his peers thought he was guilty, so he took himself off for another employer."

Lady Blackwood gave herself a little shake. "Enough of this ghost talk. I don't think I'll be able to sleep tonight. Sir Dyngley, what are the state of the roads? Do you think they are safe?"

He shook his head. "I will have my man check, but it is unlikely. After a long rain like this, the road leading to the estate is often washed out, and it can take days to dry. But do not trouble yourself. You are welcome to stay."

"You must all stay." Miss Penwrith entered the room with a large smile on her face. She smiled at each of them, even more so at Poppy. "For those of you who haven't heard, Henry and I are engaged."

Susan and Lady Blackwood looked at Poppy, then at each other. Mr. Faulkbourne dropped his knife and fork, and Sir Dyngley coughed. He looked at Miss Penwrith and she held up a hand. "It is true. He could not honor his… connection with Miss Morton any longer. Just ask John, he was there."

Heads turned toward John. "It is true. They are to wed."

The members of the group offered their congratulations, and Poppy sat back in her seat, silent. The room had suddenly become stifling, as people avoided looking at her. She rose from her seat, the chair creaking. "Excuse me."

She turned to leave the room and walked around Sir Dyngley and Miss Penwrith, when a hand snatched her wrist.

Miss Penwrith said sweetly, "Don't forget, you are invited too, Miss Morton. To my wedding. I know Henry looks upon you as a dear friend." Her eyes were full of amusement.

There was a gasp from someone at the table, and Poppy's face warmed. She shook her wrist free and fled the room. Once standing outside in the corridor, she heard John's voice say, "That was rude, Miss Penwrith. Especially coming from you."

"I was being polite, John. Besides, now she knows where she

stands here. If the roads are as bad as Sir Dyngley says, then we are stuck with her and that wretched aunt of hers. It would be mean for me to exclude them on such a happy day. Now, is there more toast? I'm famished."

CHAPTER SEVENTEEN

HENRY ROSE LATE. He'd missed breakfast, he knew that. The effects of too much to drink the night before and the whirlwind of emotion had taken their toll and he awoke around noon, feeling wretched and with a sore head. He rose, dressed, and washed his face in the cool water awaiting him in the china basin, but still felt groggy. A light rain pattered against the windows and as he looked outside, the courtyard was a sea of mud. The roads ahead had surely washed out. No one would be traveling for at least a day or two.

Then he remembered the events of the night before and sat on the edge of his bed and put his head in his hands. He recalled the moments vividly, but like elements in time, almost in the space of heartbeats. Him, suggesting he and Poppy elope. Her, refusing him. Him marching out and slamming the door behind him, his curses ringing in her ears. A foul dinner. Then finding that note, and all his hopes had been restored. Him finding Poppy waiting for him in the carriage, swathed in a veil like an unholy bride. Then standing in the pouring rain to find out he'd besmirched not her honor, but Miss Penwrith's. It was all like a bad dream, but one he could not wake from.

He recalled Miss Penwrith's gloating smile in contrast to Poppy's horrified expression, and the pang of regret he saw pass over her face. He was a fool. He knew that now. But what was to be done?

There was a knock at his door and he looked up. "Come in."

His manservant, Geoffrey, entered the room. "Good to see you're up, sir. And my congratulations, at your engagement to Miss Penwrith."

Henry groaned.

"We heard about it last night. It's all the maids can talk about."

Henry ran a hand through his hair. "What else have you heard?"

"Only that Miss Penwrith is delighted and said we are all to celebrate with a glass of punch."

"She has no right to be making orders to the servants," Henry said curtly.

"No, sir." Geoffrey quietly offered him a cup of tea.

Henry drank it, feeling the hot liquid knock his senses awake. He smiled at Geoffrey. He was a good valet in that way. Henry thought, and then realized that was not his worst problem. He was in love with Poppy but engaged to Honoria. Nothing short of death would break that connection.

"Miss Morton, how is she? Is she all right?"

"Best as can be, sir. Some say Miss Penwrith was lording it over her at breakfast." He shrugged.

Henry felt the ghost of a smile cross his face. Geoffrey was the sort of man who was quiet, hard-working, and looked honest, so many people trusted him and said things they shouldn't while in his vicinity. He was ever a good source of servants' gossip.

"Your father wished to see you, sir. Once you had risen for the day."

"Of course he does. Very well, I'll go directly."

"Sir. Perhaps you might wish to shave, first?" It was a delicate question, and one which made it clear that he needed a shave, but at that moment he didn't care.

"No. That can keep." He marched out the door and down the corridor, up another flight of stairs until he reached his father's study. He knocked and boldly walked in.

Sir Dyngley sat at his desk with a glass of wine. Not his first, from the look of it. "Henry."

"Father." Henry walked in and closed the door, nodding to John, who stood leaning against the windows that faced his father's large wooden desk.

"Am I right in the knowledge that over the course of last night, you have disengaged yourself from Miss Morton and now are to wed Miss Penwrith? Is that correct?"

Henry's shoulders sagged. "Yes, Father."

"I see. May I ask what led to this turn of the heart?"

Henry's eyes darted to one of the hard, wooden uncomfortable chairs in his father's study and he took a seat, his hands resting on his knees.

John said, "Miss Penwrith tricked him. She led him to believe she was Miss Morton, and had planned to run away with him."

"Is this true?"

"Yes, but not in the way you think. It was all my idea to run away," Henry said.

"Is that so? So you proposed eloping to Miss Penwrith," Sir Dyngley said, steepling his hands.

"No. I had suggested this to Miss Morton and she refused."

"Quite rightly," John said.

"But I received a note later that night after dinner, saying she'd changed her mind. But when I entered the carriage I..."

"Took advantage of the young woman's charms," Sir Dyngley said coldly.

"No, Father. I mean yes, but I didn't realize it was her. I thought it was Miss Morton."

Sir Dyngley frowned. "I don't know what to make of you, Henry. First, you bring this girl here under false pretenses and try to hide her low birth, then you practically ruin a girl we have all known for years and who has declared her love for you, many times." He sat up in his chair, the wood creaking. "I know you do not love her, but I don't see any other way except for you two to marry."

"But Father, Miss Penwrith was dishonest. She wore a veil," John said. "I saw it. You should have seen it, she was so jolly, as if she'd won at the horses, or at cards."

"Does it matter? She was the one in the carriage and the one who is ruined. I'll not have our family's name dragged in the mud by seeing Henry not do right by a girl he has wronged." Sir Dyngley looked at Henry. "I am sorry things have turned out this way. But there is nothing else to do. You must marry the girl."

"And if I don't?"

"That is not even a consideration. If you do not, our family name will be worthless. It will be the gossip on everyone's tongue. Miss Penwrith will be kicked out of society for the shame of it, and debt collectors will come calling. You, John, and Petunia will have no place in polite company, for who would want to socialize with a family who ruined an innocent young woman?"

"I wouldn't call her innocent."

"I wouldn't call you that either, from where I'm sitting," Sir Dyngley snapped. "Now. I know you are… unhappy. But pull yourself up, Henry. You must take account of yourself and act as befitting a Dyngley. There is more at stake here than your wounded pride."

Henry stiffened as if he'd been slapped.

"Now. You will continue on as before, just with a different bride."

"I cannot believe you just said that," Henry said.

"You have only yourself to thank for the predicament we are in," Sir Dyngley said. "Once the roads are clear, we will hold the wedding. Miss Morton's uncle is a clergyman I am told, unless that is false as well."

Henry shook his head. "He is a clergyman." But that would be the ultimate insult, for Poppy's uncle to be asked to officiate over a wedding meant to be hers. Henry looked at his father and saw no comfort there. There were no kind words to be had, only decorum and duty. Woe be it to him to act in an undignified manner. "I need a drink," Henry said.

He and John walked out of his father's study, only to bump into Lord Blackwood. "Sir," Henry bowed.

"Good morning. Is your father in?"

"He is. But I would not disturb him at the moment," Henry said.

"Son, I think the time for not disturbing each other has passed." Lord Blackwood strode in and closed the door.

Henry passed by the billiards table and spotted Tom and Mr. Faulkbourne playing. The men nodded hello as Henry sank into a chair and watched the game. John stood by and helped himself to a drink.

"Well this is a pretty sort of mess you've landed in, Sergeant," Mr. Faulkbourne said.

"No one asked your opinion," Henry said.

"Now now, don't be rude. The way I see it, you've got a few cards up your sleeve."

"What do you mean?"

"The man's stuck, Faulkbourne. He might as well be married already," Tom said.

"Why are you here, Mr. Faulkbourne?" John asked. "It must be uncomfortable for you here, to see your family's old estate in the hands of someone else."

"Yes and no, John," Mr. Faulkbourne said, earning a look of dislike from his host. "I did want to see the old place, so when Mrs. Greene offered an invitation, I couldn't say no."

"That was very kind of her," Henry remarked. "A bit too kind. And presumptuous."

"Henry…" John started.

"I know. Apologies, Mr. Faulkbourne. I am not myself to-day." Henry glanced at the old glass pane windows, where the wind could clearly be heard howling outside, despite the windows being shut.

"We are in for another storm, it seems," Mr. Faulkbourne said.

"Yes indeed."

"Henry," John said. "You should check on the families. The Taits, the Habbeshaws, and the others. See how they've survived the stormy weather. It could be they need help or repairs."

"And what, I am a carpenter now?" Henry asked gloomily.

"No, but it might give you something to occupy yourself, rather than drink yourself into a stupor." John glanced at the empty wineglass in Henry's hands.

Henry looked down. He hadn't even realized he'd been drinking, much less where it had come from. He set down the glass on a side table and got to his feet. "I will go."

"Have you considered the possibilities available to you, Henry?"

"I'd appreciate you calling me Sergeant Dyngley, Mr. Faulkbourne. What are you talking about?"

"You would not be the first man trapped into marriage by a cunning woman, nor the last. But what do you plan to do about it?"

"There is nothing to do. I will marry Miss Penwrith."

"And no doubt, live unhappily ever after for the rest of your life. But there's no need. I mean, there are things a man could do."

"Like what?" Henry asked.

"Don't listen to him, Henry. I dislike the way this conversation is going," John said.

"Then you need not stay for it," Mr. Faulkbourne said, polishing the tip of his pool cue.

"Tell me," Henry said.

"Well, you might look into the background of this young woman. Your families have been long acquainted, have you not? Where is her family now? Perhaps something in her past might shed some light on why she has pushed for you as a suitor so much."

"But we know what happened to her," Henry said, "Her family moved away some years ago, and—"

"Henry. I'm sure Miss Penwrith would not want her circumstances to be commonly known," John said.

Henry quieted. "What else would you suggest, Mr. Faulkbourne?"

"Well, you might demonstrate to others her ill character. It is one thing for us to witness her ill dealings with you and Miss Morton, but it all relies on Sir Dyngley's opinion as to whether or not the marriage can happen. Without his consent, it might not occur," Mr. Faulkbourne said.

"We have to apply for a special license in any case. And with Miss Morton's uncle unable to reach us due to the storm…"

"You will have ample time to convince your father of Miss Penwrith's unsuitability as a daughter-in-law. No marriage can take place anyway."

"I don't like that. She's already thrown away her virtue. Would you have us add insult to injury?" John asked.

"No, but neither would I willingly stand by while he is made a fool of by a woman, and trapped into marriage, no less."

"I've heard enough. Henry?" John asked, moving toward the room's entrance.

"I'll be a moment."

"Suit yourself. But I do not like these ideas." John quit the room, followed by Tom.

"There is one more thing you could do, but you might not like it," Mr. Faulkbourne said.

"And what is that?" Henry asked.

"You could kill her."

CHAPTER EIGHTEEN

AFTER BREAKFAST, POPPY found her aunt and told her what had transpired the night before. As she expected, her aunt was spitting mad and had to be consoled with hot tea and biscuits. As Poppy sat by her, there was a quiet knock on the door of Aunt Rachel's room.

"What is it?"

Petunia stuck her head in. "I'm sorry to disturb you, Mrs. Greene, but… Oh. I see you are not alone."

"Hello, Mrs. Dyngley."

"Miss Morton." Petunia inclined her head. She wore a severe purple dress and had her smart black hair pulled back in a bun beneath her frilly mob cap. Her sloping nose and angular face reminded Poppy once again of a hawk. "Mrs. Greene, I am lost. Can you look after Arthur? He's quite inconsolable without you, and I haven't the skills for childrearing." She held the wriggling babe at arm's length.

"Yes, of course. Give him here. Although I should say no, considering how you all have treated my Poppy."

Poppy blushed. Petunia gratefully handed over Arthur and said, "Yes, well."

Poppy rose. "I'll leave you to look after him. Excuse me."

"Miss Morton, I wonder if you might join me on a turn of the house. Perhaps you might wish to view my private parlor," Mrs.

Dyngley suggested.

Poppy blinked. Was she hearing her hostess correctly? It almost sounded like she was being polite. Civil, even. She swallowed. "I would be glad to join you, Mrs. Dyngley."

"Good." Petunia walked out.

Poppy gave a shrug of her shoulders in answer to her aunt's questioning look and joined Petunia in the corridor. Once they were alone, Petunia said, "I must speak with you alone. Come."

Poppy followed her hostess down the corridor and up a set of back stairs, that wound around a spiral staircase. It led to the servants' quarters on the right, and to the left, a series of rooms. Petunia led her into the first room on the left and shut the door behind Poppy.

It was a room that had recently been dusted and cleaned, but the sofa cushions were worn and tawdry with age, the small side tables were fragile, and the curtains looked as if they might disintegrate at any moment. Nothing matched, and the sunlight was dim, due to the stormy skies outside. But Petunia sank onto the sofa cushions with a sigh and eased herself down. "Sit. I assure you, they are old but quite comfortable."

Poppy sat.

"This used to be a storeroom, but I had the maids clear it out of most of the junk." She gave Poppy an even look. "You can be at no loss as to why I have asked you here."

"No, Mrs. Dyngley, I am not sure at all. I can only guess that you wanted privacy for our discussion," Poppy said.

"Quite right. The matter is, I wish to convey my regret for the situation at hand."

"You're saying sorry?"

"No. Of course not. I did nothing wrong. But I can see that Miss Penwrith, while she may love Henry, she went about it the wrong way, seducing him like that. It was wrong and frankly, she should have stood aside. Once it was clear his preference was for you but that Sir Dyngley would not sanction the match, she could have waited until Henry's mind was clear. But now, well. I am not at all convinced she is the young woman of quality I thought she was."

"What do you mean?"

"Women who are bred well do not do that sort of thing. Not the decent ones, anyway. We do not ensnare husbands by seducing them. Can you imagine the indignity of it? Pretending to be you to get his attention? It reeks of desperation."

Poppy sat back and waited for Petunia to get to the point.

"In any case, I mean to ask what you plan to do about it."

"Me?"

"Yes. In the time I have known you, you have proven yourself to be smart, resourceful, and… not dishonorable. Your choice of company is rather wanting, but you have a good heart, and are sensible I think. It is a shame you are not from a better family, but that is not your fault. So I ask, what do you plan to do about Miss Penwrith?"

"Nothing. I feel it is over and done with. They are engaged. Once the rains stop and the roads are safe again, I will go home," Poppy said.

"Is that all? Resignation and dull acceptance? Your aunt did a poor job of raising you if that is your attitude to heartbreak, Miss Morton."

"What would you have me do? Lower myself to schemes and petty pranks like Miss Penwrith? She won. She has her prize."

"Let me be frank. Do you love Henry?" Petunia asked.

"Yes."

"And he loves you. I will help you prevent his marriage to that girl, however I can. But I cannot stand by and watch as you do nothing while he goes through with this mindless plan. It will be his ruin."

Poppy blinked, stunned. Petunia Dyngley, help her? The world was coming to an end, surely.

"Why would you offer to help me? I thought you were Miss Penwrith's champion."

"I was, but… As much as I disapprove of your relationship, I think he would be unhappy with Miss Penwrith. And I have seen her do things which are… untoward."

"Like what?"

"I… Oh, I might as well tell you. Otherwise, the servants will gossip and you'll no doubt hear the wrong version of it anyway. John took Miss Penwrith aside to speak to her about her treatment of you, and her seducing Henry. I had… told her in confidence about John's past indiscretions. When John took her to task, she threw this knowledge in his face, and suggested that I might leave him or worse, that little Arthur is not actually his son, but a stable boy's."

Poppy's eyes grew large. "She didn't."

"Oh yes. I could hardly believe it myself until I suggested taking a ride to get some fresh air and John just about had a fit. Since then he will barely look at Miss Penwrith, much less talk to her unless civility demands it. So there you are. I have reason to dislike Henry's fiancée as much as you do."

"And here I thought you liked her," Poppy said.

"I did. I admit I was mistaken in viewing her as a person of quality. But then any good friend of the Dyngleys should be of good character. In any case, the Christian part of me hopes still that she is but a good girl who has made some bad decisions." Petunia gave Poppy an even glance. "I can see your mind squirreling all this information away. You are worse than a bloodhound, you know. You'll chase down her secrets with barely a whiff of information. Anyway, that was all I had to say. Close the door behind you on your way out."

And Poppy was dismissed. She rose and quit the room, her mind all astir. She had basically been given carte blanche by Petunia to ruin Henry's engagement to her rival, and would even help her. But would she act? Would she stoop to Miss Penwrith's level and make her the victim of her schemes? If it worked, she might separate Henry from her. But would he appreciate or understand if more deception was required to free him from an unhappy engagement? Or would he see her as no better than the woman who had seduced him?

Dazed, Poppy walked back down the stairs to find her aunt.

AN HOUR LATER, after playing with little Arthur, Poppy strolled down the corridor and found herself lost amongst the rooms. There were a number of them, and she found herself in a room that reminded her of the Royal Academy, in that it was rather like an art gallery, with the walls adorned with pictures. The room must have seen renovations in earlier days, for it had new-looking large windows that let in the sunlight, side tables and display cases that bore knickknacks, curios and old jewelry that looked far too fragile to wear. She was just peering into a display case that bore old broaches on crushed velvet when she heard a familiar voice behind her.

"Makes you wonder, doesn't it? Why they don't sell the finer pieces and use that to live on."

Poppy turned around. "Tom."

He bowed and looked around, then hurried forward to give her a hug. He lifted her up in the air and set her down with a smile. "There you are. I've not had a chance to properly say hello."

"Oh Tom, I am glad to see you."

"And I, you. What's this mess you've gotten into, then? Why are you and Henry not already married, or at Gretna Green?"

Poppy sat him down on one of the chairs nearby and told him everything. He let out a loud whistle. "I've never heard such a thing. Who is this girl?"

"A young woman they have known for years. She and Henry grew up together."

"I shall write to my friends in London and make inquiries. Someone must know something about her."

"Tom..." Poppy glanced toward the windows, which revealed dark gray skies and rain that batted at the windows.

He let out an expletive. "Sorry. It's just I hate to be cooped up here and yet if it weren't for Susan, I'd be gone at first light..." He stopped at seeing her face. "What?"

"Tell me. Have you two formed an attachment?" Her eyebrows rose, and he laughed.

"You might say so." He rubbed the side of his face. "Dash it, Poppy. I know she's your sister and all—"

"Half-sister," Poppy corrected.

"Yes, I know. But you don't mind my courting her? After we met that night, when you saved her life, we started to bump into one another in Town, and then I found we not only frequented the same places, and enjoyed the same entertainments, but were both making an extra effort to be at these places at the same time. Once I realized that, I asked her to dance at balls, we were much thrown together at parties, and all seemed well. Except…"

She waited.

He leaned down, resting his elbows on his knees, much like the young man she had first met in London a year ago. His light brown tousled hair looked rakish and unruly, giving him a rough air, but that could also be down to the fact he needed a shave, and she spotted a bit of fuzz on his chin and his sideburns needed a trim. He looked up at her, his eyes earnest. "Her brother doesn't know me, but your father does. Although our paths did not cross often. Once a man indicates he is not interested, I leave him be. But…"

"He knows you from your profession?"

"Yes. When I was first starting out years ago, I encountered him and your mother, although I didn't know it then. Just thought they were a handsome couple. She was a beauty, enough to stop a man in the street and forget what he was doing."

Poppy smiled. With her mother having died months earlier, she was happy to hear positive tales of her, even if it was as the long-term mistress of her father.

"Anyway. I introduced myself to him as a procurer of womanly flesh, and he told me to clear off. Said if I ever came near him again, he'd wallop me. So I left him be. He saw me here and there of course, but I never troubled him or his lady. I suspect that if your father were to take a good hard look, he'd recognize me from our earlier run-ins at the Shakespeare's Head. And then, of course, there's the letters."

Poppy's eyebrows rose. "You've been writing to each other, I heard."

He blushed. "Yes. To be fair, I asked Susan's permission if I may write to her, and she said yes. So we've been writing to each other ever since. For months."

"Months?"

He shrugged. "I would like to make her an offer but I only have my name as the third son of the Earl of Markham. To the average observer, I have nothing. No income to support myself. Except I do. I've saved for years. I have a pretty sum saved away. But I don't dare make my addresses to her father when he might recognize me."

"You're scared?"

"What if he were to refuse? If he recognizes me then he will know what I am and how I have supported myself these past few years. That's not a worthy income for a suitor of a girl of quality."

"That's not like you. Where's the bold young man I met in Town, who rescued my reticule from a thief and protected me and the other girls?"

She heard a noise outside the room. "Did you hear something?"

"No. But Poppy, what am I to do? I must do something. Susan has been dropping hints, and if her family get wind of her carrying on with a man below her, they'll marry her off faster than the dog racing, or worse, put her through a London Season."

She heard it again. A rustle of cloth, a floorboard that creaked. Were the servants listening?

She rose from her chair and moved toward the room's exit, but the floorboards gave her away. She peeked out the door when she caught a glimpse of a skirt disappearing around a corner.

"Come back, Poppy. It's likely just a servant."

She wasn't so sure, but she returned to him. "Why did you come?"

"She wrote to me. When she told me of your wedding to that prig sergeant of yours, I knew I had to come. I'd come and celebrate with you, and then if I could show myself in a good manner, if he might see me in the polite company of others, he might not dislike me so much. Or forget that we'd met in the first place. I say, I'm a bit hurt you didn't send me an invitation yourself."

"I'm sorry, I should have done. My aunt, lady's maid and Sergeant Dyngley handled those arrangements."

He shrugged and gave her an easy smile. "It matters not to me. I'm glad to be here with you, and to have a friend to talk to you. I think you could use the same. Will you do anything about the poor sergeant?"

"Henry? No. I love him, but I feel wretched about the whole business. I lost him to Miss Penwrith through trickery, I would not gain him again through a similar means."

Tom sat back in his chair. "That's the Poppy I know. Honorable to a fault, it seems."

"Is that so wrong?"

"No. But I think sometimes a little wrong can be done in order to affect a right. Especially in matters of the heart."

"How does Susan feel about this? Does she return your feelings of affection?"

"She does. I am sure of it. Will you help me convince her parents that I am worthy of her?"

"I'll try."

A FEW HOURS later, Poppy was relieved to be alone. She sat on the sofa in the Dyngley family library, a large grand room with floor-to-ceiling bookshelves, comfortable chairs, books, and bookcases that were regularly dusted, and high windows that let in the sun, with heavy drapes in case it became too bright. A smart writing desk sat in one corner of the room, facing the windows, and a series of chairs sat across from a sofa, to encourage conversation. The moment Poppy stepped into the room, she felt at ease, which was a blessed relief after the luncheon.

The meal had started off innocently enough, until Miss Penwrith had entered the room and demanded to take a seat across from Henry, as her fiancé. Then over plates of cold ham and pork, and salad with cucumber, Miss Penwrith chatted about her bridal clothes and what luck it was that the manor was already preparing for a wedding, so nothing would go to waste. It was all Poppy could do not to tear her hair out, but any stern words she had disappeared, for thought of Henry, who was missing.

"You should not speak so, considering." Petunia glanced at Poppy.

"Nonsense. It is my wedding coming up, and I am happy. Now where is Henry today?"

No one seemed to know, until John spoke, "He has gone to check on the tenants."

"Tenants? You have families living on the estate?"

"Yes. They've lived here since before I was born. He's gone to check in and see if they're all right from the storm."

"But why would he leave now? Why couldn't you go?" she asked John, who blinked.

"He's got more of a way with them than I do. Besides, I suspect he wanted the fresh air."

"That's very thoughtful," Miss Penwrith said. "But reckless. What if he were to fall and break his neck, or his horse were to slip in the mud? Besides, I thought the roads were too muddy to travel on."

"They are. The rain had let up this morning, so he took a horse out. I daresay he'll be back when he can."

"I hope so. I don't want him to miss a bit of excitement in planning our wedding," Miss Penwrith said, smiling at Poppy. "I've got the perfect dress. It's a beautiful blue gown of light silk. I remember once growing up, Henry and I sat by the lake together, and he told me I should always wear blue, for it matched my eyes."

And so it went on. Poppy was keen to leave, and soon after lunch ended, she found her way into the library. She selected a book of verse from the shelves and sat down on the sofa, instantly relaxing against the fine stuffed cushions. Despite the light patter of rain against the windows, dull sunlight streamed into the room, marking another hallmark of English weather; raining while the sun shines. After lunch and being in the warm room, she soon felt her eyelids droop, and the book fell into her lap.

In her dream, a woman was screaming. Poppy's eyes flew open.

A scream rent the air.

She jolted and dropped the book to the floor. She looked around the room and realized she'd fallen asleep in the library.

The scream came again.

She ran out of the library and bumped into John. "Did you hear that?"

"A woman screaming. Where is it coming from?" he asked.

They ran toward the sound. The shrieks came from the first floor, where the guest rooms were. They hurried toward the source and joined a crowd of people at a doorway. At the entrance of the guest room stood Petunia, Mr. Faulkbourne, Tom, Susan, and Lord Blackwood. In the room stood Miss Penwrith, holding up the tatters of a blue silk dress. She turned a tear-stricken face toward them. "It's ruined. My beautiful wedding dress is ruined. How could you?"

"Who are you talking about, Miss Penwrith?" Mr. Faulkbourne asked.

"Who else? Miss Morton, of course. She cut up my dress. She wants to kill me."

Chapter Nineteen

"Y OU THINK I did this?" Poppy asked.

"Who else would have? No one else here bore me any resentment. Everyone else has been kindness itself to me, except you. I still ache from the other night at dinner when you attacked me." Miss Penwrith wiped away a tear. "But now this? Trying to kill me wasn't enough, you had to scare me as well, is that it?"

John walked forward. "Miss Penwrith, I assure you, this is a silly prank. A joke someone is playing on you. The servants perhaps. Miss Morton would not have done such a thing."

"Wouldn't she?" Miss Penwrith asked.

"No, I would not," Poppy said, her voice sharp.

"A likely story. We all know you're jealous of me. Admit it. Ever since Henry and I got engaged you've wanted revenge on me for stealing him under your nose," Miss Penwrith said.

Poppy laughed, a harsh sound. "If you mean seducing him while pretending to be me, no. I don't like your way of finding husbands. It's a bit too sly for me."

"Are you insulting me?"

Poppy cocked her head. "I feel sorry for you."

"You feel sorry for me? That's a laugh. I have Dyngley." Miss Penwrith tossed the shredded remains of her dress on the bed and put her hands on her hips.

"You talk about him like he is a trophy, when he is a person."

Miss Penwrith spotted someone in the crowd. "Darling, are you going to stand there and let this girl talk to me like that?"

Heads turned to reveal Henry at the back of the group. His clothes were stained with mud, he had dark circles under his eyes and his gaze was dull. "Miss Penwrith, if it were a man, I would. But this is a matter between yourselves, and honestly, if you cannot verbally defend yourself from another woman, I don't see why I should."

"I think we should take this seriously," Lady Blackwood said. "Someone destroyed this poor girl's dress."

"Yes. And I think we all know who." Miss Penwrith looked at Poppy.

"When did you last notice the dress before it got damaged?" Mr. Faulkbourne asked her.

"This morning. I'd laid it out after breakfast to admire it. It was around noon, after lunch, when I went walking around the house and spoke with the servants. Then I came back and discovered it." Miss Penwrith looked tearfully at Poppy.

"And Miss Morton? Your whereabouts today?" Lady Blackwood asked.

Poppy stared at her. "You think I did this? How was I supposed to know which dress she was going to wear?"

"She did mention it at lunch," Susan said. At a dirty look from Tom, she said, "What? I'm just trying to be helpful."

"Well, I didn't do this. In the morning I was with my aunt and the baby, then after lunch, I sat in the library, where I fell asleep," Poppy said.

"Did anyone see you?" Mr. Faulkbourne asked.

"I don't know. I was asleep," Poppy said irritably. "I woke up when I heard the scream."

"So no one saw you, to your knowledge, and no one knows where you were."

"No." Poppy paused. "You make it sound like I'm hiding something, or like I'm already guilty."

"No one is saying that. We are just trying to ascertain who could have done this." Mr. Faulkbourne asked the group, "Did anyone see Miss Morton in the library?"

"I did. But she looked so peaceful asleep, I did not wish to wake her, so I left," Tom said, earning a frown from Susan.

"When was this?" Lady Blackwood asked.

"It doesn't matter, does it?" Poppy asked. "You all think I did it, don't you?"

"I don't think so," Henry said.

Poppy flashed him a smile and his gaze softened. She saw he moved slowly as if weighed down with worry, and had a streak of dirt on his chin. He needed a bath and a shave. "Thank you."

"Anyone who knows Miss Morton will know that she would never do such a thing. She is not one for scheming or pulling pranks, especially on her rivals. It's not in her nature."

"You're saying she's perfect. Like a saint," Miss Penwrith said.

"She is to me." Henry and Poppy shared a smile, then Poppy looked away. It started to hurt, seeing him, and her chest felt heavy.

Miss Penwrith gasped. "Go away. Leave me alone!"

People left and Petunia shut the door behind her.

POPPY STOOD OUT in the corridor with the others. "I hate to ask, but did anyone here do that to her?"

Heads shook, others looked around for signs of guilt. "I don't think any of us did, Miss Morton," Tom said.

"Could Miss Penwrith have done it herself?" Henry asked.

"Why?" Petunia asked.

"To cast suspicion on me," Poppy said.

"It's possible, but why would she?" Petunia asked.

"If so, she's ruined a perfectly good dress," Susan shook her head. "It seems unlikely."

"Let us retire. We are getting nowhere with these questions and it is not long before dinner. Come, Susan," Lady Blackwood ordered and beckoned her to follow.

Petunia and Susan left, followed by Mr. Faulkbourne and John. Tom hurried after them, leaving Henry and Poppy alone, almost as if by circumstance, although she knew it was meant to be a kindness by design.

"How are you?" she asked.

"As you see. I've been out all day with the tenants. Some of the families that live on the estate's lands."

"Are they all right?"

"Yes. Some needed emergency repairs to the roofs, windows, and doors. I'm no carpenter but I was able to help, a little. It's messy work, though." He looked down at himself as if just realizing he was covered in layers of mud.

"It was good of you to do that," Poppy said.

"I needed the distraction." He looked at her in the eyes. "Poppy, I—"

"Don't. Whatever you're going to say, don't. At first, I thought I would be fine, but I'm not. It hurts just being around you."

He touched her arm with a dirty hand.

She pulled away. "It hurts to see you, and know you have to marry her instead."

"Poppy." He came closer, and pushed a stray strand of hair out of her face.

The touch was too personal. She took his wrist and gently lowered it. "Enough, Henry. I can't. It hurts too much." She blinked back tears, and when she looked into his eyes, saw she was not alone. His dark brown eyes, like hers, were wet. "I'm sorry."

She released his wrist and hurried down the corridor after the others.

AT DINNER, MISS Penwrith had recovered her spirits. Dinner was a nice affair of salad with leafy greens, veal seasoned with rosemary from the garden, along with potatoes, scarlet beans and asparagus. Over fresh bread and glasses of red wine, the group's mood improved and became almost congenial, until Miss Penwrith opened her mouth.

"I have an idea," she said, chewing asparagus while talking. "I was thinking about my predicament."

"Your predicament?" Petunia asked.

"Yes. My wedding dress has been ruined. I have decided it is only fitting that I should wear Miss Morton's dress."

Poppy dropped her fork. "What?"

"I did not think you were hard of hearing. I said—"

"I heard what you said. We all did. What do you mean, my dress?" Poppy asked.

"Poppy…" Aunt Rachel murmured at her side, but within seconds, Poppy was fuming.

"Well the way I see it, you ruined my wedding dress."

"I did not," Poppy said.

"And even though you were going to get married, you no longer are. So you have a dress that's not being used. It's going to waste."

"This is my dress. Why would I loan it to you?" Poppy asked, her temper rising. She could feel an angry red flush rise up her neck.

"Because you won't have a use for it, and it's only fitting since you ruined mine," Miss Penwrith said.

Sir Dyngley coughed. "Ladies, what is going on?"

"Miss Penwrith had a dress of hers damaged and believes Miss Morton to be the culprit."

"Yes, she is."

"No, she is not. That is unproven," Henry said. "Now she seeks to play a cruel trick on Miss Morton by demanding to wear her own dress she would have been married in."

"That *is* rather cruel," Petunia said.

Miss Penwrith shrugged. "I call it justice."

"I call it mean. Why should my niece give you her dress? It's not her fault yours got cut up. I heard what happened and I say you brought that on yourself. You'll find few friends here with behavior like that," Aunt Rachel said, giving Miss Penwrith a stern look.

"But it's not fair. She has a dress and I don't. She's not getting married and I am. What else am I to do?"

"That doesn't mean you deserve her wedding dress, or that she has to give it to you," Petunia said, shaking her head. She gave Miss Penwrith an odd look.

Poppy read her glance to mean, *This sort of behavior is very odd.* She agreed.

"This can be all cleared up easily," Lady Blackwood said. "Miss Morton, will you agree to give your dress to Miss Penwrith to wear?"

"Absolutely not," Poppy said.

"There, you see? All sorted, I thought–oh." She gave Poppy a look. "Whyever not?"

"Amelia, how could you expect her to, when she did nothing wrong? It seems to me that Poppy is the victim here, and to make her do such a thing is not only heartless, it's also cruel," Lord Blackwood said.

"You would take her side. She reminds you of that whore, her mother. Doesn't she?"

"That's enough," he snapped, his voice frosty. "Please excuse us, Sir Dyngley, we have had enough to eat and shall retire." Lord Blackwood rose from the table.

Lady Blackwood stared daggers at her husband and her mouth clamped shut. A dull red flush rose up her neck and she rose, quietly, feeling the weight of everyone's gaze upon her. The very air was heavy with her humiliation. "Yes, I am feeling tired. Do excuse me." She removed herself from her chair and stalked out of the room without another word, her heeled shoes stamping across the floor tiles in the foyer.

Lord Blackwood nodded to them all and went after her.

Tom asked Poppy, "Are you all right?"

"Yes, I'm fine. Should you go after them?"

"No," Susan said, "She has a foul temper when roused, my

mum. I'd leave her be."

The others made light conversation over the dessert course, while Poppy did her best to ignore the glowering looks from Miss Penwrith.

BUT THAT NIGHT after dinner and a polite evening's entertainment of conversation over games of whist, Poppy returned to her room with her aunt and found the door slightly ajar. In the dim corridor, their attention was caught by a slim candlelight flickering within the room.

"Did you leave a candle burning, Poppy?" her aunt asked.

"No, I don't think so."

They entered the room and saw the hearth stone cold, there was no fire. Poppy looked and saw a small candle in a candle-holder, having burned almost down to its bottom. Hardly any flame was left and as they walked further into the room, the breeze from the door blew the candle out, pitching them into darkness.

Once they'd lit a fresh candle, Poppy gazed around the room. Nothing seemed to be disturbed and yet, something was out of place. She couldn't put her finger on it until she walked over to her closet, when she stumbled. She landed on a dead body on the floor.

CHAPTER TWENTY

POPPY SCREAMED. AUNT Rachel screamed.

Poppy leaped back to her hands and knees, then came to her senses. "Fetch help, Aunt. Go!"

Aunt Rachel ran from the room.

Sir Dyngley lay on the floor, a small pool of blood on the carpet at his head. A thin iron fireplace poker was missing from the fireplace and lay a few paces away from him.

Poppy approached Sir Dyngley and touched his hand. "Sir Dyngley?" she asked. "Sir Dyngley?"

He lay unresponsive.

She touched his wrist. His skin was cold but still had a pulse, barely. She could feel it, however thready.

John, Tom, and Mr. Faulkbourne arrived first.

"What happened?" Mr. Faulkbourne asked, stopping in his tracks.

"Oh my God." John ran to her side and fretted. "Father? Father, wake up."

"Move, that's not doing anything. Let me," Mr. Faulkbourne said. He moved John and Poppy aside and bent to Sir Dyngley's side. He felt his temples and placed two fingers to the side of his neck. "We need to move him. What is he doing here?"

"I don't know. I—" Poppy started.

A scream came from the doorway as Petunia and Henry

arrived, with Aunt Rachel, Susan, and Miss Penwrith in tow.

"Father," Henry said, coming toward them.

"Stay back, all of you. You're not helping by crowding him." Mr. Faulkbourne said, his face serious.

"What are you, a doctor?" Henry asked.

"No, but I studied under one for a time, at St Bartholomew's Hospital in London."

"Look, there's blood on the back of his head." Petunia pointed.

She was right. Sure enough, there was blood on Sir Dyngley's gray hair, matted darkly against his head.

"Is that blood?" John paled.

"Oh no," Petunia said, as John keeled over in a faint. "Not again."

John had toppled over in a boneless fall to the floor, his limbs splayed across the carpet.

"Oh, for God's sake," Mr. Faulkbourne muttered.

"Really, Mr. Faulkbourne," Aunt Rachel tutted.

"Sorry." He looked at John. "Does he usually faint at the sight of blood?"

"Every time," Petunia said, bouncing little Arthur awkwardly in her arms.

"Mrs. Dyngley, get Arthur out of here. This is no place for a child," Henry said.

Petunia opened her mouth to argue, then shut it. "Mrs. Greene, I need you. Miss Penwrith, you too."

The three women quit the room, leaving Poppy alone with the men. She had little thought of the impropriety of such a moment and decided she didn't care.

"Help me lift him," Mr. Faulkbourne said, taking a gentle hold of Sir Dyngley's shoulders. "Slowly."

The group lifted him onto Poppy's bed and supported his head upright with pillows.

"Fetch me some water and clean linens or rags," Mr. Faulkbourne ordered Poppy.

"She's not a servant," Henry snapped.

"I don't care what she is, we need help."

"It's all right, Henry," Poppy said. She moved to the vanity table and brought over a basin of water and a washcloth, then dashed down to the servants' quarters and relayed what had happened. In minutes she returned with maids, footmen, and armfuls of cloths.

Poppy stood back as Mr. Faulkbourne and the maids made quick work. Under his direction, the women cleaned and bandaged his wound, and propped him up on the pillows until he lay as comfortably as possible.

Henry asked, "What now?"

"We wait for him to wake up," Mr. Faulkbourne said.

"What if he doesn't?" Tom asked.

"Will you see to Mr. Dyngley, Mr. Faulkbourne?" Poppy asked.

"Oh, yes. I forgot." Mr. Faulkbourne procured a bottle of smelling salts from a maid and held them under John's nose.

In moments his eyes fluttered. John gasped and said, "What happened? Why are you all looking at me like that?"

"You fainted," Mr. Faulkbourne said.

"Fainted? I don't faint."

"You saw some blood."

John swallowed. "I… oh yes. There is that. But it's an ordinary thing to do, you know. Plenty of men topple at the sight of blood."

Mr. Faulkbourne and Henry exchanged looks as John sat up. "Sir Dyngley is comfortable enough, for now. We should speak in another room. Let's not disturb him."

Once sat in the library, the women joined them. The grand room was dimly lit but for a few candles that played shadows across their faces. The rain continued to patter outside, pelting the windows with a steady rhythm that gave no sign of letting up.

Poppy shivered and sat down on one of the sofas, rubbing her arms. She had at first thought this room comfortable, but now she practically jumped at the lurking shadows, imagining them like great dark arms, reaching for her.

"What about my father? What's wrong with him?" Henry asked, taking a seat near Poppy on the same sofa.

"He's had a nasty knock to the back of his head. I can only guess someone hit him with that poker I saw lying next to him on the floor. He's lost some blood."

"But he is alive," John said.

"For now," Mr. Faulkbourne said seriously.

"Well, what I want to know is who did this? He didn't get hit by that poker by himself. And how did he end up in Miss Morton's room?" Petunia asked.

Heads turned to Poppy.

"My aunt and I were walking back when we saw the door to my room was open and a candle was lit from inside. We thought it odd since I wouldn't leave a candle burning unattended. But when we walked inside, I could tell something was different. We walked in to see and found him, as you saw."

"What was he doing there?" Henry asked.

"I don't know."

"Why would he have been in your room?" John asked.

"I couldn't say."

"I don't believe you," Petunia said. "There's something fishy about this."

"It's true, he was in her room," Aunt Rachel said. "I was there. I saw the whole thing."

Petunia frowned as John said, "But it doesn't make sense. How did he get there? What was he doing in your room in the first place?"

"Your guess is as good as mine," Poppy said.

Miss Penwrith laughed, a mocking sound, and heads turned to her. "Are you serious? It's obvious, is it not?"

"What do you mean?" John asked.

"Pray, tell us, Miss Penwrith, for you seem to know something we do not," Henry said.

"Why, it's clear as day to me, even if you all are willfully ignorant or too polite to say anything," Miss Penwrith said, "It's obvious what he was doing in her room. Miss Morton invited him."

"What? Why would I invite Sir Dyngley to my room?" Poppy asked.

"Or any man, for that matter?" Aunt Rachel said.

"To convince him, of course. To let him allow her to marry Henry," Miss Penwrith said, her eyes narrowing at Poppy. "First you would try innocence, and then use your womanly wiles to get his attention. Perhaps you promised him a little extra affection as his future daughter-in-law."

Poppy's eyes blazed. "You take that back. I would never."

"It sounds like you're speaking from experience, Miss Penwrith," Petunia muttered.

Aunt Rachel gasped.

Miss Penwrith carried on as if Petunia hadn't spoken. "And looking at you, of course, he said no. So you hit him with the poker. You hit him hard enough to hurt him, maybe even kill him."

Poppy tensed. "Now you're accusing me of murder?"

"Then when you realized what you'd done, you'd pretended to come out and with your aunt, found him again so you'd have a witness to your innocence."

"How could I do that? I was with the others all evening," Poppy said.

"It's true," Henry said. "I watched her."

Miss Penwrith bristled at that. "A woman can always slip away unnoticed if she wants to, darling. Anyway, she could have done it and then come back and fetched her grandmother—"

"I am her aunt," Aunt Rachel said sharply, "I'm not that old."

Miss Penwrith shrugged as Petunia hid a smile. "And then with Mrs. Greene, you could pretend to find him and your innocence would be clear. She would back you up."

"It seems you have it all figured out, Miss Penwrith," Mr.

Faulkbourne said.

She smiled. "I was always good at solving puzzles."

"Except for one thing. I too, watch Miss Morton closely. She was never alone all evening. But I daresay you were."

Miss Penwrith glared at him. "Once again, you all blame me for something that is Miss Morton's fault. I see how it is. She is the favorite who can do no wrong and I am the villain. When will you not see that she is in the wrong? She could have killed Sir Dyngley and instead, you're all pointing fingers at me."

"But I didn't," Poppy said. "I didn't do it."

"Says you," Miss Penwrith mocked.

"Well I don't know who or what to believe, but we all need to calm down," John said.

"That's the first bright idea you've had all day," Petunia muttered.

John shot her a hurt look and she quieted. "Sorry. My nerves."

"I need a drink," Henry said, walking to a small wooden sideboard with crystal decanters and small glasses.

"Make that two," Mr. Faulkbourne said.

"Me too," Aunt Rachel added. At people's looks, she said, "What? This has been a stressful evening."

As Henry served glasses of port, Lord Blackwood came into the room. His normally smartly combed silver hair was in disarray and his typically immaculately tied cravat was loosened. The harried look in his eyes and tightness around his mouth meant one thing: trouble.

"I don't mean to disturb you all but we need a doctor. Immediately," he said. His face was pale.

"I have medical training. What is the problem?" Mr. Faulkbourne asked.

"My wife has been poisoned."

❧ ❧ ❧

CHAPTER TWENTY-ONE

POPPY STARED AT her father. "Poisoned?"

"Oh my lord," Aunt Rachel said, as Mr. Faulkbourne left with Lord Blackwood.

"What is happening here? What sort of a place is this?" Miss Penwrith asked.

"You do not have to stay. There is no one keeping you here," Petunia said.

Miss Penwrith looked wounded. "I would have thought you would support me, Mrs. Dyngley. It would have thought you understood my plight."

Poppy snorted. Aunt Rachel repeated, "Your plight?"

"Yes. Since I arrived here everyone has treated me like I am a villain. When all I have done is come to marry the man I love," Miss Penwrith said.

That makes two of us, Poppy thought.

"Of course now that we are engaged, there is no need to wait. I don't see why we can't be married immediately," Miss Penwrith said.

Henry blinked in surprise.

"Well you'll have to apply for a special license," Aunt Rachel pointed out. "Especially as the banns have already been read for Sergeant Dyngley and Poppy."

"Yes, I know." Miss Penwrith frowned.

"And of course, there's no clergyman here, so you'll have to wait until the rain stops and the roads are clear."

"I know that too," Miss Penwrith said, her mouth set in a grim line. "Anyway, that is my plight. It is very hard. But I wouldn't expect someone like you to understand."

"What is that supposed to mean?" Poppy asked as Aunt Rachel's face turned pink.

As Miss Penwrith opened her mouth, Petunia said sharply, "Miss Penwrith. You are a guest here. I'll thank you to keep a civil tongue toward my other guests. If you cannot keep such remarks to yourself, I suggest you stay in your room, where no one will hear you."

Poppy's eyebrows rose. Petunia Dyngley, defend them? Perhaps she'd had too much to drink.

Miss Penwrith turned pink as a sweet pea, inclined her head to Petunia and quit the room.

Poppy said to Petunia, "Thank you."

Petunia gave a sharp nod, her dark eyes flashing at the door Miss Penwrith had gone through. "I cannot abide rudeness. Miss Penwrith has long outlived her usefulness as a guest. I am… sorry if she has made you feel unwelcome."

"That is very good of you to say, Mrs. Dyngley," Aunt Rachel said, cooing to little Arthur.

"What did you mean, she had outlived her usefulness?" Poppy asked.

"Why, numbers, of course," Petunia said.

"Numbers?" Aunt Rachel repeated.

"Yes. She evens out the numbers at dinner. That is to be appreciated, for I cannot stand an uneven table. Excuse me," Petunia left, taking little Arthur with her.

Aunt Rachel asked, "Well what do you make of that?"

"I think something is starting, and more trouble is on the way," Poppy said.

"What do you mean?"

"Miss Penwrith's dress. Sir Dyngley attacked in my room, and

Lady Blackwood poisoned. It's one thing after another. It's all leading to one thing."

"What is that?" Aunt Rachel asked.

"I'm not sure. But these little events, they're all connected somehow. I just haven't figured it out yet."

"Oh no, not more investigating. I'd hoped you would give that all up, once you were married. Settle down like a nice young woman," Aunt Rachel said.

"I'm not married yet, Aunt. And I never promised to stop investigating. Besides, it's doing no harm."

"No, but you will get entangled in these things, I just know it."

Poppy went to the Blackwoods' room and was met outside by Henry and John. "How is she? Is it very serious?" Poppy asked.

Mr. Faulkbourne left the room, shut the door behind him, and nodded to them. "Lady Blackwood is not well. Something has made her very ill."

"Was it something she ate?" Poppy asked.

"What did she have for dinner?" Henry added.

"Lord Blackwood says she had the soup, the veal, the potatoes, wine, and dessert, after which she started to complain of feeling unwell," Mr. Faulkbourne said.

"Did she have anything none of us tried?" Poppy asked, earning an odd look from Mr. Faulkbourne.

"This is not a conversation for a woman."

Poppy frowned.

Henry said, "I assure you, Mr. Faulkbourne, you may speak freely in front of Miss Morton. She has a quick and discerning mind and a talent for solving crimes. She has experience in these matters."

Poppy shot Henry a grateful look, but felt annoyed at having a man speak for her in order to give her credibility. It was not his fault, and he was trying to do her a service, but it rankled all the same. What a world they lived in.

Mr. Faulkbourne looked askance at her. "Very well, but Miss

Morton, you may find it all a bit shocking for your taste. If you happen to feel overcome and need to excuse yourself, I will not think any less of you."

Poppy tried not to wince and smiled instead. "Please continue, Mr. Faulkbourne. I am sure if I feel overcome, you will be the first to know."

"Right. Lady Blackwood ingested some food that at least everyone else in the party also consumed. We all ate the soup, some of us drank the same wine she did, and others had dessert while some did not."

"So what does that mean?" John asked.

"That more of us are going to get sick, which is what I hope."

"You want more of us to be ill?"

"Of course. That would mean it was either the food or drink," Poppy said.

"Yes, that's correct." Mr. Faulkbourne looked slightly perturbed. "Or there is the alternative."

"What's that?" John asked.

"That someone poisoned Lady Blackwood intentionally," Henry said.

THAT NIGHT, POPPY had a bad dream. Sir Dyngley had been moved into his own room and her sheets and bed coverings had been replaced by the maids. But in the middle of the night, lying in bed, her eyes opened with a start.

She was not alone.

She looked around in the darkness but nothing was there. That didn't stop her breathing from growing quiet, her body tense, and the hair on the back of her neck stand up. She could hear the gentle rustling and crack of the dim fire in the fireplace and sat up. Lightning crashed, briefly lighting up the room.

A dark specter stood at the foot of her bed, watching her. Something about it suggested it was dripping wet. It had the rounded shoulders of a feminine figure, and it slowly raised its arm. It pointed at her, making her breath catch. It rasped, "I'm coming for you."

Poppy shrieked and threw a pillow at it.

And woke up.

Sunlight streamed into the room through the windows. Shading her eyes, she gazed blearily around the room and peered over the side of the bed, but no one was there. She rose, dressed, and looked around behind her with sudden jerky movements, then jumped.

Miss Cooke stood in the doorway. "Hello, Miss. Do you need help dressing?"

"I..."

"Let me fix your hair." Miss Cooke helped Poppy out of bed, helped her dress and arranged her mouse brown hair into soft curls. She stepped back to survey her handiwork. "There now. Oh."

"What is it?"

"Did you spill a drink?"

"What do you mean?" Poppy asked.

"Well, it's just there's a wet patch here on the floor. Looks like water."

Poppy slowly turned back to see. There were two damp patches on the carpet, just by the foot of her bed. She shivered and quickly left the room with Miss Cooke. Had someone really been there?

AT BREAKFAST, POPPY joined the others, taking little more than a cup of tea and a slice of toast. "Poppy, did you sleep all right? You look pale," Aunt Rachel said.

Henry looked at her with concern.

"You do look terrible," Miss Penwrith agreed.

"I'm fine. Just a bad dream," Poppy said.

Henry asked, "Are you feeling all right?"

"I'm well, thank you. What about everyone else?"

The others murmured agreement of their good health.

"What about Mrs. Dyngley?" Poppy asked.

"She usually takes breakfast in her room," John said, helping himself to some toast and jam.

"And Lady Blackwood?" Poppy asked as her father and Susan sat down to join them.

"Not well. She keeps to her bed."

"Perhaps we might visit her later and keep her company," Aunt Rachel said.

"It might be better if you were to postpone your visit until later. Her condition is rather delicate at the moment and I am not sure she is up to visitors just now."

John nodded his agreement and bit into his toast with a loud crunch.

Mr. Faulkbourne sat at the table. "How is my father?" Henry asked.

"He's awake but very weak. He hasn't spoken about what happened and seems very confused about the events of last night. One of the maids is sitting with him right now."

Henry gave a sigh of relief. "Then he is out of danger."

"For now. But I do not like it. Aside from the fact that we do not know what he was doing in Miss Morton's room, someone struck him on the back of the head with a poker. I can only think they meant to hurt, if not kill, Sir Dyngley."

This was met with silence.

"You think it was intentional?" Henry asked.

"It could hardly be an accident," Mr. Faulkbourne said.

"The question we must ask ourselves is who would attack Sir Dyngley and why? Who had reason to want to hurt him?"

"Perhaps he disturbed a thief," Mr. Faulkbourne said.

"In Miss Morton's room? He must have been lost." Miss Penwrith grinned.

"Lost?" Aunt Rachel repeated.

"I can't imagine our dear Miss Morton would have anything worth stealing. That is why she resorts to trying to steal other women's beaus."

Aunt Rachel's mouth opened in a foul response when Poppy

put a hand on her aunt's, stilling her. She bore Miss Penwrith's remark with good grace and said nothing, determined not to react to Miss Penwrith's jibes.

"Well I still think it's Miss Morton's doing. Why else would he be in her room?" Miss Penwrith asked.

"Yes, that is one suggestion," Mr. Faulkbourne said, seeing Henry and Poppy's looks of anger and protest. "But that may not be the only option. Who else might want to hurt Sir Dyngley?" He looked at Susan. "I have not heard you voice an opinion yet, Miss…"

"Blackwood. Susan Blackwood."

"Charming. What do you think of this business?"

Susan pondered this and blushed at being the center of attention. She patted her soft ash blond ringlets and said, "Miss Morton is the most obvious suspect. But if it wasn't her, I would think…" She paused. "I would guess that Mr. Dyngley might have done it. Sergeant Dyngley, I mean."

Seeing their faces, she added, "I'm sorry. It was just a guess. You did ask."

Henry frowned. "Why would you think I would hurt my own father?"

Susan blushed harder. "It's just that everyone knows you and Miss Morton were courting. You needed your father's consent, same as I would if I were to get engaged." She spoke rapidly, avoiding looking at anyone but the table. "But since he refused the match, I would think that gave you a reason. I'm not saying you did, only that it gives you a reason to want to do so."

Henry shot her a dark look, while Poppy said, "I don't think this is getting us anywhere. We're just pointing fingers at each other."

"For once, I agree with Miss Morton," Miss Penwrith said.

The group broke up after a quiet breakfast, after which Poppy wandered down to the servants' quarters when she heard a noise behind her and whirled around. It was Henry.

"Oh, hello," she said.

"Miss Morton." He nodded.

They had an awkward moment of silence, and Poppy said, "I was just on my way to ask the cook a few questions."

"So was I." He smiled briefly and asked, his voice hesitant, "Would you like to go together?"

Her heart felt full at the sight of him. His dark hair was ruffled, his face needed a shave, and shadows hung beneath his eyes.

He looked tired, but she was too polite to say so. His expression was so full of hope, she knew that to say no would be a stinging rejection of him and his suit, and he would ask again. Men were funny creatures, she decided. So strong one moment and fragile the next.

"I'd like that," she said.

His face lit up with surprise, then pleasure. "Very good. This way." He led her down a narrow spiral staircase into the kitchen. Maids were scrubbing, footmen and youths doing odd chores, bringing in firewood, polishing silverware and cooks pounding wet dough down onto a hard worktable. The slap of the bread and the smell of it made Poppy's heart warm at the knowledge that soon the kitchen would have a delicious scent, and they would dine on fresh bread that evening.

He began telling her tales of his childhood scrapes he'd gotten into as a boy, filching cakes and eating all the strawberry jam, to putting frogs in the main housekeeper's shoes. As they rounded a corner he introduced her to the housekeeper, Mrs. Ewing, and the head cook, Mrs. Piggott.

"It's a pleasure to meet you both," Poppy said, "My room is very comfortable and the food here has been delightful."

The older women nodded. Henry said, "I'm sorry to disturb you ladies, but we wanted to ask about last night's dinner."

Mrs. Ewing looked alarmed.

"You may have heard that Lady Blackwood is unwell," Henry said.

"There was nothing wrong with that meal, Master Henry. We had the same food and leftovers and none of us got sick,"

Mrs. Piggott said.

Poppy asked, "Was there anyone in our party, one of the guests, who came down here last night?"

The two servants exchanged a look. "Well, there was Master John, Miss. He did come down to fetch some tea for Mrs. Dyngley, she does like that raspberry jam so."

"And then there was Sir Dyngley earlier, he came for a plate of biscuits, and then Miss Blackwood for a cup of warm milk. So did your aunt, as a matter of fact. And there was Mr. Faulkbourne for a cup of tea. In fact, the only ones who didn't come by are Mr. Markham and yourselves."

Henry and Poppy looked at each other. "It could have been anyone."

"But how?" Poppy wondered. "We were served by footmen. If anyone had tried to doctor Lady Blackwood's food or drink, we would have noticed."

Henry asked, "Could one of the guests have paid the footmen to add something to her food?"

Mrs. Ewing pursed her mouth. "It's unlikely, Master Henry. Not if he wanted to keep his post."

"Have you hired anyone new?" Poppy asked. "For the wedding celebrations?"

Mrs. Piggott looked nervous that Poppy had even asked. "There were a few that were supposed to come and help on the day, but not yet. The only staff members here are those in the Dyngley family's regular employ."

"You trust them?" Henry asked.

"I trust they wouldn't dare think of doing such a thing, Master Henry. Not in my kitchen."

"Nor in my household," Mrs. Ewing added.

Henry smiled. "I don't doubt it."

They parted ways and returned upstairs when Mrs. Ewing called to Henry. He left Poppy and returned a moment later.

"Everything all right?" she asked.

"They wanted to share their concerns about my father, and

say they don't believe I or John would hurt him."

"That's good of them," Poppy said.

As they walked back upstairs to the main floor, Henry said, "It is as I thought."

"What do you mean?"

"The servants are all trustworthy, and if they weren't, Mrs. Ewing and Mrs. Piggott would have sniffed them out by now."

"Which means?"

"Whoever is behind all of this, is one of us."

CHAPTER TWENTY-TWO

THAT AFTERNOON, POPPY spent time with Petunia, Aunt Rachel, Susan, and Miss Penwrith in the large parlor, while Mr. Faulkbourne, John, Tom, and Henry played billiards, with regular intervals of checking on Sir Dyngley and Lady Blackwood.

Poppy investigated her room. The poker indeed had blood on its edge, which gave her a shiver. She looked around and wondered, why would he be in her room in the first place?

She opened the closet and looked around, then realized something.

Her wedding dress was gone.

POPPY MARCHED INTO the parlor, her hands trembling. The women looked up as she entered the parlor. Aunt Rachel said, "Poppy, you're back. Did you want to play with little Arthur?"

Poppy shook her head furiously. She said in a shaking voice, "My wedding dress is missing."

Heads turned to Miss Penwrith, who looked evenly back at her. "So? What are you all looking at me for?"

"You took it, didn't you?" Poppy asked.

"Would you believe me if I said I didn't?"

"Where is it?"

"How should I know?" Miss Penwrith said, her voice nasty.

"There is no reason it would go missing. Especially when you are the only one who wanted it," Poppy said, "Did you take it?"

"No, of course not. Don't be ridiculous. You're as tall as a tree. It wouldn't fit me anyway."

"I don't think she is being ridiculous at all, Miss Penwrith," Petunia said, "No one else would have wanted it. We all were present when you asked for it. It leads to reason that you would be the one to have taken it."

"I'm surprised at you, Mrs. Dyngley. A good and proper hostess would never suspect a guest of hers of thieving," Miss Penwrith said.

"A good and proper guest wouldn't give me a reason to."

"Well, I didn't do it. Can't you see that this is what the person wants? To turn you all against me?"

"Why would anyone want that? You're doing a fine job all by yourself," Mr. Faulkbourne said, leaning against the entrance.

"Well I don't know, but I think someone is going around pulling pranks. First my dress was cut up, and now Miss Morton's is missing, Lady Blackwood is ill, and I could have sworn I saw a figure standing in my room last night."

"So did I," Poppy said. "A figure all in black, a woman, at the foot of my bed."

"Ugh, this sounds like something out of a gothic novel. Stop it, both of you," Petunia said. "This is nonsense."

"It's not, someone is trying to cause trouble," Miss Penwrith said.

"Maybe it's the ghost," Susan said.

Everyone looked at her.

"Could it not be the ghost of that maidservant, Nell? Sir Dyngley said the story goes that she was spurned by her lover and thought she was going to get married. What if she is taking revenge on all of us because Miss Penwrith is having the wedding that she did not?"

Aunt Rachel shivered. "Lord, I hope not. What a horrid thing to think."

"I agree," Petunia said. "That's nothing but an old ghost tale meant to frighten you. I'm surprised you believed it."

Susan colored. "He said it so convincingly, I thought it was true."

"Perhaps, but there is no ghost. Specters don't exist," Petunia said.

"But what if they do?"

"They don't," Petunia told her.

"But if they do?"

Petunia rolled her eyes. "Can someone talk sense into this young woman?"

"I believe you," Tom said.

"Ugh," Petunia groaned. "There is no ghost."

Poppy said, "A ghost would not have taken my wedding dress."

"A tall one could have," Miss Penwrith muttered.

Poppy glared at her and left, tears stinging her eyes.

"Poppy, wait," Tom said, catching up with her in the corridor.

She turned around. "What is it, Tom?"

"Are you all right?"

"No. I'm furious. I'm hurt, sad, and I'm angry."

He put a hand on her arm. "Walk with me."

She walked, too emotional to think straight. They walked along the corridor, passing pedestals with flowers, family portraits darkened with age that decorated the walls, in addition to well-executed landscapes and framed embroidery on silk. Such neat scenes of domesticity somehow made it worse, and she stood and rested her hands on the balcony railing that overlooked the large staircase that led to the foyer. She gripped the hard wood, and said, "It's not fair. I've just about had enough of this. If it's not bad enough that she has taken Henry, she's now stolen my wedding dress. And she's lying to my face about it, although I should have expected that. It's just… I can't take it, Tom. I just can't."

He put a hand on her shoulder. "I know. It's wrong, and we

all know it."

"I'm sorry you came all this way for nothing."

"Well, I had an ulterior motive, as you know." He smiled sheepishly.

"How is that going? Your courtship I mean."

"Not very well. Every time I try to steal a moment with her alone, she is guarded by her mother, father, or someone else. It's a wonder young people are actually able to see one another before they are married."

Poppy smiled.

"You know, as much as I dislike him, your sergeant is a fool if he doesn't fight for you."

"But he's engaged. He's stuck. She entrapped him."

"So what? If a man doesn't want to get married, he won't. And especially one trapped into a false engagement against his will, he won't stand for that."

"He doesn't seem to be doing much."

"Give him some time. He's reeling. His father was almost killed, he's lost you and now is stuck in an engagement to a woman he doesn't want. It's enough to drive any man to drink." He paused. "Did he really ask you to elope?"

"Yes. I turned him down."

Tom smiled. "Good on him. I never would have expected that from him."

"You sound like you approve."

"Let's just say I'm coming around to his way of thinking."

"Tom…"

"Don't worry, I'm not going to steal your half-sister away. I mean to do this right."

Poppy looked at him with a sly grin. "Is she going to make an honest man of you?"

"Something like that. I've had enough of that lifestyle anyway. I'm going to ask her father's permission to court her formally. Enough sneaking around corners and trying to meet her out of sight," he said.

"Well done, Tom. You've got my support, if that means anything," she said.

"It means a lot." He gave her hand a gentle squeeze. "I won't give up if you won't."

"Agreed." She watched and nodded as Lord Blackwood and Susan walked into the library. "I think there is your chance."

"It's as good as any." Tom rubbed the side of his face and tugged at his cravat, then straightened it, then tugged at it again. "I look all right?"

"Yes. Go on."

He dashed into the library. Poppy tiptoed down the corridor and stood by the side of the door. It was open, so she could hear.

"Sir, I wonder if I might have a word," Tom began.

"Eh? Oh. This isn't the best time," Lord Blackwood said.

"Father, please," Susan said. "It's important."

"Very well. What is it?"

Tom cleared his throat. "I would like permission to court your daughter."

"My Susan?"

"Yes, sir."

"So you're the one who has been writing her letters."

"Yes, sir."

"And skulking around corners. And are the reason my wife brought her here in the first place, is it not? To escape you."

"Sir, I… That is true. But I have a fondness and affection for your daughter, and I believe she returns my regard," Tom said.

"Does she?" Lord Blackwood's voice was stern. "Susan?"

"I do, Father. I… care for him."

Poppy's heart rose and she grasped her hands with joy. Susan, in love. Her half-sister, admitting she was in love with one of her friends. What pleasure there was to be had. She could practically picture their wedding now.

Lord Blackwood laughed, a harsh sound, shocking Poppy out of her reverie.

"You are young. You are eighteen and with barely more sense

than a child. And you, sir. I feel I have seen you before some-where in London. Are we acquainted?"

"Our paths may have crossed. You may perhaps know my father."

"Who might that be?"

"Lord Markham, the Earl of Markham, in Wyck, near Tisbury in Wiltshire."

"And you, you are the heir?"

"Er, no. I am the last of his three sons. Harris, although I dislike the name, so everyone calls me Tom."

"I see. And what was your business in coming here? To this place?"

"I am friends with your daughter, Miss Morton."

Poppy heard the loud breathing in of Lord Blackwood's nose. "Do not drag her into this."

Poppy tensed. Drag her? Was he ashamed of her? Was he embarrassed by her? She fretted when she saw Miss Penwrith approach, and held up a finger to her lips to stop her. Miss Penwrith froze, and took a spot on the other side of the door, listening.

Tom said, "But it is true. I count her as one of my friends. A good, kind young woman. When I heard she was to be married, I wanted to celebrate with her."

"So you came uninvited."

"No, sir. I wrote to her aunt who confirmed the happy news and was invited."

"And you knew my other daughter was coming."

"No, but I will not lie, I did hope she might be amongst the company."

"Father," Susan's voice took on a slightly pleading note.

"All right. You have my permission, but I will be watching you, Mr. Markham. And—"

"You cannot allow this to happen," Miss Penwrith strode into the library before Poppy could stop her. "I heard everything and cannot stand while you allow this schemer to fool you."

Poppy's mouth dropped open and she darted in after her. "Excuse me."

"What are you both doing here?"

"She was listening at the door, and I happened to walk by when I heard this man's false statement. I knew I could not let it stand," Miss Penwrith said.

"What is she talking about?" Lord Blackwood asked.

"Nothing," Poppy said, her blood rising. She saw then the scene before her. Tom and Lord Blackwood stood almost as if they were to begin fighting. Susan perched on one of the sofas, wringing her hands.

"She lies. They're all lying to you. You have met this man before, Lord Blackwood. In London. He is a procurer of womanly flesh, and sells women's charms to the lowest bidder."

"You're a ruffian? A pimp?" Lord Blackwood said, the blood rushing from his face. He looked as pale as a ghost.

"No," Tom said, as Miss Penwrith said, "Yes. That's exactly what he is."

"I don't know what to say, I have never met this girl before, sir. Not before I came here," Tom said.

"And yet her words ring true. Why would you say such things, Miss Penwrith?" Lord Blackwood asked.

"Because they are true, and I would not wish you to have a pimp escorting your daughter around town, or worse, as a son-in-law."

"No," Susan said, her face becoming pinched. "She's lying."

"Mr. Markham? Is what Miss Penwrith says the truth?"

"It is. I heard him and Miss Morton talking about it earlier. They thought they were being secret and could fool the lot of you."

Poppy blinked hard. "No, that's not—"

"I want to hear it from Mr. Markham. Do you deny what this girl has said?"

"No," Tom said.

"Tom," Poppy said, as Susan's hands darted to her mouth.

"It's true. But if you would hear me out—" Tom started.

"There is nothing to hear. I have heard all I need to know. My answer is no. You are not allowed to court my daughter, and furthermore, you will keep your distance from her. If it were not for the rains, I would ask you to leave immediately, but this is not my house. Keep away, Mr. Markham."

"But sir—"

"No. I have enough to worry about without Susan getting in trouble with a man of low standing. You may come from a good family, but I think your father would despair at seeing what you have become. Shame on you for attempting to drag my daughter to your level," Lord Blackwood said, and gestured to the door. "Susan?"

Susan turned a tear-stricken face toward him. "Father…"

"Go check on your mother. Right now."

Susan fled from the room. Lord Blackwood turned toward Poppy. "I am disappointed in you, Poppy. It is one thing to find yourself in lowered circumstances and to try and make your way, but quite another to allow a man of ill-repute to socialize and hope to court my daughter, when you should only have her best interests at heart."

"Father—"

He held up a hand. "I do not want to see or speak to you right now. We will talk later." He walked away.

Poppy leaned against the doorframe, feeling the hard wood jam into her back. It hurt, but she didn't care. She'd managed to ruin Tom's relationship with Susan.

Tom sat on one of the sofas and stared at the floor. "I should never have come."

"Tom, I'm so sorry."

"It's not your doing. It's my own fault. I should have been honest from the start."

"That's on you," Miss Penwrith said.

Poppy rounded on her. "You have a nasty habit of inserting yourself into other people's affairs."

"I was doing my Christian duty."

"Christian? That's not what I would call it. What you did was cruel," Poppy told her.

"You're the niece of a clergyman, you should know better. I couldn't stand by and let such a scandalous thing occur. Petunia Dyngley would be shocked."

"I rather think Mrs. Dyngley can think for herself," Poppy said.

"Well, I bid you congratulations, Miss Penwrith," Tom rose and offered her a mocking half-bow.

"What do you mean?"

"Only this, that you have the singular consequence of having offended literally every guest at this party. If anyone were to push you off the roof, I would wish them well," he snarled and stalked away.

Miss Penwrith gasped, her hand darting to her mouth.

"He didn't mean it," Poppy said to her, before going after him. She only hoped Miss Penwrith would not cause more scandal by spreading rumors of Tom's ill words.

Was it a trick of the light, or did she spy a slight smile on Miss Penwrith's face?

CHAPTER TWENTY-THREE

P OPPY TOOK A hot bath, and as she sat in the ordinary tub behind a screen, facing the hearth in her room, she pondered the weather outside. The rain poured steadily, most unlike an ordinary summer in England. She had grown up with the summers having a rainy season, but it was also a common feature of the English weather to rain for five or ten minutes, only to be sunny, warm and dry again within a quarter hour. This weather was so strange. For days it had been raining and it was hardly safe to go out.

She stepped out of the bath, dried herself and rubbed her damp hair with a towel, before slipping on her shift and tying on a warm dressing gown. Miss Cooke knocked and entered, and attended to her hair, motioning for footmen to remove the tub. Once they were alone, Miss Cooke helped Poppy into a comfortable dress of purple cotton, printed with small flowers. A small sash went around her waist, and Miss Cooke pinned her hair back into a bun and tied a light purple headband on her head, weaving hair around it to keep it in place. The effect was pretty.

"You're not letting that Miss Penwrith get to you, are you, Miss?" Miss Cooke asked.

"What makes you say that?"

"Your look. I can see it on your face."

Poppy gave a tiny snort and a smile. She could always trust

her lady's maid to speak the truth, however plainly.

"She has gotten on all of our nerves, and those of us she does speak to, she has offended."

Miss Cooke laughed. "That sounds like her. She's spent time downstairs too, giving orders for what she wants."

"And what is that?"

"She's been telling us what she likes to eat, and how she wants things done, for when she is mistress of Faulkbourne Manor she will turn us all out who doesn't obey."

Poppy's eyes widened. "My word. I wonder what Mrs. Dyngley will say to that."

"Don't think she knows, Miss. Perhaps you might tell her?"

"What about her lady's maid?"

"Mrs. Dyngley don't have one. The girls take turns looking after her. She's gone through three in the past month alone, along with the wetnurses for the baby."

"Good lord."

Poppy glanced at her reflection in the looking glass above the wooden vanity table, that revealed her long neck, pale skin and hooded eyes, as if she'd been haunted. The look was true enough, she thought. She was just gazing out the window as Miss Cooke chose a necklace for her to wear, when she heard a scream.

Poppy and Miss Cooke stared at each other. "What was that?" Poppy asked.

"Did you hear a—"

The scream came again.

Poppy jumped out of her seat and ran out of the room, Miss Cooke at her heels.

It was a woman's voice, a ragged cry that shrieked again and again. Poppy and Miss Cooke ran down the corridor, stopping at Aunt Rachel's room.

There inside stood Aunt Rachel, who stood back by the fireplace.

"Aunt, are you all right?" Poppy asked.

"L-look! It's the ghost." She pointed.

"Where?" Poppy asked.

"Where did it go?" Miss Cooke said, rolling up her sleeves.

"It's gone. But look!" Aunt Rachel pointed at the bed.

There on Aunt Rachel's bed, lay a mess. Her bed was covered with feathers. And there in her pillow, was a knife.

Poppy swallowed. The very sight of it sent a chill down her spine.

"What's happened? I heard a scream," Henry said, at the door, trying to catch his breath.

He was soon joined at the door by John, Tom, and Mr. Faulkbourne, as well as Susan and Miss Penwrith.

"Look at that," Miss Penwrith said.

"What have you done to your bed?" Henry asked.

"It's not me. I didn't do that," Aunt Rachel said.

"Then who?" John asked, walking toward the bed.

"It was… I think it was the ghost," Aunt Rachel said.

"I knew it," Susan said, eyes darting around the room. "It's the ghost of that maid, Nell, come back to take her revenge."

"Oh lord, don't say such a thing. Where is my fan? I feel hot," Aunt Rachel said, her face becoming flushed.

Miss Cooke crossed the room and fetched a fan, handing it to Poppy's aunt. "Thank you." Aunt Rachel began fanning herself madly.

"Did you offend someone?" Henry asked.

"No. Not a soul," Aunt Rachel said.

"What were you doing when this happened?" he asked her.

"I'd just put little Arthur to sleep in the nursery, when I came back here. Saw the door was open and there were feathers on the floor. I looked and saw that mess." Aunt Rachel fanned herself. "Is it the ghost, Sergeant?"

"Ghosts don't exist." Henry joined John by the bed and examined the scene. "And they certainly don't stab letter openers into pillows."

John pulled out the offending weapon. "We normally keep this in the library."

"I am sorry that happened to you, Mrs. Greene. Miss Cooke, if you would call for the servants to assist in cleaning this up," Henry said.

"Yes, sir." Miss Cooke curtsied and quit the room.

Poppy stood by with her aunt as the others left, servants cleaned up the feathers and tidied the room. Aunt Rachel took a seat by the fire and fanned herself. "You don't think…"

"It wasn't a ghost, Aunt."

"No, I know. Do you think it was that girl…"

"Miss Penwrith?"

"No, Susan," Aunt Rachel said. "The last time we met was at London where she had thrown wine at you and I'd slapped her across the face. Do you think she did this, to take her revenge?"

Poppy blinked. "That was months ago, Aunt."

"Well it wasn't Mrs. Dyngley, she and I are on very good terms. Lady Blackwood is indisposed. Unless you think one of the men did it? But who would want to torment me?" Aunt Rachel fretted. "Do you think it's a warning? That I am next?"

Gone was her aunt's solid self-confidence and no-nonsense manner. This had shaken her, to be sure.

"I strongly suspect it was Miss Penwrith."

"But why? I haven't done anything to her."

"You haven't done anything to anyone, Aunt. This was a senseless prank, that is all. I'm sure of it."

Petunia knocked on the door. "Mrs. Greene, are you all right? I heard from John what had happened. I cannot imagine this happening to you under our roof. It's unpardonable."

"Oh don't worry, Mrs. Dyngley. It's quite all right. I'm made of strong stuff. A little nonsense like this won't bother me," Aunt Rachel said with false bravado.

"Do you need anything? There's no need for you to stay in here, we have more rooms if you would prefer. I am shocked this happened, honestly."

"I will be fine. But… whoever did this knows where I sleep. Poppy, if I might share your room tonight?"

"Of course."

"That is very good. Miss Morton, a word." Petunia beckoned Poppy out to join her. Once they were alone in the corridor, she said, "Do you know who was behind this attack on your aunt?"

"I wouldn't call it an attack."

"I would. A knife in her pillow? It's a wonder she didn't faint. I'm sure I would have. Who do you think did it? She hasn't annoyed the servants, has she?"

"Not that I know of. It could have been anyone. Sergeant Dyngley thinks the servants are above suspicion, so the likelihood is, it's one of the guests who is behind this," Poppy said.

"In that case, we can guess who did it," Petunia said.

"You think it was Miss Penwrith?"

"Who else? She's been a thorn in everyone's sides since she arrived, and I have only recently seen her for what she is. Did she inquire after your aunt?"

"No, but she was present when we all came to see what had happened."

"Regardless, I shall speak with her," Petunia said darkly and walked away.

Poppy installed her aunt safely in her room. They would share a bed, but that was no matter of consequence to Poppy. She more dreaded the possibility of her aunt snoring during the night and keeping her awake.

THAT NIGHT AT dinner, Lady Blackwood was back amongst them, and wished Henry and Miss Penwrith congratulations on their engagement, when footmen brought in slices of cake.

"What is this?" Petunia asked. "Dessert was to be ices."

The footmen began slicing the cake, serving pieces to each person. It was a decadent fruit cake dusted with sugar.

"How delicious looking," Aunt Rachel said.

"I asked the cook to prepare a sort of wedding cake, as a taste of what's to come," Miss Penwrith smiled as a footman placed a slice before her.

"You should not have given an instruction to the servants without discussing it with me first," Petunia said sharply.

"I wanted it to be a surprise," Miss Penwrith said.

Poppy looked at Henry, who was as dumbfounded as she, then at the slice of cake placed in front of her.

He gazed at the slice before him, looking decadent and delicious. He could spy the delicate fruit in the sponge, and detected the rich scent of orange. The cake had not been resting long, it was practically fresh out of the oven. But what it represented, sickened him. From her wanton ways in the coach, to being positively vile toward Poppy and the other guests, to ordering around the servants, and now this. This was the final straw. It stared him in the face, and he viewed it like a sort of snake. To take even a single bite would signify his acceptance of Miss Penwrith's interference with their daily lives, and that he could not accept.

"No." He pushed his slice away. "I am not hungry. And this is inappropriate, Miss Penwrith."

"What do you mean? We are engaged. I thought it a nice touch, since we have to wait for the rain to stop and to apply for a special license." Miss Penwrith speared a piece of it and touched it to her tongue. "And it's delicious."

Poppy rose from the table. She couldn't sit there and make polite conversation while eating a wedding cake for Miss Penwrith and Henry. Her face flamed with embarrassment. She felt like a fool, and to have to pretend like nothing was wrong…It bothered her, deeply. "Excuse me, I… Excuse me." Poppy fled from the dining room.

Henry glared at Miss Penwrith. "That was poorly done. You have been insensitive, callous and cruel." He threw his napkin down on the chair and went after Poppy.

She stood outside the dining room, in the foyer, leaning against the staircase. She looked up as he entered. "Oh Henry."

He took her in his arms. He held her close, breathing in the clean scent of her damp hair. He whispered sweet words of comfort against her and felt himself relax as he clasped his hands around her slim body. When he released her, her cheeks were wet with tears.

"I've been such a fool. It all feels like it's coming to a head now, and she's lording it over me that you… you…" she started.

"I'm not going to marry her," he told her.

"What? You're not?" she blinked hard.

"No. I could never marry anyone who is so heartless toward others. What she did tonight was unpardonable. No wife of mine would ever be so cruel." He used his thumb to dry her left cheek, feeling her warm salty tears. Her brown eyes were the color of melted chocolate, and what with her mouse brown hair, now dark and damp, he wanted to tell her more than ever that by God, they would be together.

So he did.

"I will marry you, Poppy. Do not doubt it. I will not let anyone persuade me otherwise. Will you believe me?" He took her by the shoulders.

"Yes."

"Then stay constant, and so will I."

"But how? You are engaged to her." She made the word *her* sound like an insult.

He felt the small of her back and pulled her close. "Let me worry about that. Look after your aunt."

He kissed her, gently, like the barest touch of a butterfly's wings. He felt her lips, soft and yielding at first, then salty from tears, and kissed her harder. He pulled her against him, trapping her in his arms, and he didn't care if anyone from the party came to see or happened to come across them. He loved her, she loved him back, and he would not be denied this most innocent of touches.

And then he heard it.

A cough.

And again. *Cough cough.*

A nasty one, a pregnant cough that grew and grew, to the

sound of raised voices.

"Miss Penwrith, are you quite all right?" Lady Blackwood asked from within the dining room.

Henry released Poppy. Her eyes were dark with worry. "Something's wrong."

Together they hurried back into the dining room where Miss Penwrith stood, coughing, clutching at her throat as her face turned red and she stumbled, her dress dragging down the tablecloth and scattering plates and glasses as she crashed to the floor. Women shrieked and men stood as she coughed and hacked, crawling on the floor toward them, her head raised to see Henry and Poppy together. Her eyes narrowed in anger and she reached for his shoe.

"Stay back," Henry stood before Poppy, his arms in front of her as Miss Penwrith gasped for breath, when a piece of food shot out of her mouth and she collapsed.

"Is she all right?" Petunia asked.

Henry bent to her, moving the tablecloth away. "I can't tell."

"Let me," Mr. Faulkbourne said, moving him aside. He supported Miss Penwrith's head and leaned in close.

"What is he doing?" John asked.

"I'm listening for her heartbeat," Mr. Faulkbourne said.

"Well, your head is very close to her chest, it seems most improper," Aunt Rachel commented.

"Ssssh, he's listening," John said.

Henry backed up and stood, feeling Poppy slip her hand into his. That was improper, but he didn't care. "Is she…"

Mr. Faulkbourne sat up and said, "Miss Penwrith is dead."

CHAPTER TWENTY-FOUR

PETUNIA SCREAMED. LADY Blackwood jumped. Tom swore. Aunt Rachel fell off her chair. John faltered and leaned back against the table. Susan gasped and clutched Tom, who held her close. Poppy leaned against the doorway for support.

Lord Blackwood turned pale. "I can't believe this. She's dead?"

Mr. Faulkbourne stood. "She is."

Footmen came and stood at attention. One servant asked, "What would you have us do?"

John rubbed the back of his neck. "I don't know."

Poppy glanced at the body of Miss Penwrith. She lay with her eyes closed, her hands still splayed out.

Mr. Faulkbourne said, "We need to move her. Put her back in her room. We need to discuss this."

Tom and a footman carried her away, supervised by Mr. Faulkbourne.

"I don't understand. What happened? She choked?" John asked.

"It looks that way," Henry said.

"This is terrible. Simply terrible," Lady Blackwood said. "Sergeant, I'm so sorry for your loss."

Everyone looked at her.

"What are you all looking at me like that for? I love a wedding," she said.

Petunia breathed in and pinched the bridge of her nose. "I think we can safely say this meal is over. Would everyone please join me in the drawing room?"

Once everyone was seated, she rang for a footman to attend, and ordered drinks to be served. She clutched a glass of wine and sat down on one of the sofas.

Poppy took a moment to appreciate the room. It was a large room that gave off a cozy sort of feeling. It bore light red wallpaper, almost with a burnt sienna tinge, and more than one set of deer's antlers hung on the wall. Small, squat side tables bore large, heavy candelabras made of iron with marble bases. These served as ornamental and functional, and the many candles scattered around the room offered a dim warmth.

The footmen immediately built a fire in the fireplace nearby, and the ladies took seats on the aged, dull yellow overstuffed sofas and wide chairs, while the men stood by in attendance. Once everyone was either seated or served, Poppy caught Henry's eye.

Miss Penwrith was dead. Her rival was gone. What did this mean for her and Henry? She scarcely dared think, much less hope. Then she felt instantly guilty for her thoughts. She was being selfish.

Henry looked at her but said not a word.

Lady Blackwood said, "What an unfortunate run of bad luck. First I am ill, Sir Dyngley is attacked, and now this. And Susan tells me there is a ghost walking around."

"There is no such thing. It is just a story," Petunia said.

"Even so. Now an innocent young woman is dead. It's a terrible accident. Someone should write to her family."

"Her parents are dead. She has no more family," John said.

"She was staying with us until she found her way," Petunia said.

"And now she never will, the poor thing," Lady Blackwood said.

"Well someone needs to look into this." Petunia downed her drink, set it aside and crossed her arms.

"You can't think it was anything but an accident?" Lady Blackwood said, "We all saw it. She choked to death."

"There is no reason to think it was anything malicious," Henry said. "Lady Blackwood is correct."

"But Henry, I would have thought that what with your experience, you could look into this."

"There is nothing to investigate. The girl had an unfortunate accident." He frowned. "I fear the ground is too wet to bury her. We will need to leave her in her room for now."

"Oh, how horrid. A dead bride." Lady Blackwood shivered, then looked pale, clutching her abdomen. "Oh my. I need the— excuse me." She rose from her seat and dashed out of the room.

Lord Blackwood glanced at them all. "Excuse me, she's still not very well." He went after her, Susan following in his wake.

Mr. Faulkbourne re-entered, along with Tom. "Well, it's a sorry thing that's happened. I've only ever seen a thing like that once, a person choking like that."

"It's good you were here. Are you a doctor, Mr. Faulk- bourne?" Petunia asked.

"No. Once upon a time my father thought I might become a surgeon, and I studied medicine for a bit at university. Even did a brief stint at St Bartholomew's Hospital in London, but I felt it wasn't for me." His eyes took on a faraway look, and for a moment, he looked haunted. "In any case, I have some medical training. Not so much I would profess to be a doctor, but I have some. I can manage in a pinch. Muddle my way through, as it were."

"What do you do now, Mr. Faulkbourne, if not medicine?" Aunt Rachel asked.

"I have no profession."

This was met with silence as Aunt Rachel daintily sipped her drink. "Um, I hate to be a bother, but is it possible she was poisoned?"

Mr. Faulkbourne winced.

"No, certainly not. We do not go around poisoning each other in this household," Petunia said.

"It was an innocent question," Aunt Rachel said. "Considering…"

Petunia frowned. "I won't hear of it. First ghosts, now this. There is nothing wrong with this manor."

John touched her shoulder. "It's been a long night. It's getting late. Perhaps we should adjourn, yes?"

"Yes, that's a good idea." Petunia accepted his hand and bid them all goodnight.

Poppy nodded good evening to the others and joined her aunt upstairs. As she ascended the staircase after her relative, she glanced down over her left shoulder. Henry and the others stood there talking, but Henry's eyes were on her.

Poppy was smart to be wary, she realized in the middle of the night. She had thought kindness toward her aunt was boundless, but as her aunt rolled around in her sleep and tore the blanket off of her, Poppy decided her good will only went so far. She loved her aunt, but not in that moment. The woman snored and talked in bed and took up far too much of the blanket, when she wasn't stealing it altogether. Poppy looked at her aunt in the darkness. The woman had now wrapped it around herself like a cocoon, snoring happily.

Poppy sighed. She shivered in her shift, as the fire in their room had burned low. She got up, pulled on a dressing gown and tied it around her for modesty, when she heard a noise.

She put on a pair of slippers and quietly crept out of her room.

She didn't know what time it was, but knew the hour was late. The rain pattered against the windows and she shivered, when she saw a shadowy figure walk across the landing at the stairs. Poppy's breath caught in her throat. Was it a ghost? Were the others right? Did ghosts walk at Faulkbourne Manor?

She walked down the corridor to the landing, but whomever

was there had gone. Disappeared into the darkness.

Poppy shook herself. "You're being silly," she told herself, and walked back to her room and went to sleep.

THE NEXT DAY, Poppy didn't see Henry or John at breakfast. She went looking for them and found them upstairs, but not playing billiards. Instead, Tom and Mr. Faulkbourne played, and nodded hello. "Beastly weather, this," Tom said, glancing out the windows.

"What are they up to?" Poppy asked, nodding toward the open door of Sir Dyngley's study. "I wondered where you all were."

"Seems Sir Dyngley's study was disturbed during the night," Tom said.

"It was? What was disturbed?"

Henry came out of the study and stood against the leftmost sliding door. "Good morning, Poppy. We can't tell. Papers have been moved and his chair was knocked over, but we can't tell if anything has gone missing. You didn't see or hear anything last night, did you?"

Poppy turned pink. "I did actually, but you'll think it silly."

"Why is that?" John asked, joining the group. "Tell us."

"Well…" She realized she had all of the gentlemen's attention on her. "I woke in the night and thought I heard a noise, so I went out of my room. I thought I saw a woman by the staircase."

Henry's eyes widened. "Did you go after her?"

"I did, but didn't see where she went. By the time I got there she was gone. I rather wondered if…"

"Don't say it," Henry told her.

"You really think?" Tom asked.

"It couldn't possibly," Mr. Faulkbourne said.

"Could it have been a ghost?" John wondered.

Everyone looked at him.

"What?" John asked. "I'm just saying what we're all thinking. And before you tell me that ghosts don't exist, I disagree. You're all trying to convince yourselves that you don't believe, but I do. And I trust Miss Morton. If she believes she saw a ghost, I reckon she is telling the truth."

Poppy smiled at John, but also half winced. She did not believe in ghosts or spirits of any kind, but then why had the woman disappeared before she could reach her? "I told you it was silly."

Henry frowned. "Who could it have been?"

"Perhaps Mrs. Dyngley was awake?"

"No, she's a heavy sleeper. Fast asleep all night," John said.

"Could your aunt have…." Henry started.

"No," Poppy said, and blushed. "She was the reason I woke in the first place. What about Lady Blackwood, or Susan?"

"We'll need to speak to them both, although what with Lady Blackwood being indisposed so much of this week, I doubt she would have gone walking around the house in the middle of the night," Henry said. "Mr. Markham, would you care to speak to Miss Blackwood about her whereabouts last night?"

"Me?" Tom dropped his pool cue and picked it up. "No, I'd better not. Things are… I'd rather not if it's all the same to you."

"Very well." Henry raised an eyebrow. "Poppy, would you talk to her? She's your sister."

"Half-sister," Susan entered the room. "And I'll thank you to remember that. I was fast asleep in my room anyway. I didn't go out." She avoided looking at Tom, who colored.

Miss Cooke appeared and curtsied to the group. She coughed and said, "Miss Morton, might I speak with you?"

"Of course." Poppy followed her lady's maid out of the billiards room and into the small open space that faced the stairwell. To their left stood the entrance to the east wing. There was a corridor and a door had been hastily constructed over it, but it exuded an odor of subsidence and decay.

"Begging your pardon, Miss Morton, but the servants downstairs are worried. Someone's been rifling through the kitchens and Mrs. Piggott is fretting. Would you come down and talk to them?"

"All right." Poppy went back to the group and paused, then said, "Susan, I wonder if you might join me."

"For what?"

"It's a secret."

Susan rolled her eyes. "All right. But you're not being very subtle, whatever it is."

Susan joined Poppy and Miss Cooke. "What is it?"

"What would you say to a little investigating?"

"Oh, no. Not me. Not after last time. Do you not remember? One of your friends turned out to be a madwoman and kidnapped me. I almost died."

Actually, I almost died, but never mind, Poppy thought. "Fine, if you could walk with me a little, I would appreciate it."

"Very well. But only because I've been sitting for too long. And I don't want to be in the same room as him." Susan glanced back at the billiards room.

Miss Cooke walked on ahead, leaving the two half-siblings alone. Poppy said, "I thought you had an understanding with Mr. Markham."

"You thought wrong. And I don't want to talk about it," Susan said grumpily, walking down the stairs.

Poppy hurried to keep pace with her. "How have you been? I've hardly seen you but at mealtimes."

"Yes, well... I'm fine." her face took on an unhappy look. "Mama found my letters, and the letters between you and Papa, and learned about the engagement. She was so angry, so we had to come."

And you did nothing to stop her, Poppy thought.

"She didn't actually like Miss Penwrith," Susan was saying. "I think she just thought that by supporting her cause, she'd be actually hurting you and Papa."

"What about you and Mr. Markham? He came here to see you."

"He did? I mean, I know, of course he did. He'd hoped we

would see each other at the wedding. He told me so himself." She looked at Poppy. "Is he really a…?"

"A procurer of women? He was. But I don't think he is anymore."

"So it's true then." Susan's pretty face twisted angrily. "He was a pimp. All this time I've been a fool."

"Not at all. I've never seen him so besotted."

"You would know."

"Yes, we became friends. I think if you asked him his story, he would tell you," Poppy said.

"I don't want to know. What do I care about a pimp?"

"Even a reformed one?"

"I don't care. I'm done with him. He should have told me from the start."

"Would you have paid him any attention once he'd told you?"

"Of course not. I…" Susan glared at her. "Whose side are you on?"

"I want you both to be happy."

"Well, you've got a funny way of showing it."

They passed Aunt Rachel, who said, "Oh hello, girls. I'm on my way to Miss Penwrith's room."

"What for? "Susan asked.

"To pay my respects. I thought I'd say a little prayer, if you both want to come along?"

"I'd rather not. I have other things to do," Susan said.

Poppy added, "I'll come by later."

The girls continued to head down the stairs when there came a dreadful scream from above. Poppy, Susan, and Miss Cooke hurried, holding their skirts as they ran. Poppy led the way as she came to recognize the scream that rang out again. She went down the corridor and crashed through the open doorway of Miss Penwrith's room. "Aunt? What happened? Are you all right?" She stopped and stared.

"L-l-look!" Aunt Rachel pointed.

Susan and Miss Cooke arrived a second later, slightly out of breath. "What is it?" Susan asked.

John, Tom, Henry, and Mr. Faulkbourne joined them in moments. "What happened? We heard a scream."

"Henry, look," Poppy said.

"What is it?" he asked, "Are you all right?"

"I'm fine. It's Miss Penwrith," Poppy said.

"What about her?" John asked. "I don't see anything."

"Exactly. This is her room. But her body, it's gone. Her corpse has gone missing."

CHAPTER TWENTY-FIVE

HENRY FROWNED. "WHAT do you mean, she's missing?"

"Her body, it's disappeared." Poppy turned to Tom and Mr. Faulkbourne. "When you brought her up here, I presume you laid her on the bed. Is that right?"

"Yes. We did. She was still warm," Tom said with a shiver.

"Well, she's gone now. Where could she be?"

Petunia walked into the room. "What is going on? Has something happened?"

John said, "Nothing to concern you, my love, why don't you go on—"

"Stop it, John, I'm not a child." Petunia pushed by him. "What are you all doing in here?"

"Miss Penwrith's body is missing," Henry said.

"Where is it?" Petunia asked.

"We don't know," Poppy said.

"I don't understand. Corpses do not just get up and walk away," Petunia said, crossing her arms beneath her chest.

"Where is little Arthur?" John asked.

"In his crib, asleep."

Poppy asked, "Mr. Faulkbourne, could you have made a mistake when you examined Miss Penwrith?"

"What are you talking about, Poppy? Miss Penwrith choked to death, we all saw it," Susan said, shooting a dirty look at

Poppy. "You're just trying to stir up trouble, aren't you?"

Poppy reddened. "Not at all."

"You owe Mr. Faulkbourne an apology. He's a doctor, after all." Susan gave Mr. Faulkbourne a winsome smile. Tom's face fell.

Mr. Faulkbourne cleared his throat. "There is no apology necessary, Miss Blackwood. I was only trying to help. But you are correct. Miss Penwrith choked and died, I confirmed it. When I got to her, she was no longer breathing," Mr. Faulkbourne said.

"Then how do you explain this?" Henry asked.

"I don't. Someone is playing a trick on you all and moved her. Maybe to fool you. Or maybe the footmen moved her elsewhere so as not to alarm the ladies."

"It's possible," John said.

"Well, what do we do?" Petunia asked.

"Nothing. I will speak with the servants to see if they moved her body. Mr. Faulkbourne, I wonder if you might—"

"I need him. Mama is still feeling poorly and he should check on her," Susan said, standing close to Mr. Faulkbourne. He nodded his acquiescence and held out his arm to Susan, who took it and followed him from the room. Petunia and John went after them, which left Poppy, Tom, Henry, and Aunt Rachel.

"I'm going to go lay down. That was truly frightening," Aunt Rachel said.

"Miss Cooke, would you bring my aunt a cup of tea?" Poppy asked.

"Yes, Miss." Miss Cooke bobbed a curtsy and walked out, as Aunt Rachel nodded and quickly left the room.

Tom's expression was grim. "What can I do?"

"Not much for now. Keep an eye out for anything strange," Henry said.

"This entire past few days have been strange. Please, Sergeant. I need something to do. I can't bear to…"

Henry took pity on him. He didn't like Tom Harris, or Markham, whatever his title was. But he recognized the signs of pain, for it was as obvious as if someone had scrawled it upon Tom's face. "Come with me. Perhaps you can help me question the servants."

"My pleasure."

Henry turned to Poppy. "Will you look after your aunt?"

"Yes. Although I should tell you, Miss Cooke informed me right before my aunt screamed, that the servants reported the kitchens had been tampered with overnight."

"They were? Why did they not report it to me?"

"I don't know. I was on my way downstairs to speak to them when we were interrupted."

"I see. Leave this to me, I'll find out." Henry looked at Poppy, his chest heavy with feeling. He had conflicting thoughts about Miss Penwrith's death, and what it meant for his relationship with Poppy, but there was too much to do to think about that now. "Excuse us."

But when Henry and Tom went down to speak with the servants, Tom tapped his nose. "Let's part ways. I'll learn more if I'm on my own."

"As you wish," Henry said, with dislike. Trust that Tom would find a way out of doing real honest work.

Henry passed through the servants' hallway and knocked on the private study of the family's butler, Mr. Newell. An older gentleman with thinning gray hair and a stiff-backed bearing, the man looked positively ill at ease at Henry's questioning. The older man mopped his head with a handkerchief.

Mrs. Ewing knocked, entered, and pulled out a chair. "Mr. Newell?"

The butler gratefully took a seat and leaned his chin on his hand. "This woman is missing? I thought she had died."

"She did. We are wondering if one of the footmen might have moved her."

"Them, touch a body? No indeed. No one would dare do that. What reason would they have?" Mrs. Ewing said.

"No reason. But she was left there yesterday evening and

now she is gone."

"Was she really dead?" Mrs. Ewing asked.

"That is not under debate. Yes, she was. Is. So the matter remains, did one of your household move her?" Henry asked.

"Not a chance." She crossed the room and shut the door behind her, leaning against it. "I wonder, sir. Did you know that someone was in the kitchens last night?"

"I heard about that from Miss Morton. Why did no one tell myself or John?"

She looked down. "At first Mrs. Piggott thought one of the maids had been careless and had gone rummaging in the pantry for a late-night nibble. I told her that if she fed the staff properly, then they wouldn't go feeling peckish late at night. I—"

"Mrs. Ewing," Henry started.

"Right. Yes. Well, she questioned the girls and none of them were down here last night after hours. She trusts them all, so you can take that as her word."

"And the footmen, Mr. Newell?"

The butler roused himself. "Alfred and Rupert wouldn't do that, nor Simon. They're good lads."

"They wouldn't have gone into the kitchens?"

"More like the cellar to get at the wine. I've caught Simon in there more than once when he thought I wasn't looking. But never late at night. They wouldn't."

"And you're sure none of them would have moved Miss Penwrith's body?" Henry asked.

"No," the butler said.

Henry thanked them and walked out, when Mrs. Ewing caught his sleeve. "Yes?"

"Master Henry, I think it best we do not mention the news about Miss Penwrith and all. These maids, their heads are always full of stories and they love a good gothic tale. If you go asking about her body and whatnot, they'll be seeing her ghost everywhere they look, and I'll never hear the end of it."

Henry smiled. "I'll not mention it." He climbed the stairs and met Tom, who nodded to him. Once they were above stairs and stood in the open foyer, Tom said, "I spoke with the maids."

"Did you learn anything?"

"Only that whoever broke into the kitchens helped themselves to a little feast last night. They left a dirty plate and made off with some ham, potatoes, and iced buns."

Henry snorted. "I wonder if it was one of the guests."

"After Miss Penwrith choked last night? I doubt anyone would've had an appetite after that," Tom said.

Fair point, Henry thought.

He returned to his room to find the door ajar and a fire roaring in the hearth. That was odd. The room was blazing hot. As he stepped inside, something was amiss. Writing papers on his writing table were flung onto the floor and a quill lay out of his inkstand, dripping black ink. Someone had scratched a letter, and the fine indentations of the quill were hard pressed into one of the sheets of parchment, so heavy he could almost make out a message, but couldn't.

He tidied his desk, got ink on his fingers and realized he'd touched his collar. He picked up a small looking glass on his table to check if there was a stain. But he did not like his reflection, nor the thought of feeling vain, when his breath caught. There was something written on the glass. He breathed again and again, watching as ghostly letters began to form.

HENRY

He shivered and set down the looking glass. glanced at the fire and opened one of the windows to let cool air in. Rain poured steadily down outside, harking no end to this wet weather disaster. As he turned, he spotted some ash on the floor by the hearth and scraps of paper.

He walked over and picked up one of the scraps. It read:

—ot what —e see—

He puzzled over it and put the scrap in his pocket. He certainly didn't write anything. Then a chill ran down his spine. Was Miss Penwrith writing him messages from beyond the grave?

AT A QUIET lunchtime meal, Henry proposed the idea of splitting into groups to search for Miss Penwrith's body. Petunia was disgusted, and Lady Blackwood felt too ill to eat much beyond a few bites of cold ham before retreating back to her room. Lord Blackwood had a tray sent up to his room, and a servant brought up some warm broth for Sir Dyngley. Susan teamed up with Mr. Faulkbourne and Aunt Rachel, Poppy investigated with Miss Cooke and Tom, while Henry, his valet Geoffrey, and John explored together. Henry did not like the idea of Poppy alone with just Miss Cooke for protection, but the rules of society dictated that she be escorted by a close family member if she were to be in the company of other men, and to be alone in a group of men was even worse.

John soon left to check on their father, so Henry and Geoffrey explored the library, the parlor, the sitting room, even the attic where the servants slept, but found nothing. There was no trace of Miss Penwrith. It was as if she'd never existed. He found it very strange. As they stood outside the library, Geoffrey said, "Sergeant, I wonder, is it worth checking your mother's room?"

"No. Why would she be in there? Besides, it's in the east wing. Everyone knows to stay out of it. It's unsafe."

"Should we look?"

"No, leave it. No one would go there. They know to stay out," Henry said.

Geoffrey nodded and they looked in a handful of rooms, but did not find any trace of Miss Penwrith. "Sir, the servants are wondering."

"Go on."

"Now that Miss Penwrith is no longer with us, will you and Miss Morton…"

Henry blinked. "I don't know. It's hard to say. Why, is that what they're talking about?"

"Yes. Mrs. Ewing is trying to keep the maids and footmen from talking about a ghost, so they're discussing that instead."

Henry snorted. *Of course they were.* "You can tell them I have no plans at present." He glanced around the display room they stood in, that reminded him of a museum. "Geoffrey."

"Sir?"

"Where are the games?"

"What games?"

"My father had a chess set in here. It's gone. Did one of the maids take it for cleaning?"

"Not that I know of, sir."

"Find out."

Geoffrey left, and Henry stood, puzzling. Where would a game have gone, and why?

THE RAIN PELTED down all day, with regular intervals of letting up, and coming down hard again. Henry had never seen so much rainfall at one time. The grounds around Faulkbourne Manor were green and saturated, and the lake was full. The road had washed out, and it still wasn't safe to leave. The very ground was brown and muddy.

That evening at dinner, the company was quiet. Lord and Lady Blackwood kept to themselves, while Susan sat by Mr. Faulkbourne, hanging on his every word. If it weren't for the fact that she was so obviously trying to make Tom jealous, he would think she didn't like Mr. Faulkbourne at all. But instead, she laughed at his jokes, smiled at him, and batted her eyelashes, flirting as much as she dared under her parents' watchful gaze. Mr. Faulkbourne was delighted at the attention, and together they carried the dinner conversation.

Henry looked at Poppy. She appeared tired, with dark circles under her eyes. Her mouse brown hair was in a bun and had little pretty tendrils of hair that curled by her face, but her skin was a trifle too pale, and she moved with jerky movements and darting glances, as if she expected Miss Penwrith's body to jump out at any moment. He wished to comfort her but could not. They were not engaged, they were... he didn't know.

"How are you feeling, Lady Blackwood?" Henry asked.

"Much better, thank you," she said, over a glass of wine and a bowl of rich broth.

"I say, why don't we have some entertainment tonight after dinner?" John asked.

"Is that really appropriate? A girl has died," Aunt Rachel said.

"It's the perfect time. We need something to lift our spirits, or else we'll be hiding from shadows and seeing ghosts everywhere. A small dance would be just the thing," John said. "Who will join me?"

Poppy looked at her aunt. "I will."

"That's the spirit," John said.

"I will too. I love to dance."

"Excellent. Lady Blackwood?" John asked.

"Well I don't know. Perhaps. I have been told before by some people that I am rather graceful on the dancefloor..."

"I don't doubt it," John said with a smile. "Petunia, would you care to play the pianoforte?"

She nodded.

In seconds, John had the ear of a footman and gave him instructions to prepare the drawing room for dancing and entertainment. Once the meal ended everyone adjourned to the drawing room, where the sofas and chairs had been moved down to one side of the room and a small pianoforte and chair had been brought in. The room wasn't overly large, but well suited to a small party. In no time at all Petunia sat down at the instrument and began playing a concerto.

Henry stood back, amused. His sister-in-law was a talented piano player, but this was not quite what John had had in mind.

After listening to the opening movement John clapped and said, "Perhaps you might play something a bit more suited to dancing, dearest."

"Oh yes, of course." Petunia began to play a country tune, which gave way to a reel.

Soon everyone was dancing. Henry danced a reel with Poppy, a quadrille with Lady Blackwood, and a country dance with Susan, before going back to Poppy. It was a pleasure to touch her hand and lead her in the formation, even if they did not speak. He did not know what to say and for that matter, neither did she.

Henry did not know when he'd had so much fun, certainly not for some time. After an hour or so the dancing broke up, and people began to bid each other goodnight. Soon the only ones still in the room were himself, John, and Poppy.

Henry stood by the windows drinking a glass of wine with John, who remarked, "I say, look. The rain has stopped."

Henry said, "You're right."

A maid entered the room and cried, "I've just seen the ghost of Miss Penwrith! She was walking upstairs."

Henry shook his head. "You're mistaken, there is no ghost."

The maid was young, and wrung her hands, her face drawn close to tears. "Please, sir. Won't you see? I know I saw her, clear as day."

Henry set his shoulders and let out a sigh. "All right, let's go see."

Then they heard a piercing scream. It was a woman. Henry froze and looked at John, when a dark figure flew past the window and smacked into the ground below. The maid squealed and fainted dead away.

"Oh my god," Henry said.

"Did you see something?" John asked.

"See to the maid, help her wake up." Henry ran, taking a candle with him.

"Wait!" John called after him.

Poppy also took a candle and ran after him, as he dashed out into the corridor and down the stairs, his feet taking him as fast as he could go. The servants were beginning to blow out the candles and the foyer was lit with darkness, when Henry ordered, "Open the door!"

A footman turned and jumped, then opened it immediately.

Henry dashed out, followed by John and Poppy. He heard voices and footsteps behind him. He held the candle out, but its tiny flame had already blown out.

John stepped into the muddy courtyard beside him. "Where did you see it fall?"

"Over there, I think." Henry led the way.

He walked, his eyes gradually adjusting to the night sky and the gloom from the dark clouds that had pervaded much of the day. He walked ahead, as John called out, "Who's there?"

Henry tripped. He landed on something solid and wet. He got to his feet, his hands dirty and muddy as John came up behind him, Poppy at his heels.

"Poppy, stay back," Henry warned.

Poppy didn't listen, of course. She came right up to see and gasped. "Henry, your hands."

"Yes, I know, it's been raining," he said irritably.

"No. There's blood on you," she said.

He looked down. His hands were covered in blood. A chill ran down his spine.

"John, hold up your candle. Poppy, you too."

Together they knelt and held their candles down to reveal…

The dead face of Miss Penwrith, staring into the sky. Her glassy eyes reflected the moon as they stared into nothing.

CHAPTER TWENTY-SIX

HENRY STARED AT the body of his former childhood friend and fiancée. She was gone.

John scrambled back, falling. "Good god!" He dropped his candle in the mud and ran off toward the house, his boots splashing the puddles with each step. "Get help! Someone, get the servants out here. Get the doctor, call Mr. Faulkbourne!"

Poppy stood next to him. "Are you all right?"

"No."

She stood by him, not speaking. He ran a hand through his hair, then realized his hands were bloody, muddy, and lowered them. He needed a bath.

"She's dead, isn't she?"

"Yes."

Poppy reached down and touched Miss Penwrith's wrist.

"What are you doing?"

"I want to see if she has a pulse. I've seen doctors do this before." She felt her wrist and gasped. "Henry."

"What?"

"She's still warm."

"What?"

"See for yourself."

Disgusted, he swallowed his revulsion and leaned down to touch Miss Penwrith's wrist. Sure enough, her skin was warm.

Just, the warmth was fading.

"Do you realize what this means?" Poppy asked.

"What has happened?" Mr. Faulkbourne came outside with John, Tom and a pair of footmen along with the butler, each holding lanterns and candles.

"Miss Penwrith is dead."

"Of course she's dead, she died the other night at dinner," Mr. Faulkbourne said.

"Touch her. Feel for her pulse. You'll see she is still warm."

Mr. Faulkbourne stared. "What?" He leaned down and touched her wrist. "How is this possible?"

"I can only assume that she was not dead before," Henry said.

"But she was. I examined her. She was dead."

"Then how do you explain this?" Henry held up his hands and gestured to the blood that pooled out of her brain. He could see grisly bits of her body and decided not to look too closely, for the sight made him queasy.

"She's dead."

"But she bled. Dead bodies do not bleed," Henry said.

John turned his back, wincing at the mention of blood.

One of the footmen tried to take hold of Miss Penwrith's shoulders and dropped her.

"Careful, man!" Henry admonished.

"Sir, might we fetch a sheet to wrap her in? The sight might disturb the women," the footman said.

"Yes, go on."

The footman fled. He returned minutes later with a bedsheet. They wrapped her up in it, blood, mud, and dirt already staining through the sheet.

The group followed as the footmen brought the body in and took her upstairs, back to her room. They laid out towels and put her on her bed when Petunia, Susan, Lord and Lady Blackwood, and Aunt Rachel came to the room. "We heard a scream and came to see. Is that– oh no."

Lady Blackwood walked into the room. "Miss Penwrith. She's

wrapped up in a sheet. What happened?"

"We don't know. We too heard the scream and went outside, where we found her."

Lady Blackwood walked over and pulled the sheet back. "My god. She's…"

"Dead," Henry said.

"But how?"

"I think she fell," Henry said.

"From where? Her room?"

People looked at the windows, but they were closed.

"No, but…" Henry's mouth set into a hard line. "A short time before, a maid came in shouting about having seen her ghost. We were going to investigate when we heard the scream and saw something fall, then found her."

"So she really is dead this time."

Mr. Faulkbourne turned angrily. "She was dead when I examined her before."

"She couldn't have been. Not to have her be dead a second time. People can only die once."

His face turned red. "It's possible she was thrown."

"No, her body was still warm when we found her. She was alive when she fell," Poppy said, earning a glare from Mr. Faulkbourne.

"I don't know. She was cold when I examined her. We had all witnessed her choke. I believed her to be dead."

"So you admit, you could have made a mistake," Lady Blackwood said.

"I won't deny it is possible."

"You couldn't just admit to it? She was still alive when you pronounced her dead," Lady Blackwood said.

"What is the point? The girl is dead now. Why does it matter whether she was dead before?" he asked.

"Because *if* she was still alive, then we could find a clue, perhaps, about what happened to her," Poppy said. "Could anyone have come in while she was resting and hurt her?"

"No, no one. Who would have wanted to see a dead body?" Mr. Faulkbourne asked.

"Anyone who wanted to pay their respects," Aunt Rachel said. "I was going to."

"Then you could have done it."

"What? Me? No," she protested.

Poppy stood in Mr. Faulkbourne's way. "My aunt would never do such a thing."

"I'm not saying she did, just that she could have." He looked at Aunt Rachel. "You look strong enough."

"To do what?"

"Hoist a dead body up and throw it out of a window."

"The windows aren't open."

"You could have closed it when you finished, then pretended to come with the others. Everyone would believe you."

Aunt Rachel's eyes blazed. "Now see here–"

Everyone started talking at once.

"Everyone, please. We're not accomplishing anything by pointing fingers at each other," Henry said.

The group looked at him.

"What we need to figure out is whether Miss Penwrith's death was an accident. Could she have taken her own life?" Henry asked.

Lady Blackwood frowned and stood by the bed, looking at Miss Penwrith's body wrapped in the sheet. "I think it is possible. She has had to put up with so much these last few days, from what I've seen. But I also think it equally possible that someone caused her to have an accident."

"An accident? Mama, she fell, she didn't trip over her own shoes," Susan said.

"I know. I'm just saying, it could be either."

"Surely if she meant to take her own life, she would have left some sort of note. Don't people do that sort of thing, so that others know why they did it?"

"Sometimes, other times not," Mr. Faulkbourne said.

"Let us work on the assumption that she killed herself. Why would she do it?"

"She was desperately unhappy." Lady Blackwood said.

"Was she?" Poppy asked.

Lady Blackwood did not dignify her with a response.

Poppy said, "She had everything she wanted. She'd reconnected with the family, she had her fiancé—"

"She even got your wedding dress," Aunt Rachel said.

"What?"

"Look. She's wearing your missing wedding dress. I knew she'd taken it," Aunt Rachel said, pulling the sheet open. "See?"

Poppy watched as the sheet was tugged aside to reveal the pink gown she was going to wear as a bride that had been stolen. It was much too long for Miss Penwrith's shorter body, and the hem of the dress was muddy and damp. Seeing the proof of her suspicions there for all to see was disheartening, and she sighed.

"I knew it. The girl was a thief. She lied right to your face."

"It doesn't matter now, Aunt." Poppy's voice was dull.

"Did you know, and did you do something about it?" Lady Blackwood asked.

"Amelia," Lord Blackwood started.

"Stop me if you know something I do not, but these two girls have been at odds since we arrived. And from what Susan tells me about her background, any animosity this young woman incurs upon herself is well deserved..." She glanced at Susan and gave Poppy a stern look.

Poppy snorted. Considering her half-sister's thinly veiled dislike of her, the knowledge that she and her mother would have spent hours together in a carriage with little to discuss, it was no wonder Lady Blackwood arrived with such an ill-conceived notion of her. What a shame she took no time to make up her own mind, rather than let someone else decide her opinion for her. In that moment she decided not to worry about Lady Blackwood, for there were some people whose good opinion she would never have, and some whom she would never change.

Poppy asked. "I don't see why Miss Penwrith would kill herself. She had everything she wanted."

"Not the marriage contract," Henry said.

"What contract?"

"When she first came to us, she referred to a marriage agreement of sorts, between her mother and ours, promising us children to be married if we were both in our twenties and still single. I did not know such an agreement existed until she mentioned it, but neither of us know where it is, or would be." He paused. "With it, Miss Penwrith could finally prove her case and legally push for us to marry."

"But that didn't matter, she'd already trapped you into an engagement."

"True."

"I think you are all forgetting something," Aunt Rachel said. At their questioning looks, she added, "A knife was stabbed into my pillow a day ago. It was terrifying. Am I supposed to forget about that?"

"No. You're right, we still don't know who did that or why."

"I think she did it herself, out of an inability to do anything else. A woman could well feel powerless in such a situation as Miss Penwrith found herself. She came to your door looking for love and instead found…" Lady Blackwood glanced at Poppy and sniffed. "No doubt Miss Penwrith felt betrayed by you, Sergeant, for wanting to marry another woman, expressly against both your mothers' wishes."

Petunia looked at her thoughtfully. "She does have a point, Henry."

"If that were so, then why would she trap me in the carriage like that and compromise her honor?" Henry asked.

"She likely felt she had no other option than to demean herself in that way. Men often fall to their lusts and lower base natures. She just needed to remind you that she too, was a woman," Lady Blackwood said.

Tom snickered.

Lady Blackwood rounded on him. "You think that's funny, do you? Well, I know exactly how you are and what you do, Mr. Markham. Wait until I spread word of your misdeeds to my friends. You'll be a laughingstock. No one will accept you. You'll be barred from all good society. You'll be a social outcast."

Tom stood back. "You seem to have the measure of me, madam."

"I'm just amazed you had the audacity to make an offer for Susan. As if we would accept a man like you."

Susan looked pained. "Stop this. Stop it, Mama."

"What for? He is nothing to you."

"No. He is… He is… I care for him."

"Poppycock. You're too young to know what you want."

"No. I do. And I…." she heaved a breath. "I like him. I want you to give your permission to allow him to court me."

"Absolutely not. Have you been listening for the past five minutes? He's a miscreant. A blackguard. A rake. He's–"

"You're right. I am. I'm all of what you said. But I care for your daughter," Tom said, his face earnest.

"Stay away from her. You have no right to even speak to her."

Tom looked glum. "Will nothing convince you of my good conduct?"

Lord and Lady Blackwood shook their heads.

"Then I wish you the very best." He nodded, bowed to Susan, and turned to go.

"Tom, where are you going?" Susan paused, touching his arm.

"Home. Back to London. I'll go as soon as it's light enough and if the roads are dry."

"Tom, please."

"Susan, don't talk to him," Lady Blackwood said.

Susan ignored her mother. "Please don't go."

Tom patted her hand. "It's all right, love. It wouldn't have worked out anyway. They're right. You're too good for me."

"No, I'm not, I…" She glared at them all. "I know who did it. I know who is behind all of this."

"You do?" Petunia asked.

"Tell us," John said.

"No, not yet. I'm going to give the person a chance to come clean. They have until midnight to admit to what they've done. Otherwise, I'm going to the authorities at first light."

"You do have a sergeant here. Why not just tell him?"

Henry said, "Susan, if you know something, tell me now and we can put an end to this."

"No. It would be unfair to the person. Come clean before it's too late. I know what you did."

"You say it like they're here," Petunia said.

"But they are. They're in this room," Susan told her.

"You mean…" Petunia started.

"Isn't it obvious? The person who is behind all this, and Miss Penwrith's murder, is one of us."

CHAPTER TWENTY-SEVEN

POPPY WENT TO her. "Susan, if you know who did this, you have to say so, immediately. Don't play games."

"Spare me your good advice, Poppy. I don't want to hear it. We may be related but not by my choice." Susan walked off, going after Tom.

"Susan–"

"Let her go," Henry said, at Poppy's shoulder.

Poppy stood by as Susan went out of the room. The rest of the group quieted, talking amongst themselves. They could hear Tom and Susan's voices clearly.

"Tom, where are you going? Why didn't you stay and say something?"

"There is no point. Your parents have already made up their minds about me."

"So you won't even try?"

"What for, when they're right? Do you know, last week I was invited to a country party, where I thought the host wanted to introduce me to his eligible daughters. Instead, he wanted me to meet his maid and see about finding a girl for him in town. He knew my name and yet didn't care, he just wanted my services." His voice was annoyed.

"I don't care."

"You have no idea how wretched it was. I don't want to bring you into that world, Miss Blackwood. I won't. Your parents are right. I'm… bad for you."

"You're not."

"You cannot want to be dragged into my schemes and lifestyle. I've given all that up, but it doesn't matter, men know me for what I am, not who I am. I want to be honest with you."

"Then make a dishonest woman out of me."

"Susan!" Lady Blackwood lunged for the door.

"I won't do it, Miss Blackwood. I won't." Tom left.

Lady Blackwood stood in the doorway. "Susan, come away from there, right now."

Susan must have ignored her, and walked away, for Lady Blackwood went after her, saying, "Susan, come back here."

Lord Blackwood sighed and looked at Poppy. "An honorable pimp. Who would have thought it?" He quit the room.

Poppy stood beside Henry and glanced down at Miss Penwrith's body. "Do you really think Susan knows?"

"I doubt it. I suspect she thinks to rile the person into a confession. But it won't work. It never does. It only causes more trouble."

Poppy waited for the others to go, then glanced at the room. It was a small, decent room suitable for a guest. The wallpaper was white with blue patterns, and the curtains were of a similar white and blue material. The dressing table was surprisingly free of anything, aside from a looking glass and a small basin for washing.

Poppy took the edges of the sheet and covered Miss Penwrith, until she was decently covered up again. It worried her to see the sight. The young woman was so full of life and yet, her final days had been full of manipulation and scheming. Was that truly the way she wished to carve a life for herself with the Dyngleys?

As she pulled the sheet tight, she spotted a sheet of paper curled in Miss Penwrith's right hand. "What is that?"

"What do you see?"

"A bit of paper." Poppy gently pulled it from Miss Penwrith's stiffening grip. She read its contents and gasped. "Good lord."

"What? Let me see."

Petunia read over Poppy's shoulder:

I, Mrs. Anne Dyngley, being of sound body and mind, do so hope that if my son Henry is yet unmarried by age twenty, that he and Miss Honoria Penwrith will marry, if she too is unwed. But if they are engaged or married already, I hope they are happy, and will always stay good friends.

Signed this first Thursday in October, in the year of our lord, seventeen hundred and ninety-two.

Anne Dyngley
Violet Penwrith

"My god, it's that blasted marriage contract Miss Penwrith was going on about. She really did find it," Petunia said.

"But it's nothing but a few lines of hope and happiness. It's not a contract at all. It's not notarized or witnessed," Poppy pointed out.

"How awful. The girl pinned her hopes on nothing but a little note between friends. What a shame," Petunia said. "She must have been distraught when she found out."

"Indeed. But would that be enough for her to want to kill herself? Surely if she found it, she would destroy it, or else hide it. It's proof that her claim to Henry is null and void."

"I'm not sure. We'd better tell Henry. What are you think-ing?" Petunia asked.

Poppy turned around. "Only that we know so little of Miss Penwrith. I don't think her death was an accident, but neither do I think she would have killed herself."

"We know a little of her history. She and Henry practically grew up together. If it weren't for that dratted marriage agree-ment, I would have thrown her out the next day," Petunia said.

"But you seemed to champion her cause, particularly against

me. Why the sudden change of heart?"

Petunia paused. "I disliked her way of treating you and Henry. A woman does not trap a man into marriage, at least no honorable woman does. She could not expect to keep him. I would think it a matter of days before you found Henry at your door, wanting to pay court to you."

The ghost of a smile flitted across Poppy's face.

"I also think you have been blind to Miss Penwrith's faults and actions toward others."

"What do you mean?"

Petunia looked at the bed with the corpse, and said, "In her own way, Miss Penwrith has managed to offend or annoy almost everyone here. Aside from Lady Blackwood, she had no friends here. And that is only because Lady Blackwood was ill and Miss Penwrith had not managed to insult her yet. I'm sure she would have found a cause soon enough."

Poppy glanced at Miss Penwrith's traveling trunk, which had seen better days. It bore her initials. "Do you think it inappropriate if I were to examine her things?"

"Highly. But I could not possibly comment on such a thing if I did not see it." Petunia turned her back.

Poppy almost grinned. She almost laughed. Instead, she jumped as Petunia asked, "Well, have you found anything?"

Poppy went to Miss Penwrith's trunk and opened it. Such an unlikely ally, Petunia Dyngley. But inside she found dresses, gloves, and letters. Nothing out of the ordinary.

"What's that?" Petunia asked, pointing at the vanity table and drawers. A bit of paper stuck out of one of the drawers and ink had spilled, dripping down the front of the drawer.

Poppy pulled open the drawer and examined its contents. Inside was an overturned inkwell, stained quills, and a piece of parchment paper. "This is strange."

"What is it? Let me see." Petunia came to peer around her. "That is odd."

On the page it said over and over:

Mis Honora Penwrith

Miss Honoriia Penwrth

Misz Honoria Penwrith

Miss Honoria Penwrith

Miss Honoria Penwrith

Miss Honoria Penwrith

"Why would she write her own name multiple times? And with such mistakes? There are inkblots on the paper," Petunia said.

"I'm not sure, but I have an idea."

"Well, do tell. She was rather self-absorbed. Perhaps she enjoyed little pastimes like writing her own name?"

"No, I don't think that's it. Not entirely."

"Then what?"

Poppy said, "Wait here."

"With a murderer around? Not likely."

"Fine, come with me." Poppy took the sheet and walked to the library, where Henry and John sat.

"Look at this, Henry, we found the marriage contract." Petunia waved it like a miniature flag in the air.

Henry started. "Let me see that." He read its contents. "Where did you find this?"

"In Miss Penwrith's hand. It fell out as Miss Morton was fastening the sheet around her body."

Henry breathed a sigh of relief. "I'll put this away. This proves she had no claim at all." A slight smile lit his face for the first time in days.

"I wonder, do you have any recent letters from Miss Penwrith?" Poppy asked.

"Yes. Why?"

"May I see them?"

Henry frowned at her request. "Whatever for?"

"I want to examine something."

"Just do it, Henry, we're investigating," Petunia said.

John's mouth quirked into a smile as Henry walked to a writing desk and pulled a letter from a drawer. He handed it to Poppy. "Are you going to share your theory with me?"

"Not just yet."

Poppy walked over to the nearest candle and held up the two letters.

"What do you see?" Petunia asked.

"Look at the handwriting."

"Yes, what of it? They're different."

"Exactly."

"So? That's no great concern—oh."

Poppy smiled. "Why would Miss Penwrith have different handwriting in her letters?"

"I don't know. Do you?"

"I think I might," Poppy said with a smile. "If I didn't know better, I'd say she was practicing."

LATER THAT DAY, Poppy went up to visit Sir Dyngley, and knocked on the door. As she opened the door, she spotted her father before her. "Ssssh, he's resting."

Her father ushered her back into the corridor and shut the door behind him.

"How is he?" she asked.

"Recovering. That knock on the head has addled his mind somewhat, but I think each day he grows better. And he's eating, which is good."

"Is he talking?" she asked.

"Oh yes."

"That's good. I'll go speak with him then."

"You shouldn't." He stood in her way. He said, "I've tried talking to him about the accident. But whenever I bring it up, he becomes confused and distressed. You asking questions won't help, you'll only bother him more."

"Oh. All right. Could you tell me when he is feeling well

enough to talk?"

"Yes, but really that's a matter for Mr. Faulkbourne. You should ask him."

Poppy raised an eyebrow. "Father."

"Yes?"

"Is there something you're hiding?"

"No. Of course not. What a thing to say."

She flashed a smile at him. "Sorry. I've been investigating with Mrs. Dyngley and am seeing suspects everywhere. I'm just glad we're talking again."

He smiled briefly, then frowned. "You shouldn't be investigating anything."

"But Father, it's–"

"No buts, Poppy. You shouldn't be sticking your nose where it doesn't belong. Nor should you be dragging Mrs. Dyngley into it. If you're bored, read a book. Do some embroidery. But leave these matters to the men."

Poppy glanced at him, taking in the fine lines around his eyes and laughter lines at his mouth. She curtsied and excused herself, walking down the corridor.

It made her sad to disobey him and to have to mentally put him on the same shelf as other men who viewed her as an oddity at best, and at worst, an interfering busybody. But investigating to her was as easy as breathing, and it gave her a thrill. She wouldn't stop investigating until she was dead, and knew it. She only hoped she found out who was behind these little crimes before it was too late.

THAT AFTERNOON, POPPY sat with Petunia, Henry, and John, and mulled over the facts. Or rather, she and Petunia stood back and watched as the men played billiards. It wasn't that they weren't encouraged to join the men's game, but Petunia turned up her nose at the idea and Poppy's mind raced too much for her to focus on a game.

"So who could have done it?" John asked. "Who killed Miss

Penwrith?"

"That Mr. Markham and Miss Blackwood," Petunia said immediately. "They clearly came here with no other reason but to see each other, and court beneath her parents' noses. When I think about the insult they have shown to our house." She shook her head.

"You think my half-sister is a murderess?" Poppy asked. "I don't believe it."

"Maybe not her, but they both had reason to want her dead. If Miss Penwrith hadn't opened her mouth, they might now be courting, or even engaged. I think they were heartbroken when their secret was found out."

"I think you're mistaken, my love," John said. "I'd put my money on Lord Blackwood."

"My father? Why?" Poppy asked.

"Sorry, Miss Morton. I know he's dear to you, but he did mean to marry you into our family and keep the intricacies of your relationship a secret from our father. I'm all for happy endings, but you must admit, it was somewhat... duplicitous."

"What about Mr. Faulkbourne?" Poppy asked. "He has medical training, or is a doctor, or something. How good a physician is he, considering his assessment of Miss Penwrith when she choked?"

"It's called human error, Miss Morton." Mr. Faulkbourne joined them. "It happens, even to the best of us. And I certainly do not count myself amongst the best in my profession."

Poppy turned pink. Henry and John glanced at him, while Petunia gave him an even look.

"Apologies for the intrusion. I heard voices and wanted some company. I can go if you'd rather," Mr. Faulkbourne said.

"No, stay. We are just trying to figure out who is behind Miss Penwrith's murder," Petunia said.

"Ah. If I had to guess, I would say the good woman herself."

"You think her death a suicide?" Poppy asked.

"Definitely. She came here knowing of your engagement and

yet did everything she could to put an end to it. I think all of us knew she wouldn't succeed. Any scheme she tried was doomed to fail." He leaned against the wall and surveyed the game. "Think about it. Everything she did and said was done out of spite. She turned everyone against her, and for what? All to marry a man who did not love her back. I think that's enough to turn anyone's heart to stone."

"It's possible. If we're pointing fingers, we might as well blame each other," Henry said. "I had as much a reason to want Miss Penwrith dead as anyone else. More so, I'd say, considering her actions."

"Same as me," Poppy said. "She made a mockery of reading the banns, did her best to ruin our engagement and did, and even trapped you into marrying her. If she hadn't died…"

"We might be married within days," Henry said.

"So there you have it. We all had a reason to want Miss Penwrith gone. Who have we missed?" Mr. Faulkbourne asked.

"My aunt. But she would never do such a thing," Poppy said.

"Wouldn't she? Would she stand by and do nothing while an upstart, devious young woman tried to ruin her niece's happiness? I'd be surprised if she didn't do something."

There was a knock, and Miss Cooke appeared alongside Henry's valet, Geoffrey.

"Yes, what is it?" Henry asked.

Miss Cooke had a funny look on her face, as if she had eaten something that had disagreed with her, or like something was terribly wrong. "Begging your pardon, sir, but there's a visitor at the manor."

"Oh?"

"She says she is Miss Honoria Penwrith, and she's come for the wedding."

CHAPTER TWENTY-EIGHT

Henry's jaw dropped open. "What did you say?"

Miss Cooke winced, and Geoffrey said, "It's true, sir. A woman named Miss Penwrith has arrived. She's asking to see you."

"Good God. Another one?" Mr. Faulkbourne said. "First she's dead, then she's not. Now she's alive again. What is this? A circus of horrors?"

Henry said, "Show her to the parlor. I will meet her straight away."

"Me too," John said.

"And me," Petunia said.

The group went en masse downstairs and were introduced to Miss Penwrith, a pale, frail, fragile-looking creature of twenty years of age. She might have once been considered a beauty, but sickness had ravaged her body and she still bore the traces of it. Her cheeks were hollow and her black eyes dull; her dress hung on her body. Where once she might have filled it out with womanly curves, she had her corset laced tightly, and yet even that seemed loose on her bony form. Her hair was brown and thin, but she held herself with a dignity and poise that Henry immediately recognized.

"Miss Penwrith," he bowed.

"Henry." She curtsied and looked at him. "Hello again, after so many years. John, hello."

"Hello Miss Penwrith." John bowed and gave her a smile. "You're looking well. It's good to see you again."

Miss Penwrith snickered and shot him a knowing look. "You can end the forced politeness, John. I'm Honoria, not a solicitor. And I know exactly how well or ill I look. It's why I've come. How have you been? And where is my wayward nursemaid?"

"I beg your pardon?" Petunia asked.

Miss Penwrith gave her a deep curtsy. "Forgive me, madam, for I have known these two gentlemen since they were boys and catching frogs by the pond. I am Honoria Penwrith, an old friend of the Dyngley family."

"I've heard that before," Petunia said.

Miss Penwrith cocked her head, confused.

"Never mind. Tell us what you're doing here. Please, sit." She gestured toward one of the large comfortable chairs and rang for tea.

"I am sorry I did not keep up the correspondence over the years, but you recall that our family moved away from Essex," Miss Penwrith said.

"Yes, we remember. It came as a bit of a surprise, as I recall."

"Well, the fact is, our family fell on hard circumstances. My father did the best he could, but gradually our prospects soured. He attempted to get a leg up over his debt by making some investments, but, well… I won't go into the particulars."

At that moment a servant brought in tea, and Petunia served everyone. Honoria Penwrith gratefully accepted her cup and held the steaming hot china cup in her hands, gripping it as if she'd been cold for a very long time. She continued, "Needless to say, when he died, it was just my mother and I… and my mother, already in a weakened state from taking on work and looking after my father, I think she died of a broken heart once he passed. Truth be told, once she died, and her funeral effects used up all our money, I did not know what to do with myself. All I had were the tales of my childhood and the fond memories of our times with your family for comfort. Once I caught a fever, I did not expect to live long. Neither, I suspect, did my nursemaid, Lizzie Bethamy."

"Your nursemaid?" Petunia repeated.

"Yes. Lizzie was a dab hand at making homemade remedies, and as she'd looked after mother and father when they fell ill, she took to looking after me too. She loved hearing tales of us as children and of the manor, and especially of my time spent getting into childhood scrapes. She even loved hearing about the little marriage arrangement my mother had drafted with Mrs. Dyngley. Where is she? I'd like to say hello. And Sir Dyngley, is he around?"

"Our mother is dead. She died a few years ago."

"Oh. I'm so sorry. And Sir Dyngley, is he…"

"He's resting upstairs. So Miss Bethamy looked after you," Henry said.

"Yes. No thanks to her medicines, I became sicker than ever. I think she may well have had something to do with that. My health took a turn for the worse and I think she feared I would die. As it happened, I drank her medicine one night and when I woke up later, my clothes and all my money was gone. Miss Bethamy had disappeared. I was too weak to do much and depended on the kindness of strangers until I got my strength back.

"When I looked for my things, I realized that she'd taken everything. My personal effects, my clothes, even my letters and notes from my family. Everything that made me, me. Even my necklace, the silver locket I'd received as a birthday gift, the last one we'd shared together before my family moved away. You remember it, don't you?"

"I do."

"When I woke it was gone too. I wouldn't doubt it if Miss Bethamy sold it. In any case, I'd hidden some money away for emergencies and used the last of it to make my way here." She looked at John, Henry, and Petunia. "I have nothing and no family in the world. This was the closest thing to home I ever knew."

John's expression softened, but Petunia put a hand on his arm. "I'm sorry, but I've never met you before. How do I know that you are who you say you are?"

Miss Penwrith glanced down at the floor. "I should have expected this. Henry, when you fell in the pond and I fished you out, you were afraid you'd get in trouble, and so I said I'd pushed you."

"I remember."

"The real Miss Penwrith could have told you that," Petunia said, "Henry, ask her something only the real one would know."

"When we first met, you commented on my appearance. What did you say?"

She smiled. "That you had big ears."

He gave her a warm smile. "It is a pleasure to see you again, Honoria."

"And you, Henry. Now do you believe me?"

"Yes." He turned to his sister-in-law. "It's her, Petunia."

"Very well. So why have you turned up at our doorstep now?"

"I have come to ask your help in finding my errant nurse-maid. She not only robbed me but she took my locket, which was a keepsake. Could you help me? I can't pay you, but I could work as a servant for a time, or—"

"Are you good with children?" Petunia asked.

"Yes, I love children."

"And you can tolerate their crying and demands for constant attention?"

"It's never a matter of tolerating."

"And I suppose you can provide references?"

"I could always write to the innkeeper who looked after me, I watched his little Maisie from time to time."

Petunia waved a hand. "I don't care. When can you start?"

"Um, now, I could–"

"Excellent. Mrs. Greene can show you everything."

"Now wait a moment, Petunia–" Henry started.

"Honoria, you need to sit down," John said.

Honoria sat. "I work hard, and I don't ask for much. You won't even know I'm here, honest."

"It's not that. Honoria, your nursemaid came here."

"She is? Where is she? I'll have words with her…."

"She's dead."

Miss Penwrith stared. "Dead? How? When?"

"It's a bit of a long story…"

AFTER HENRY INFORMED Miss Penwrith of what had transpired, Poppy said, "That's it. Miss Cooke, would you call everyone down?"

"Whatever for?" Petunia asked.

"I know who is behind these little incidents and I think it's time we shed some light on the subject."

In a matter of minutes, everyone was called into the drawing room. Poppy began, "Forgive me for disturbing you, but I thought it important we all meet in the open and discuss what has been happening. A woman is dead, and I think it's necessary to clear the air."

"Go on," Aunt Rachel said, helping herself to a ginger biscuit with her tea. "When she's like this, it's always good to have something to nibble on."

Petunia rolled her eyes and took a biscuit. "Well?"

"Since I was first engaged to Sergeant Dyngley, Miss Penwrith had been doing her utmost to wreck the engagement. But now she is dead and we cannot go on thinking it was a harmless accident.

"Firstly, Miss Penwrith's mutilated wedding dress. While I didn't do it, I think she wanted us to find her with it, so as to cast suspicion on me. Second, Lady Blackwood fell ill."

"I was poisoned," Lady Blackwood said.

"And yet, all of us had some of the same food as you did that evening, but none of us became ill. Can you guess why that is?"

"It's obvious. Whoever killed Miss Penwrith thought I was a dangerous person to come against and were afraid, so they decided to poison my food. It could have been anything, a drink, a bit of off-meat…"

"I'm glad you said that, Lady Blackwood. For you see, after you became ill, I visited the kitchens and spoke with the staff. The servants told Sergeant Dyngley and I that some of the food that had gone bad, had also gone missing. It had disappeared overnight. Almost as if, someone had helped themselves to a midnight snack."

Heads turned toward Lady Blackwood, who blushed. Lord Blackwood said, "Amelia? You…"

"I was peckish after the meal and found some food had been left out. It was so dark, I helped myself. I didn't think anything of it."

Lord Blackwood ran a hand through his silver hair.

"Let me get this straight, you poisoned yourself?" Petunia asked.

"She's done this before," Susan said, earning herself a dirty look from her mother. "It's true."

"That doesn't mean you need to be airing our dirty linen to strangers," Lady Blackwood snapped, her face pink. Seeing the others' looks, she said, "I admit it. I did go down to the kitchens. But the food was there, I didn't think it would be bad."

"You didn't judge by the smell or taste?" John asked.

"I've had a cold recently and my senses were dulled. I thought it was fine until… I got sick."

"So that's why you've been keeping to your room this visit," Petunia said.

"Yes. Now please can we discuss something else?"

"Yes. Next my wedding dress was stolen," Poppy said, "But we know Miss Penwrith, or I should say Miss Bethamy, took it. We found it on her body the night she was killed."

"Why was she wearing it? How morbid," Lady Blackwood

wondered.

Poppy shrugged. "The better perhaps to keep up the ghost facade. While she was pretending she was dead, she could wear whatever she wanted."

"And what, decide to suddenly pop up and declare she was alive again? It seems odd."

"I think this wasn't the first time she was in Miss Morton's affairs," Henry said. "When my father was found in her room, there is no proper reason for him to have been in there."

"When we found him, he was lying face down in front of the closet. It's very odd."

"I suspect he found Miss Penwrith there in the middle of trying to steal my dress," Poppy said.

"But he was hit on the back of the head. For her to have hit him, she would have had to walk around and get the poker from the fireplace, and be facing him from behind. It doesn't work out. Unless he somehow slipped and fell and hit his head," Petunia pointed out.

"Yes," Lady Blackwood said, "it might all be completely innocent."

"I think it unlikely. Why else then would the poker be beside him, away from the fireplace? He wouldn't have struck himself, and I cannot imagine Sir Dyngley to be the type of person to threaten another with a poker."

"You think he was struck from behind," Mr. Faulkbourne said. "I agree with your theory. But who did it?"

"Whoever did, they're the murderer," Poppy said. "I believe he caught her stealing and confronted her. Someone else came in and struck him, allowing her to escape with my dress. I noticed it was gone after we'd found Sir Dyngley, but it seemed less important at the time."

"But then, my pillow was attacked," Aunt Rachel said, her mouth slightly full of ginger biscuit. She took a quick sip of tea and swallowed. "Someone stabbed a knife into my pillow. Why would they do that?"

"Erm, that was me." Susan raised her hand.

"You? Why?" Aunt Rachel asked. "I was terrified."

"I'm sorry about that. It was meant for Miss Penwrith. I got the rooms mixed up and thought it was her room."

"Disgraceful. Why would you do such a thing, Susan?" Lady Blackwood said.

"Can you not guess?"

"No, I cannot."

"Miss Penwrith ruined Tom's proposal of courtship for Susan. I was there, I saw it. We were all in the library when it happened. Where there also happens to be a letter opener made to look like an ornamental dagger," Poppy said.

"Oh, my goodness," Aunt Rachel said, having another sip of tea.

"But then Miss Penwrith died, the first time. Who caused her to choke like that? Was it an innocent accident?" John asked.

Aunt Rachel colored. "I um, might have asked Miss Cooke to assist me in that."

"What? You tried to kill Miss Penwrith?" Henry said.

"No, don't be silly. Of course not. I would never."

"I think you'd better explain yourself, Mrs. Greene," John said.

"Well, it's just, Miss Cooke did mention to me how that young woman was getting very high and mighty with the servants downstairs, even telling them to switch out the dessert planned for the night and instead serve up slices of her wedding cake. I thought it was in very poor taste, so I thought, why not give the girl a bit of her own medicine."

"What did you do?"

Aunt Rachel paused.

"I can guess," Poppy said, "You asked Miss Cooke to put a little something on Miss Penwrith's cake slice. Not anything dangerous, just something to disturb her. Something to make her need the necessary, if I had to guess."

"You are good at this, Poppy. Quite good," Aunt Rachel said.

"That's it exactly."

"You make it all sound like a game, but it is not. The young woman choked and later died." Lady Blackwood shot a dirty look at her husband, as if to say, *And you wish to be allied with this family?*

"So when she choked, she played dead. Then later, she died again. Do we know why she pretended to be a ghost?"

"I think she did it to scare us, namely me. I woke up from a dream one night to see a woman standing at the foot of my bed, pointing at me. And then later, walking around at night. I think it was Miss Penwrith, pretending."

"But something was wrong. I found a scrap of paper in the fireplace of my room with the words *not what eeesseee*, or something like that. And in my looking glass, Miss Penwrith left a message for me."

"Her ghost left you a message?" Susan asked, her eyes wide.

"What did it say?" Lady Blackwood asked.

"My name. It was hard to tell," Henry said, "I must admit I had thought it a prank of some sort."

Lady Blackwood turned pale. "Miss Penwrith was leaving you messages from beyond the grave, and you speak of it as casually as if you're discussing what to have for dinner. My god. Hugh, let us leave, at once."

"Yes, dear. We will."

"But that wasn't the only thing she wrote," Petunia said. "We found it, didn't we, Miss Morton? In her room. She'd been writing her name, over and over."

"Why would she do that?"

"Because she wasn't Miss Penwrith at all, but an imposter," Poppy said. "And we have the real Miss Penwrith here to prove it."

Honoria nodded and looked a trifle embarrassed at the attention, and settled for bouncing little Arthur on her knees.

"There is the matter of Miss Penwrith, or Miss Bethamy's, untimely death," Poppy said. "Someone had had enough of her schemes and killed her."

"Yes, we were in the drawing room when we saw her fall," John said. "But in her bedroom later, there was no sign of anything out of place. The window was closed, her things were in order. If she had climbed out and committed suicide, wouldn't her window be left open for us to find?"

"Yes. She didn't fall from there. I went to the roof and inspected it. There were two sets of footprints in the mud and tatters of the stolen dress on the railing. She either had spoken to someone shortly before she died and fell, or they pushed her," Henry said.

"Then it's murder. If it was an accident or suicide, then whoever spoke to her last would have said so," Petunia said, "There's also the matter of the marriage contract."

"That old thing? I thought it was just a joke between our mothers, almost threatening us with a future of each other if we didn't behave," Honoria said.

Henry smiled. "Miss Bethamy thought it was real, and found it. We found it on her person."

"Goodness me. What did it say? It didn't actually... you know." She looked at Henry with slight revulsion.

"No. More of a note expressing their hopes for our future happiness, with or without each other."

"Well, that's a relief."

Henry grinned.

"What about the missing game?" John asked. "A game of chess, and a set of cards is missing. They're gone from the library."

"Oh. That was me," Lord Blackwood said.

Everyone looked at him. "I rather... Well. I've been laid up in bed before and it's terribly dull. Miserable, as a matter of fact. So I thought I'd check on Sir Dyngley. One thing led to another and... the man's an excellent chess player. We've spent the time playing cards and chess. Sorry, I should have said."

"And how is Sir Dyngley?" Aunt Rachel asked.

"Well enough, but something haunts him still. He looks unhappy whenever Mr. Faulkbourne is in the room, but it's clearly a case of nerves. I can't stand doctors myself." He smiled.

"We now know who's behind all of these little incidents except for one thing. Who is the murderer?" Petunia asked.

THAT EVENING AFTER dinner, Miss Penwrith had taken over the care of little Arthur and put him to bed, and the company sat chatting over drinks and cards. A number of the group had left, until it was only a handful still in the sitting room. Poppy had risen and bid the others goodnight when Petunia met her at the door.

"Have you seen him?"

"Who?"

"Arthur. He's missing."

CHAPTER TWENTY-NINE

"WHAT IS GOING on? What do you mean he's missing? I thought Miss Penwrith was looking after him," Henry said.

"She was, and I was with her when she put him to bed. Then she went to her room, but later, I heard him crying and waited for her to see to him. The noise stopped, so I thought nothing of it, but then I thought I would instruct her on the proper way to hold him. Only, when I went to his room, he was missing, and when I went to her room, I could not wake her. She's fast asleep and won't wake up. Little Arthur is gone," she said tearfully.

The group roused the entire household in a search for Arthur. Maids, from lady's maids down to the lowest scullery maid, all took part in the search. Petunia was in hysterics, Aunt Rachel was tearful, and John was almost as bad. Mr. Faulkbourne stood by and went in the direction of the kitchens.

"Why is he going there?" Petunia asked.

"To prepare a sedative. In case the ladies' nerves get the better of them."

"I am perfectly well," Petunia said, her eyebrows knit in a frown.

"What if something's happened to him?" John asked, his face twisted in worry.

The group split into pairs to cover more ground. The servants took the lower floors, kitchens, and the servants' hall on the top floor, while Petunia and John searched the ground floor. Poppy, her aunt, and Miss Cooke wandered together, as did Henry and Tom. Lady Blackwood kept to her room, while Lord Blackwood joined the search with Mr. Faulkbourne, who wanted to check on Sir Dyngley.

Every room was looked into, every corner peered at. The servants and guests called Arthur's name, but nothing could be heard but each other.

Poppy stood with Miss Cooke and her aunt on the first floor. They had tried the gallery and the library with no luck, and were about to head back downstairs when Poppy said, "Look at that."

"What is it?" Aunt Rachel asked.

The door to the east wing was open.

It stood ajar, the dust around it disturbed.

"Oh, I don't like this. Just close it and let's go back and join the others."

"Wait," Poppy said, holding up her finger for silence. "Do you hear that?"

"What is it, Miss?" Miss Cooke asked.

"There. A sound. I think it's Arthur!" Poppy flung open the door. She stared into the darkness. "Fetch me a candle, quick."

Miss Cooke took a sputtering one from nearby and handed it to her. As Poppy held the little pewter candleholder by its small round hook, she took a deep breath and walked forward. A breeze blew against her, smelling of damp and rot.

"Aunt, get the others. Someone's been in here."

"Who shall I call?"

"Anyone. Get Henry."

Aunt Rachel and Miss Cooke left as fast as they could go.

Poppy hurried the way, peering into the dark. She walked down the shadow corridor, passing rooms on her left and right. Rainwater dripped into places that smelled of mildew, which made her wrinkle her nose. Then she heard it again. A baby.

Poppy called out, "Arthur?"

"In here!"

Poppy darted ahead. She spotted the flicker of a light and entered a room. "Why, Mr. Faulkbourne, you found him. Mrs. Dyngley will be so relieved."

She stopped short. Mr. Faulkbourne stood by a table with a quill, ink, and paper. In his arms, he held Arthur, who wriggled, over a large gaping precipice as rain water dripped heavily from the ceiling, bending down the plaster. It looked like the roof might cave in at any moment.

"Mr. Faulkbourne?"

His grin was nasty. "Hello Miss Morton."

Poppy breathed in. "What are you doing?"

"What does it look like? I'm done waiting. I've come to collect what I came for."

"What is that?"

"The deed to the estate. I want it. And one of the Dyngleys is going to sign it over to me."

"But why?"

He laughed, the sound echoing over the gaping hole in the room. "Is it not obvious? I'll tell you. I grew up hearing stories of our grand estate, how rich we were, and how my fool of a great-grandfather lost it all in a card game. It was my grandfather's greatest regret losing this house in a stupid card game to the Dyngleys. It was a dirty trick, and he let it become his torment. When he threw himself off the roof, he was ashamed. It embarrassed us all. He couldn't bear it."

"But why? Half of the house is a ruin, as you can see."

"Doesn't matter. What's ours is ours. It belongs to my family. To me. And I want it back."

"Give me Arthur." She took a step forward.

"Nuh-uh, not a chance Miss Morton. You could have helped me, once. When you actually had some say in the Dyngleys' ears. But they can hardly bear to look at you, along with your precious father. No. Be a good girl and fetch one of the Dyngley men for me."

Poppy's cheeks bloomed with indignation, but she swallowed her pride. "I will. But how do I know you won't drop Arthur?"

The baby wriggled and Mr. Faulkbourne pulled him back, holding him to his side. "You don't. But I can't trust you, either. Miss Penwrith was right about you."

Poppy stared. "She was your accomplice. You were working together."

He nodded. "Took you long enough. They all said you were smart, but I didn't think it would take me to have to explain it for you to understand."

Her brows knitted into a frown. "She was helping you. Why?"

"I caught her. She was cutting up her dress to pin it on you when I walked in and told her if she didn't help me, I'd give away her little secret."

"What did you have her do?"

"This and that. I didn't tell you all that she was sabotaging herself to blame it on you, and she helped me look for the deed to the estate."

"You found it, then?"

"Eventually. But not until Sir Dyngley told me."

"What do you mean?"

"The night he was injured? He caught her in your room, taking your wedding dress, red-handed. I gather they had words, and whatever story she gave him, he didn't believe it. I overheard him telling her off. He was going to raise the alarm, so I hit him with the poker."

Poppy's mouth dropped open. "So it was you. I thought she had struck him."

"No."

"Is that why he hasn't been well enough to join us? You are keeping an eye on him."

"Yes. When that interfering father of yours isn't in the way, visiting. I have to spend time in there too to make sure he doesn't say a word about it. And when it looks like he will, I give him a sedative. As a former doctor, people will believe just about anything I say."

Poppy stared. "What did you do with the real Miss Penwrith?"

"Drugged her, of course. Everyone trusts a doctor. She was glad to have one of my little sedatives. She'll sleep like the dead until dawn."

So that was how he'd stolen little Arthur, Poppy realized. "And the fake Miss Penwrith? Miss Bethamy? You killed her. Why?"

"She served her purpose. As the real Miss Penwrith said, Miss Bethamy was entranced by her childhood tales of spending time living in luxury with the Dyngleys. She only wanted the Dyngley name and fortune. When she saw the poor straits the Dyngleys were in, she agreed to help me, but stopped when she discovered what I wanted. Then the little witch tried to stop me. I even caught her leaving notes for that sergeant of yours."

"That's right. The word in the mirror, and the scraps of parchment in the fire."

"I'm sure you'll agree, she had to go. You should thank me, Miss Morton. Now you can marry your precious sergeant and live happily ever after."

"His family would not accept me."

"Such a shame." The baby wriggled more and there was the sound of rain, creaking and falling into the room.

"So, Miss Penwrith's ghost, then?"

"Ah. You were right on that one. She didn't die. When she choked, I whispered to her to play dead. That gave her free license to wander around the house at night, looking for that damned marriage contract of hers. Then if anyone saw her, they could claim they'd seen her ghost. Smart, eh?"

"So you lured her up to the roof and killed her."

He shrugged one shoulder. "She'd found the so-called marriage contract and wanted me to change it. She thought I could rewrite it, or change the wording somehow to make it official. I told her she was out of luck. She lunged at me and I dodged. Not my fault she fell off the roof."

"You didn't try to save her?"

"She was already slipping. Good riddance to bad rubbish. You could almost call it providential."

"She didn't deserve to die."

He laughed. "Didn't she? You have no idea what she'd planned in store for you. If you'd kept hanging around, she was going to doctor your drink so you'd never wake up."

That chilled Poppy's blood. "I suppose with help from you."

"Not at all. She knows what she's doing. I suspected as much when I heard she'd poisoned herself the first time after attacking you at the dance. She wasn't really ill. Just enough to be weak. Shortly after I arrived, I overheard her chuckling about it to her maid. A great joke, she thought."

"Arthur? Arthur are you here?" Petunia walked into the space. "Arthur!" She lunged, tripped, and fell on the floor. "There you are. Hand him to me, Mr. Faulkbourne. Thank goodness you found him."

"Uh-uh-uh, Mrs. Dyngley. I want something first." He jerked his head toward the table. "Fetch your husband. As the heir, he can sign over the estate to me."

"What? Don't talk nonsense, give me my baby."

"Do it first. Then we'll talk."

"No, give him to me now." She rose to her feet and started to edge toward him, the hole in the floor wide and dark. The very air smelled of mildew, mold, and damp.

"Stop where you are, Mrs. Dyngley. One more step and I drop him. It's a long way down."

Petunia froze. A tear rolled down her pale cheek. "Please. Give me my baby."

"No. Fetch your husband."

"John!" Her voice, ragged with emotion, carried.

"Coming," came the echoing answer.

"You won't get away with this," Poppy said.

"'Course I will. I came prepared."

"Poppy, did you find—Oh." Susan appeared at the door.

A gun appeared in Mr. Faulkbourne's other hand.

"Mr. Faulkbourne, what are you doing?"

"Come over here, Susan," he said. "Do it, or I'll kill the baby."

Susan let out a breath and slowly walked around the big hole in the floor, hugging the wall, until she reached him.

"Now then," he said. "Options."

Lord Blackwood, Tom, Henry, and John all arrived at the same time.

"Mr. Faulkbourne," Henry growled. "I should have known it was you."

"You never did trust me."

"You've proven why I couldn't. A man with your name, coming here on the barest of pretenses?"

Mr. Faulkbourne made a snide face at him. "Doesn't matter to me as long as I get what I want. You have the deed. Sign it."

Henry stared. "Of course. You're the one who broke into the archives room at White's. You were looking for the agreement from the card game, where your great-grandfather lost the estate to mine."

Mr. Faulkbourne sniggered. "For a sergeant, you're very slow to catch on."

"What were you hoping to achieve by stealing it from the club? Erase all record of it? Sorry to tell you, but it was recorded, signed, notarized, and is mentioned in at least ten different legal records. But perhaps you realized that later. This has been your plan from the beginning, hasn't it? You come and try to ingratiate yourself into our social circle, taking advantage of my engagement to Miss Morton. You procure yourself an invitation and then prove your worth as a medical professional once Miss Penwrith takes ill. All the while you keep an eye on everyone."

Tom and John spread out, John coming closer.

"Don't anyone get close," Mr. Faulkbourne said, holding the pistol in his hands. "Anyone makes any sudden moves and the baby dies."

"Please, don't hurt him," Petunia said.

"Mr. Dyngley, be a chap and sign that document. Do it, and you'll get your son back."

John walked over to the table. "What is this?"

"I want what's mine back. The estate belongs to my family. Sign it over and you'll get your son returned."

"And if I don't?"

Mr. Faulkbourne laughed.

John made a move for him, but slipped and fell, almost falling into the hole. "John!" Petunia said, reaching for him. She and Tom helped him up.

"I'm all right, I'm fine," John said, glaring at Mr. Faulkbourne.

"Sign it," Mr. Faulkbourne said.

"Susan, are you all right?" Tom asked.

"Uh-huh," she said confidently, but her face was pale.

"Do it, Mr. Dyngley. This squalling baby of yours is heavy and my arm is getting tired. I wouldn't want him to slip from my fingers."

"Do it, John. Do it," Petunia said.

John edged toward the table, picked up the quill, and began to read by the light of the flickering candle. "You've added an addendum to this agreement."

"So I have."

"What does it say?" Henry asked.

"That this agreement is null and void upon Sir Dyngley's death. And that as the heir, I willingly agree to sign over ownership of the manor and its lands to Mr. Faulkbourne, executor of the Faulkbourne family." John looked up. "But my father isn't dead."

"He will be, once I take care of him."

"No. I won't sign his death warrant."

"If you don't sign, I'll drop your child. Children are tough little buggers, but that's a very steep drop and I can't imagine he'll survive. But you never know."

John grimaced, picked up the quill, and signed it. "There. I've signed your bloody thing. Now let my child go."

"As you wish." Mr. Faulkbourne dropped little Arthur.

"No!" John and Petunia cried.

Poppy was closest and dove after him, sailing into the darkness.

POPPY FELL THROUGH the air and caught little Arthur, crashing into the floor below. She cradled him in her arms and they landed with a hard thud. Arthur instantly began crying.

"Ssssh, ssssh, it's all right," she cooed, then called out, "I've got him! He's safe."

"Oh, thank God. Miss Morton, is he all right? I'm coming!" Petunia began climbing over the edge of the hole.

"No, Petunia. Stop. Let's go downstairs. Be sensible," John said. "We're coming!" he called.

"And with that, I will take my leave," Mr. Faulkbourne said.

"Not so fast. You tried to kill my nephew. You're not going anywhere but jail," Henry said.

"Oh, I disagree."

Poppy heard the click as the pistol's hammer was pulled back. She scrabbled away and picked up the crying Arthur, holding him close to her chest as she backed from the gaping hole above. Rain trickled in a steady stream down. The floorboards creaked dangerously beneath her feet, and she hustled toward the safety of the corridor, heading back.

"Let her go. She's done nothing to you," Tom said.

"But she's important to you, and therefore valuable to me. Come along, Miss Blackwood."

"Oh!" Susan gasped in pain.

"Don't you touch her," Tom said.

"Get out my way. Come any closer and she's dead," Mr. Faulkbourne said.

Susan squeaked with fear.

"You won't get away with this," Lord Blackwood said. "Stop

this. You've won. Let her go. We won't interfere."

"Speak for yourself, Blackwood. Your daughter here is my protection. Once I have a horse and am out of here, you'll get her back," Mr. Faulkbourne said. "And if you try to stop me, I'll bring her along for some company. Maybe Miss Penwrith had a good idea. Think about it, I could be your new son-in-law."

"Never." A scuffle ensued. It sounded to Poppy like the men were grappling, when the gun went off, a bullet flying into the damp ceiling.

"Tom!" Susan cried.

At that moment the roof fell in, and rained down water, wood pilings, rafters and beams, stone. It all fell in a mighty crash on Tom and Mr. Faulkbourne, sending them into the hole and crashing through the floor.

"No!" Susan said, scrambling toward the hole. "Tom, are you…"

"Come away, Susan," Lord Blackwood said.

"No, I won't," she said, leaning over the hole in the floor. "Tom!"

There was silence.

Poppy cradled the crying Arthur in her arms and met Petunia and John in the corridor.

"Oh, my baby," Petunia wept, taking him from Poppy. "My poor little one."

John stood by her, his eyes on the child. He looked up at Poppy and said, "Thank you."

"What was that noise we heard?" Petunia asked. "Did I hear a gunshot?"

"Yes. Mr. Faulkbourne shot at Mr. Markham, but missed. I think the bullet ricocheted and the roof fell in. They fell through the floor."

"Tom? Tom?" Susan called, her voice thick with emotion. "Tom?"

There was silence as the sound of Susan's quiet sobs could be heard amidst the falling rain.

POPPY JOINED THE others in the search for Tom and Mr. Faulkbourne, and found they had fallen through not one but two floors, through the lower ground floor and into a long abandoned cellar. They pulled aside timbers, fragments of stone, as well as broken pieces of wooden beams now rotted, and wet floorboards.

"Tom? Mr. Faulkbourne?"

A low cough and a groan sounded.

"Tom?"

Immediately, everyone began working to pull aside rubble.

In minutes, Tom's coughs grew louder and a footman helped him out. Tom coughed and groaned. "Thank you."

"Tom!" Susan was wild and climbed and stumbled over rubble to reach him. He held an arm back but was powerless as she ran into his arms.

He coughed and hacked, as she said, "You're hurt."

"Well, I did fall through a floor. Never mind that. Are you all right? He didn't hurt you, did he?" he asked.

"I'm fine," she said, touching his back.

Lord Blackwood said, "Let him up, Susan."

Susan helped Tom as he gingerly cradled one arm and accepted her help in climbing over the rubble.

"I think my arm's broken."

"Where's Mr. Faulkbourne?"

Tom looked back. "He cushioned my fall. Don't look, Susan. He's dead."

Susan nodded and helped Tom walk away, with support from a footman. They stopped when they came to Lord Blackwood.

"Sir?" Tom looked up.

"You tried to save her life."

"He did, Papa," Susan said.

"Do you still wish to court my daughter?" Lord Blackwood's voice was gruff.

"If she'll have me."

Susan held onto Tom tighter than ever, making him grunt.

"Then yes, you have my permission to court her," Lord

Blackwood said.

"But sir, my background. Your wife–"

"She will agree when I tell her what you have done. And when I tell the Earl of Markham that his third son is in fact not a womanizer, but saved my daughter from a murderer."

Susan smiled and led them away.

Poppy stayed and walked over to inspect Mr. Faulkbourne's body.

Henry joined her. "He's dead."

"Yes. I was so distracted by Miss Penwrith's schemes to win you, I didn't even notice his attempts to disturb your family."

"I suspect he thought that Miss Penwrith walking around when she was supposed to be dead would have scared us all into thinking she was a ghost, and in time would scare us into thinking the place was haunted and would leave. Then all he would need to do is make us an offer and he would have the place to himself," Henry said.

"I believe you're right. But Henry, look at that." Poppy pointed. "Beyond his body. Is that…?"

"Bones." He stepped forward and carefully pulled Mr. Faulkbourne's body from the mess, with the help of two footmen, who dragged the corpse away. "Will you look at that?"

There in the rocks and broken floorboards, the dripping rain that pattered down on the rubble and stone, lay the wizened skeleton of a woman in a faded maid's dress.

"It must be that maidservant, Minnie. From Sir Dyngley's ghost story. It looks like she didn't leave after all. That's sad," Poppy said.

"Yes, it is." He looked at her. "Poppy?"

"Yes, Henry?"

"Will you marry me?"

She looked at him. She was sweaty, and dirty, and they stood together in a pit, with rain dripping down, a pile of bones by their feet.

"I appreciate it's not the appropriate time or place, but I–" he started.

"What about your father? He didn't give his consent."

"After what you did for Petunia and John, I won't let him say no." He took her hand and led her away from the rubble. "Say you will? Unless your feelings toward me have changed." His eyes were dark with worry, his handsome face drawn and serious. "But truly, Poppy. I am but a poor sergeant, and if you say yes, we will have naught but my family's home to live in, or your townhouse in London."

"And what of you, Henry? I am the daughter of a gentleman and his mistress, raised by my aunt and uncle. I have never been to Town to learn painting or sketching from the masters, I know no other languages aside from the Queen's English, and I have no musical talent to speak of."

"But you have a mind and a beauty like none other. You have a practicality and good sense that will win the day. But all that does not matter, for I love you."

Hope bloomed in her chest, even as practicality won over. "I know as well as you that a relationship, even a marriage, cannot survive on love alone. We will need to figure out finances, and how we will survive." She touched his hand and gave it a squeeze. "But my affection for you is unchanged. I will marry you."

He smiled, and it was the first time she had seen a real smile on his face in days. It was warm as the afternoon sun, and made her heart fill with joy.

EPILOGUE

AS EXPECTED, THE deed John had signed was scratched out. The real Miss Penwrith awoke and once she learned of what had transpired, vowed never to sleep again. The impracticalities of this statement were gently pointed out to her, but the nature of her apologies and worry for Arthur were so genuine, Petunia forgave her on the spot.

Not that she needed any forgiving, Poppy thought, but held her tongue.

Peace had been restored to the Dyngley household. Petunia was delighted at having gained a nursemaid and governess who doted on her child, and being of a good education and appropriate background, could even see her as a future companion.

Mr. Faulkbourne's body was buried without ceremony and a note sent to his family, with condolences for his having died in a tragic accident. Sir Dyngley recovered his health. The rains stopped and with help, the road leading out from the manor was repaired and made passable. In a few weeks, Uncle Reginald was given a clean bill of health, and allowed to travel by carriage, provided it was slow.

And in a good and proper time, Poppy and Henry met again for a wedding, this time in the small, private chapel reserved for the Dyngley family. The inside of the old church was bedecked with flowers, and the sun shone through the small stained glass windows, throwing welcome light on Uncle Reginald, who wore his clerical robes and officiated while using a cane, the sunlight beating down on his balding head.

Poppy wore an elegant new dress of blue silk with lace trim, a blue ribbon in her hair, and satin shoes, while Henry wore a smart suit of navy blue with matching blue at his cravat and waistcoat.

Petunia teared up and cried in the front row, as did Aunt Rachel, with happiness. John sat beside Sir Dyngley, who remained polite and civil, if somewhat disapproving. John did his best to emulate his father and act polite and serious, but he shed a tear too, and eventually ended up using one of Petunia's handkerchiefs to dry his eyes. The real Miss Penwrith bounced the happy baby Arthur in her arms, a polite smile on her face. In the rows behind sat the Blackwoods, and farther back sat Tom, looking cleaned up and very smart, despite his arm in a sling. Somehow, despite his fine suit, the sling gave him a rakish look and he looked more like a rogue than ever. Poppy thought the roguishness rather suited him.

Poppy rather wished her uncle might announce them as man and wife, but this was a proper English wedding ceremony, and decorum and seriousness were the order of the day. She and Henry exchanged rings; Henry repeated the words, "With this ring I thee wed, with my body I thee worship, and with all my worldly goods I thee endow."

Poppy's heart soared as he spoke the words, and she almost laughed aloud as he winked at her. They signed the register and when the service had ended, led the procession out of the chapel. Once outside and into the sun there were cheers, and clapping, and the small group in attendance threw seeds and wild rice at them, along with flowers. Henry withdrew a small bag of coins and tossed them into the air, as he took Poppy's hand in his own. Then, in front of everyone, he stopped what he was doing and without a care in the world, or concern for who might be watching, pulled her toward him for a kiss. It was to be the first of many.

"Are you happy, Mrs. Dyngley?" Henry asked, releasing her.

"Yes, Sergeant Dyngley. Henry." She smiled, looking into his eyes. "I am."

And she really was. Finally, she had married Henry Dyngley. Her Dyngley. They would solve crimes together, now and forever.

The End

Historical Note

I've taken a few liberties with historical words and phrases in this novel. Apparently, the first time that "happily ever after" was used in connection to marriage dates back to 1702. Similarly, phrases like snack and peckish may not necessarily be appropriate, but they were in existence during the time this novel is set. It is complete fiction, and I hope you have enjoyed the series starring Poppy and Henry. Do let me know what you think.

About the Author

E. L. Johnson writes historical mysteries. A Boston native, she gave up clam chowder and lobster rolls for tea and scones when she moved across the pond to London, where she studied medieval magic at UCL and medieval remedies at Birkbeck College. Now based in Hertfordshire, she is a member of the Hertford Writers' Circle and the founder of the London Seasonal Book Club.

When not writing, Erin spends her days working as a press officer for a royal charity and her evenings as the lead singer of the gothic progressive metal band, Orpheum. She is also an avid Jane Austen fan and has a growing collection of period drama films.

Connect with her on Twitter at twitter.com/ELJohnson888 or on Instagram at instagram.com/ejgoth.